PRAISE FOR ALEXANDER MAKSIK

"*You Deserve Nothing* is rivetingly plotted and beautifully written . . . [Maksik] writes about the moral ambiguity of Will's circumstances with dazzling clarity and impressive philosophical rigor.

—Adam Langer, *The New York Times*

"*You Deserve Nothing* is a powerful, absorbing novel . . . Maksik is an unusually gifted writer."

—Tom Perrotta, author of *The Abstinence Teacher* and *The Leftovers*

"With writing that is reminiscent of James Salter's in its sensuality, Francine Prose's capacious inquiry into difficult moral questions and Martin Amis's loose-limbed evocation of the perils of youth, Maksik brings us back to that point in all our lives when character is molten, integrity elusive and beauty unbearably thrilling."

—Susan Salter Reynolds, *The Christian Science Monitor*

"The phrase 'brilliant debut' is much overused in our world, but Alexander Maksik's *You Deserve Nothing* is truly one of those rarest of creatures, a brilliant debut."   —Ben Fountain, author of *Billy Linn's Long Halftime Walk*

"*A Marker to Measure Drift* is a bold book . . . Maksik has illuminated for us with force and art an all too common species of suffering."

—Norman Rush, *The New York Times Book Review*

"Poetic, often mesmerizing . . . faultlessly lyrical . . . *A Marker to Measure Drift* is about compassion; perhaps it's even a masterclass in compassion."

—*The Sydney Morning Herald*

"No novel I read this year affected me more powerfully than *A Marker to Measure Drift*."   —Richard Russo, author of *Everybody's Fool*

"A sensitive and beautiful novel . . . The emotional power of this luminous and tragic story, suggestive of the work of Albert Camus, is striking."

—*Paris Match*

"Immensely powerful . . . Beautifully written . . . Jacqueline is a mesmerizing heroine . . . She is alive on the page from the outset, and with each paragraph she deepens, grows more complicated."   — *The Boston Globe*

"Haunting and sensual, Maksik's prose deftly intertwines the tenderness and torment of memory with the harsh reality of searching for sustenance and shelter."   —*Harper's*

"Beautiful . . . *A Marker to Measure Drift* will leave you breathless and speechless; it will send you reeling."   —*The San Francisco Chronicle*

ALSO BY

ALEXANDER MAKSIK

You Deserve Nothing

A Marker to Measure Drift

SHELTER IN PLACE

Alexander Maksik

SHELTER IN PLACE

Europa
editions

Europa Editions
214 West 29th Street
New York, N.Y. 10001
www.europaeditions.com
info@europaeditions.com

Library of Congress Cataloging in Publication Data is available
ISBN 978-1-60945-364-0

Maksik, Alexander
Shelter in Place

Book design by Emanuele Ragnisco
www.mekkanografici.com

Cover photo © B.Aa. Sætrenes

Prepress by Grafica Punto Print – Rome

Printed in the USA

To Madhuri in the rain.

For us back then, to live seemed almost to die.
—Galway Kinnell
Astonishment

I created you while I was happy, while I was sad,
with so many incidents, so many details.

And, for me, the whole of you has been transformed into feeling.
—CP Cavafy
In the Same Space

SHELTER IN PLACE

1.

In the summer of 1991 my mother beat a man to death with
a twenty-two ounce Estwing framing hammer and I fell in
love with Tess Wolff.

Now, many years later, they have both disappeared and I
am alone here on this pretty clearing in the woods.

Alone, save for the tar and the bird and the other thing, for
which I have no name.

2.

I'd taken my father's Wagoneer in to be serviced. This was in late August, nearly two months ago now.

Tess was in the garden when I left.

Like a miracle, we had fat strawberries all summer long and she was out there filling a basket with them. I was dressed for town, standing on the deck, looking down at her in the sun.

I said, "I'm going."

She was kneeling in the dirt and, when she heard my voice, looked up at me, shielded her eyes, smiled and raised the brimming basket.

A few hours later, when I returned home, she was gone.

Her note was held to this table by a white bowl full of berries. They were still wet, as if washing them were an afterthought.

She wrote, "I am too various to be trusted. But I am safe and I love you. T."

3.

This table, always too large for that little dining room in Capitol Hill, fits perfectly here. We have six of my father's cherrywood chairs.

Four too many. Or five by the look of it.

Before me are glass doors framed in pine and mounted on tracks so that there can be no separation between the dining room and our deck, our deck and the clearing, the clearing and the forest. It is an extravagance. In winter we lose heat.

We built this house to bring the outside in. I wanted as little separation as possible and that is what we have.

We can slide back the walls.

Our neighbors are miles away.

Through the glass I look out on our green clearing. Soon to be brown, soon to be white. And beyond that, maybe a hundred yards from where I sit, is dense, old-growth pine forest. The clearing was here when we bought the property. It's why we bought it. Why we built.

The clearing at the end of the road. Like a fairy tale, a children's story of good and evil and adventure. A knight, a damsel. A witch, two children and their great courage. One way in, one way out. No neighbors nearby. Just us and the animals. Deer. Elk. Moose. Owls. Hawks. Foxes. If you sit here long and still enough, you see them all. They come peeking out of the woods, poking their heads into the open space, sniffing the air. The elk, the moose, the deer, they come to graze. The others, they come to hunt.

It is a place we're proud of. This house on a hill. Ours. All wood and glass and river rock. One long rectangle full of light. On the second floor, like a crow's nest, is nothing but our bedroom and bathroom. All the rest is downstairs—a kitchen and a dining room and a living room all running together. There's a guest room in the back. A small office. Two bathrooms. An entire wall of books facing the fireplace. We built it ourselves. That's what we say, anyway. But, of course, we had help. Still, it's our vision. And a lot of our labor too. It is a place we love, a place entirely ours. It is quiet and calm. Which is what we wanted more than anything else. Quiet and peace above all. And logic, I think.

We wanted a place of good systems. Or I did. And that is what we've had.

4.

L isten, I am trying to survive.
    Days here I'm barely hanging on. Talking to myself.
    Talking to my parents. To Claire. To you.
    I'm trying to put it all in order, arrange it into something
with clear borders and clean logic.
    First off, you have to understand this tar and bird bullshit.
I'm nowhere if I can't translate that.
    Second, there's no single word. That's the fucking problem.
Or one of them.
    I am trying to translate into language two experiences for
which all language is inadequate.
    I'm not going to tell you everything. You should know that
from the start. I won't answer all of your questions. This is not
every single thing. It is only one version. Please remember that.
    Also, there will be no continuous rhythm.
    We the erratic keep terrible time.

5.

I was twenty in 1991, living in Los Angeles in a grim but glorious studio apartment with its balcony overlooking Pico Boulevard. Two beach chairs and a hibachi. My last year at Cal State Northridge. I was happy. As far as I knew, we all were. My parents in Seattle, my sister, Claire, in London, at LSE. The brains and ambition of our family. Aside from school, I was bartending at Chez Jay, a famous little dive on Ocean Avenue where rich kids and movie stars came slumming. More than once Claire told me to transfer to UCLA. Do something with your life. Sure, I always said, but never got around to it. I didn't much give a shit. Wasn't very curious. Didn't worry, didn't plan the way she did. Wasn't a snob the way she was. I had no intention of becoming Secretary of State. Lucky for the State. I was okay to go along, wander. I liked pouring drinks. I liked my wrecked Toyota pickup, the girls who came to see me at the bar, ruling over my little fiefdom four nights a week.

But out of the thinnest air, without warning, it arrived in my body.

Landed there.

A leaden thing, whose form and quality shifts constantly in both memory and present mind.

Then, the first time, its arrival was sharp and sudden. Came with the force and surprise of a solid sucker punch. Or as if someone had spiked my drink. Or pushed a needle into my arm, pressed the plunger.

I was on my bed, back against the wall. Me and my same constant self.

And then whatever it is took hold: a sickening, narcotic feeling of terrible weight. I don't know what to call it.

I never have.

There is that word they use, but it is severely insufficient and one I loathe.

I'm not talking about sadness.

I am not despondent.

I am talking about the body. I'm talking about invasion and possession. This is a physical thing.

I am not fucking *blue.* I am not *feeling low.* I'm not *sad.*

Look, one moment I was a strong, happy kid reading a book. And then *out of thin air* it arrived in the dead center of my chest: a dull, cold pain.

It knocked the paperback from my hand. It closed my eyes and there in the dark I saw thick tar inching through my body.

Then, as the pain sharpened, a blue-black bird, its talons piercing my lungs.

Say what you will. These were the things I saw.

It is both animal and substance.

There is no logic to this, I understand, yes. Nonetheless, I am telling you what appeared behind my closed eyes in that shitty apartment I once loved: creeping tar, blue-black bird, talons.

The weight nails me to the floor. It deadens my arms; it draws me down. The substance closes my throat. It pulls at the backs of my eyes.

Now I am accustomed to it. Now I have ways to fight. Methods of battle. But not then when I was so young, on that morning when it first arrived.

I didn't leave my room for three days. Made no phone calls. I don't remember sleeping. Only sitting on my bed, or the floor, or in one of those plastic-ribboned rainbow chairs on the balcony watching the traffic lights change, trying to decipher their codes.

And then this beast, this creeping invader vanished as quickly as it had come. The greasy film lifted from my eyes, the weight gone, the pain, too. The bird took flight. As if it had never been there at all.

I went back to work, and back to class.

I expected red wounds, dried blood, but the terror and violence of those days were like awful guests vanished in the night.

6.

In the spring my parents drove down to Los Angeles in my father's Baltic Blue Wagoneer. Claire came from London wearing expensive clothes and a new haircut.

At dinner that evening we all watched her tell stories about her friends, about her job trading commodities, something none of us understood. It seemed we were watching a woman we barely knew pretending to be Claire. She was as theatrical as she'd always been, but now she'd become a person of accomplishment and confidence. As if she were the adult at the table, and we her children. I half expected the waiter to deliver her the check and the truth is that even then she had more money to burn than our parents did, or ever would. Our parents, Claire's audience, both amazed, thinking, I'm sure, who is this odd and lovely person, and what does she have to do with us? My father, catching me looking at him, his face so full of pride and wonder and love, smiled to say, look at this woman, your sister, where on earth did she come from?

Our mother, who was going heavy on the champagne, stood up towards the end of the evening. She was wearing a fringed wool poncho, red as fresh blood. She'd bought it many years before on a trip to Guatemala, a rare romantic vacation with my father. Claire recoiled the way she always did when my mother made herself—intentionally or inadvertently, it didn't matter—the center of attention.

"What I'd like to say," she said in her voice always too loud for the room, "is that I'm proud of my son. My son stepping into the wide world just like his big sister did."

Here she raised her glass, drawing the poncho up to the right, forming a stunted woven wing and revealing a flash of red satin bra. Claire, cool in some trim black dress, red lipstick, hair drawn back tight to her skull like those women in that Robert Palmer video, winced.

"First to my daughter." Now she raised the glass high enough to break the wing and reveal a spray of brown armpit hair. My father and I laughed and raised our own glasses, but Claire only gave a tight smile and took a slug of champagne. "And second and more important, because it's his night after all, to my sweet sweet son Joey."

Here I thought my mother might sing, but Claire raised her eyes from the table and if they could have killed they would have. In all the years of those mortifying stares, I'd never seen one quite so powerful, quite so cruel.

I think it knocked her back from the table a step, but even if that's in my imagination, I'll tell you one thing, she sure didn't sing. Instead she smoothed her palms over that unruly hair, lowered her voice and said, before slumping into her seat, "To Joe."

That night remains vivid for this scene, for my mother's performance, for my sister's mean eyes. Vivid because Claire was so pretty and assured in her new affectations, her new English lilt, telling us we *must* do this, we *must* do that. But more and above all, I think now, it is because I saw, or believed I saw in my mother's eyes, the dark settling talons, the slow-flowing tar. And this vision chilled me. This quick belief that within her lived the same thing that lived in me.

In an instant I began to believe, without evidence, without reason, that this punishing bird had flown from my mother to me. We shared it. Were its host. The great leaden beast was not only mine, but hers.

Listen, I am not one to see magic in the skies. I do not pretend to see the invisible world any more clearly than another person, but this, I am certain, was both premonition and prelude.

By the end of the night we were all watching Claire hold court and I was struck by a sadness so profound I could no longer eat. Was it that I knew then that my mother and I shared this migratory animal? Was it that I understood we were fracturing, our rare and resilient family? Or that we'd never been solid to begin with, that we were just four people barely bound together by fog and blood?

When Claire and I were young, my mother told us a thousand times in a thousand ways, "Nothing arrives *out of thin air*. There are precedents and there are signs. Always indicators and histories. Only an idiot or a child is surprised."

Well, it seems to me now that ours were whispers and suggestion. They existed within the realm of the magical, imprecise, formless, and here I am looking, there between the fissures, for that faint sparkle of the other thing.

L ater, after our parents went back to their hotel, I drove
Claire to Chez Jay. We sat in the last booth at the back.
"Sometimes Mel Gibson comes here," I told her. "Sits
right there."

I wanted Claire to be impressed—by the solicitous girls
smiling from the bar, the locals who knew me, my position here
as reliable barman, my fresh degree. I was an autonomous, self-
sufficient adult. I am a man, Claire. Here is my diploma, here
is where I work. But she looked around that place as if she'd
been tricked into being there.

She shrugged and studied me the way she always did—with
tender indulgence—and raised her glass. "To the graduate,"
she said, mocking my mother.

"Why can't you leave her be?" I said.

She shook her head and looked past me to the bar. "I'll
leave her be when she stops making fools of us."

"She doesn't make a fool of me."

"Did you see what she was wearing? The way she drank?"

"A few glasses of champagne, Claire."

"Enough to show you her bra."

I changed the subject.

"Sean Penn, too," I said. "He's a nice guy. Tips well."

Claire ignored me. "So now what, Joey?"

In a few weeks I'd drive up the coast, camp with some
friends in Big Sur, go back to Seattle, find a job somewhere. I
had no other ambition, no further plan. Save for those three

mean days, I'd always been happy. Was never restless the way Claire was. I'd never wanted other things the way she did.

"And then what?"

"Roam free." I laughed.

"You're a moron."

"Maybe I'll come visit you."

"You should," she said. And then, leaning in, "Hey Joe, I met someone. We might get married."

"What are you talking about?"

"He's very, very rich."

"So what?"

"You should see our life."

"How old is he?"

"Thirty-eight."

"And I'm the moron?"

"Don't tell Mom and Dad."

"Why not?"

"Just don't, okay?"

"Thirty-eight, Claire?"

"Who cares? Come visit. You'll see."

"Maybe I will," I said. "And maybe I'll put a bullet in his head."

She smiled and looked so far away and so much older than I would ever be.

Driving back I wanted to tell her about the tar. I wanted to ask if it was in her, or even if she knew what it was, but I couldn't muster the courage.

She hated being delivered to her expensive hotel in my truck, so I made sure to pull in slow, rev the engine, tap the horn.

It was the only power any of us ever had over my sister: our ability to humiliate her. The valets, irritated by the honking, waved me forward, but I stopped in the middle of the drive, made us a spectacle, got out and walked around to her side.

"You're such an asshole," she said. "My sweet bartending graduate."

I wrapped my arms around her and said, "I'll see you in London, you little snob."

But I never saw Claire again.

8.

A few weeks later I loaded my truck, drove west along Sunset Boulevard to the ocean, and turned north. Then it was as if I'd never lived in that city at all.

Cut and run. Just like Claire. Just like my mother.

The cardboard boxes were fitted neatly into the bed of the truck. My father's old Army duffel. A blue plastic tarp covering it all, strapped down with a crisscross of orange bungee cords.

I'm in the empty apartment, all evidence of my former life erased.

"The past is dead," my mother once loved to say. "Sink or swim, kids. Fight or die."

I drove up PCH toward the future. My mother again. "Toward the future, Claire. Toward the future, Joey." Another way of keeping her children moving, never, not for an instant, glancing back.

"Joey" from a song her long-dead father once loved to sing. Not Joseph, not Joe. "Joey, Joey, Joe," she said and sang to me for so many years. "You've been too long in one place." Whispered as a lullaby and sung at great volume on so many car trips to the coast. Said it like some kind of prophecy.

"Joey, Joey, Joe. You've been too long in one place. And now it's time to go."

But it was my sister who got the message.

Me, I prefer to stay where I am.

When we were young, we had the fortune of a secure and constant life.

My parents worked. Claire and I went to school. In the evenings we ate as a family around a rectangular table beneath a yellow light. If we made mistakes we were punished for them reasonably, with consideration. Those mistakes were insignificant. An occasional fight (me), a few incidents involving drugs (both of us), academic probation (me), vandalism (Claire), violations of curfew (Claire). None of it was irreversible. None of it destroyed us, or caused our parents any real worry. Both of them had grown up rough, as they often liked to remind us. Both had been poor, both just scraping by with parents of their own who had, in one way or another, abandoned them.

My father left for Vietnam three weeks after he finished high school. His mother had died in childbirth, and when he returned from war, his father, too was dead.

My mother left home at seventeen and never saw her parents again.

"Sink or swim," she said whenever we got into trouble. "Sink or swim," she said when she was angry or, much worse, disappointed. "Sink or swim, kid," when our mistakes amused her.

And sometimes, "Fight or die, buddy," when she was in a darker frame of mind.

This the guiding principle of her life.

My father probably worried more than my mother did, but as we grew up both of them looked on with cheerful bemusement and maintained as their general parenting strategy a kind of benevolent ambivalence. I think they could barely believe that Claire and I were theirs, that they'd provided us such safe and steady lives.

With all of our comforts, our regular meals and individual bedrooms, we were strange and privileged creatures who would never sink, but always swim.

10.

My father was a carpenter who worked out of our garage, and on-site for various contractors around Seattle. My mother, Anne-Marie March, whose name you may know, was a nurse at Harborview. Depending on the year, my father was more or less often in his workshop, but she was always at the hospital, where she'd worked since graduating nursing school. Despite so many other options, she stayed in the ER where she began, and where she felt most at home.

What else of those very early years? After school there was the distant sound of my father working the band saw. The workshop smell of fresh-cut wood and orange oil. There he is standing in the kitchen dressing a cut index finger, bleeding calmly into the white sink, asking us about our homework, our friends, our teachers, our troubles. Our father surprising us with wooden knights and faeries, dragons and princesses beneath our pillows.

And my mother coming backwards through the front door with a low stack of pizza boxes. The exhilaration and relief of our reunited family in the evenings after school.

Maybe I overstate all this happiness of youth. Claire would probably say so. But I'm not so sure.

Whatever the case, ours was never a sentimental family. However happy we were, our parents always took a brutal attitude toward time.

"What's gone is gone. What's done is done. What's dead is

dead," my father said when we came home crying after some injury, slight or failure.

"And who," my mother would add.

The two of them faced us in those moments like soldiers returned from a war neither of us could fathom.

"For better or for worse," he said dealing pizza slices onto our plates.

"Mostly for the better," my mother said.

I am nine years old. I have a black eye. My mother is walking me home through the neighborhood.

"Don't be blue, Joey Boy. It is difficult, but you are strong. It is difficult, but you are strong and next time you'll fight harder."

There is golden sawdust caught in the hair of my father's forearms. Clear safety goggles perched on his head.

"There is nothing you can't do, Joe. Nothing in the world," he says, pouring oil onto a rag.

"Fly? Be invisible? Become a lion?"

"Even those, kiddo. Even those."

Then I'm wearing the goggles, too big for my face, his eyes through the scratched plastic lenses, he's lifting me up and I'm flying, arms outspread, and we're no longer in the workshop, but on the back lawn gliding to the roar of jets, the smell of his coffee breath.

I'm trying here to find some kind of order.

I want to do now what my father did in his later life. I want to see the world, our history, with peaceful clarity, find in it some pristine logic. Or no, maybe what he really did was give up on all that entirely. Maybe what he did best of all was surrender.

11.

The drive to Big Sur must have been exquisite, but what I see from here are only stock photographs. That famous bridge. The ocean crashing into craggy rocks. The highway winding along at terrifying heights, the tall pines, dramatic headlands. These are not memories of experience, but of magazines.

Still, I'm certain I drove that road, and found my friends at a campground down by a good beach. I can no longer see their faces, but I was happy to find them there, happy to be drawn out of my mind.

We waded into the cold water, tore mussels from a looming black rock and collected them in our T-shirts. Arranged them on a damp plank of driftwood, and laid it on the fire. They are sputtering and snapping open as the wood smokes and blackens at the edges. We used their shells as knives to cut the flesh free, and as spoons to eat them. The most delicious food I'd ever tasted. Full of smoke and ocean. Someone had a guitar. We sang around a bonfire. We pulled cans of beer from an enormous white cooler full of ice. We sat with cold night air at our backs and firelight on our faces. I am standing at the ocean with a blond girl, our feet in the water and she is kissing me. I remember her warm mouth and the wind coming up and she's holding me to her with such force. She's touching my neck with her cool hand and then the two of us on the mattress in the back of my truck covered in a grey and white striped blanket. We're on our sides looking out at the ocean, and she's saying, "I love you, I love you," and I remember thinking, *yes, why not*, said, "I love you, too," and the way my saying "I love you, too" closed whatever space was left between us and she pushed back and I could feel her tight and so warm and the ocean was out there and everything would be fine and I was swimming not sinking, swimming not sinking. I was slow, kept my lips to her neck, whispered who knows what, pressed my hand between her legs. She was so wet then and embarrassed.

"I'm sorry," she said, "I'm sorry."

And I said, "For what? Why are you sorry?"

She didn't answer, but pushed me deeper and I kept whispering into her neck and watching the waves.

There were days and days of this. I remember her, but not her name, and her face is only a wash of color. But I know just how she felt in my arms at the fire, and the way she put my head in her lap and stroked my hair. How I wanted to tell her about the bird and the tar, but didn't have the language, or the courage. The way the mussels tasted and the beer and someone singing who could really sing and not a single day of rain. Someone with a laugh so high it seemed invented though it wasn't.

One of us running naked into the cold ocean.

A girl gone missing and that thrill and spike of fear, and her being found just before the police were called. Then a lightning storm and loud thunder and rain for days and whatever had been was over and we left our camp and dissolved into our lives in various vehicles going on to various places.

Is it possible that the blond girl came with me? That we continued up the coast together? I can see her sitting shotgun. Her bare feet on the dash, toenails painted blue. But that may have been only for a ride to buy more beer, or someone else entirely, from another time, another place. I can see her running across a different beach, a vast beach that looks more like Oregon than California.

But perhaps not. Perhaps that too is stock art stolen from some postcard. I did love her though, on that beach, by the fire, in the back of my truck, in the cool mornings. That didn't feel anything at all like a lie.

All love being borrowed anyway.

Whatever the case, with her or without her, I drove on from Big Sur out of the storm.

Surely I'd return to all of those people again.

I must have left with that warm feeling of shared experience and friendships deepened, our years in Los Angeles together somehow confirmed and authenticated by our days in Big Sur. Not only in Los Angeles, but there too in the land of Jack Kerouac and Henry Miller we were friends.

And so we would be forever.

From my table here I watch the water on the glass, and the wipers snapping back and forth, cutting the rain to infields, and maybe that windshield was mine, and that rain was the rain coming down as I left, but maybe not.

12.

The next evening I drove into Cannon Beach in the rain. And because it was raining, or because I was tired of camping, or because it was getting dark, I paid for a room at a motel. It was too much money—thirty-five dollars a night or whatever it was—but worth it for the shower, the neatly wrapped soap, the cup sealed in plastic, and the fresh towels, and the clean sheets.

Then, naked beneath the spray of hot water: an abrupt and inexplicable detonation.

A switch thrown. I was overcome by pleasure, by a sense of overwhelming power. Rapid rise. Sudden swelling euphoria. Savage ecstasy. My heart huge. I was absent all fear. I was standing on the bed. I was dressing. The clean shirt like some kind of wonder fabric, making my skin hum, and I left that room pulsing with mysterious rapture, qualities I'd never known, and outside by the Coke machines I broke the shell and withdrew my body until there was no separation between it and myself, it and the night sky. I put my head down and flew like a fish. All my muscles fast twitch. My bones pure black oil. My blood made of gasoline. There was no cold. There was nothing I could not control. I stretched my arms and legs. Arched my liquid back and sailed. I was a traveler, a man. I had weight and fire. I found a bar and walked inside like some kind of Clint Eastwood cowboy, some fearless hero soldier on leave. I see all of it. From the hot water to the do-not-disturb sign to the wet street to the bar door. The way I began to swing upwards from happiness into something else again and then again, higher with my eyes all clear, and my body humming and my heart ever-expanding. Something like I'd never felt in my life. No drug had ever come close. Eyes huge, I saw every detail of every surface of every object. The place was full of people, but I glided past them. I was a skier, a dancer, a skater. I ordered a drink I'd never ordered in my life.

"Beam, rocks," I said.

I don't know where it came from, whether I was conjuring some actor, or some guy who used to come to Chez Jay, or what. I'd never much liked bourbon, but I was going to like it now. It was still coming on that thing whatever it was, whatever it is, and then I was the sudden scorching center of that place, the very marrow of it. I looked around and I waited and on it flowed into my blood. And when you feel it, when you've got it in you, and your eyes are like that, and your skin is humming and your heart is deadly, there is no memory, there is nothing but the present world, which pours in and pours in and all you want is more of it. You want everything and the room was full of women and it was as if they moved together in some unified rhythm, as if it were some code, some bodily language that only I could read. My heart firing, my eyes so sharp I could kill with my vision. I had perfect control of the room. I saw every inch of it rolling into me through my eyes and skin and I waited and waited and then I crossed the floor for that one woman who was something else, who was not part of the heaving mass. I wove through to her as if I were a person accustomed to crossing rooms that way, yet I know that was the first time in my life. I looked her in the eyes and said, "My name is Joey I find you extraordinary I'd like to buy you a drink and talk for a while if that would be all right," and when she looked at me as if I were a lunatic and her friends gaped, I said, "I'm not crazy by the way, I'm not dangerous, it's just that I find you so graceful and so I'd like for us to have a drink together would that be all right? Would that be okay?" She gave me her hand and laughed and curtsied and said, "Why, yes, sir, it would be just fine, just fine indeed," mocking me, putting on a bad southern accent. Her friends teased her and disappeared as if I had dissolved them myself with a flick of a finger. We drank and danced and drank and danced and I saw everything. I saw her face as whole and I saw it disassemble. I saw her tongue move over her teeth, saw her green eyes, her throat, her lips, her small breasts, her narrow hips, her bare shoulders, her big feet. I saw her turn to water. She was everywhere. All of her falling through me, her lemon smell, her liquid skin, her soft wrists, her heat, and when I found the sweat at the back of her neck hidden beneath her hair, I trailed my tongue across it, she leaned back against me, and I said into her ear, idiot child that I was, "I might die of you." "What? What did you say?" She was turning and then looking at me as if she'd seen a thing she didn't like, and right then something splintered. In my chest, behind my eyes, in the air.

"What did you say?" she asked again.

"I might die of you," I said, but it was no longer joyous, no longer drunken, no longer light. It was something else. I had lost the elixir. It was running out of me. I could feel it subsiding. She looked and looked and I thought she would leave me there. My eyes were shrinking. I was losing my sight. I was falling. All the edges were softening, but still I tried to see. Before it was too late, before it was gone, I tried to see, and then after a moment of the two of us standing still, while all those other people warped and buckled, she took my hand in her strong fingers and she pulled us from the bar.

We were changed in the air.

Or I was.

We came to a stop out on the empty street pulling our coats on with the door closing to dampen the music. Though I tried with real concentration, I couldn't get her face into focus.

I was running out of sentences.

"What did you say in there?"

I didn't want to say it again. It felt as if it had been years ago. The whole night was fading. I couldn't remember where I was. I'd forgotten the name of my motel.

She said, "What does that mean? What does that mean you could die of me?"

I shrugged again. I didn't know what it meant. I was having trouble reconciling this woman in the street with the woman in the bar.

Christ, I'd been alive barely twenty-one years.

She shook her head. She seemed angry and I was afraid that she'd leave, which I did not want. I did not want to speak and I did not want her to leave.

"You've lost all your charm," she said. "What happened to that? Where'd it go?"

"I don't know," I told her.

I noticed that the noise was gone from my head, that there was now a wonderful stillness.

I wished that we'd stop talking, but I knew that I'd need to speak to keep her there. I must have said something, made some noise.

"Are you talking to yourself?"

I looked at her.

"I thought you said you weren't a madman," she said.

I smiled.

"But you are?"

"I don't know. It's possible."

Her eyes were on mine. She wouldn't look away.

"Are you trying to decide if I'm going to kill you?"

"Yes," she said. "That's exactly what I'm doing."

I laughed. She squinted at me.

"Well?"

"No," she said. "No I don't think you will."

"In that case, maybe we can walk somewhere."

"Where?"

"I don't know. I just got here. I barely know where I am."

"Come," she said and gave me her hand.

Out on the enormous beach the sand was firm from the rain and the sound of the waves was a constant white-noise roar. It felt good to be out in the low wind with her. Even if it had all run out of me, and I was exhausted.

"What's wrong with you?"

There wasn't much light, and it was difficult to see her face.

"I don't know," I said.

"Why did you say you could die of me?"

"Just a thing to say to a pretty girl in a bar, I guess."

"Asshole."

"Not really," I said. "And anyway, why would you come out here with me?"

"I don't know."

"So neither of us knows anything."

We went on like that crossing the vast beach toward the waterline. And all I wanted was for her not to leave me. As if without her I might not survive the night. And the thing was that it seemed we were both trying to answer that same question about what was wrong with me. And then as we came to the ocean gliding silent across the sand we stopped and watched for a while. The silhouette of Haystack Rock against the sky, and the wide blue bubbling tongues of foam moving in and out of the water.

"Why would you come out here with me?"

"Because you were very charming for a while," she said. "Mostly though because you're so sad."

"Am I?"

"You were."

"I don't know."

"I do."

"And you like that?"

"Maybe."

"Well, I'm glad you're here," I told her. "I wouldn't want you to be anywhere else."

"Ah, there's the charm again."

"No," I said. "I mean it."

I looked at her dark shape.

"Are you looking at me?"

"Yes," I said and reached for her.

My uncanny mind was very quiet then and all I felt was that warm body and the ocean throbbing its gentle pulse in my brain.

Later, we walked back across the beach toward the lights of the little town softened by the blue fog. She returned with me to the motel without either of us making the suggestion and when we stepped inside it was as if we'd entered someone else's room. Someone I might have known, whose things I recognized, but were nonetheless not my own.

She undressed me and then herself. For a moment we stood together, my chest against her warm breasts, my hands moving over her smooth back.

She was lovely, but I felt no desire, no lust. I wanted only to keep her against me as if to ward off the bird, which I could sense circling. There were brief twinges of that weight, ominous contractions in my chest, but nothing that lasted. I became convinced that she was my protector.

She kissed me and then again with more passion. I picked her up and laid her on the bed. I pulled the blankets over us and then her tight to me. She reached between my legs. I was soft.

"If we could lie here tonight," I said. "If we could just be still. If we could just be quiet."

"You're a strange boy, Joey," she whispered. "Joe. Joseph. So strange."

"It's only recent," I said.

She sighed and fitted herself to me with all her warmth and I thought she was relieved to give up sex until she said, "So what, baby, you just want me to hold you?"

I laughed and closed my eyes and we lay there falling asleep, while together we battled back the bird, which circled and circled above us looking for an entry point.

I woke early from the kind of black, motionless sleep that no longer comes to me here. Cold air moved through an open window. I drew the covers over us, closed my eyes and matched my breathing to hers. The night was gone. The bar felt a thousand years ago.

She was so warm with her skin cutting the trailing cold, and I wanted nothing else to happen. I wanted nothing else but for nothing to change.

But she will open her eyes soon, and curl against me and kiss my neck and whisper, "Good morning, Joe, Joey, Joseph." She will climb out of bed and walk naked to the bathroom and close the door. I will listen to her pee and the sound will make me happy. I'll hear the toilet flush and as it refills, the sound of water running into the sink. She is splashing handfuls of it against her face and then she is reaching for one of those clean towels hanging from the cracked chrome bar.

What I see and what I saw and what I imagined and there is no difference. Not a single difference in the world between those three things. They are equal. In memory. In value. In clarity. Equal.

I love to watch her standing naked at the sink. She is twenty years old. She is unafraid. She is not careful. When she's finished, the water is everywhere. It is always everywhere when she's finished and will be forever. Her cheeks will be flushed with color. She will favor her right leg and press it against the porcelain so that when she returns from the bathroom there is a pink line across her thigh. She is fearless and she is sure.

I'd never watched anyone so carefully in my life.

She returned to bed, to her place against my body, and slid her hand between my legs and found me hard.

"So," she said wrapping her cool fingers around my cock.

I closed my eyes and moved so that my leg was between hers. She pushed against me.

"Joseph," she whispered. "Alive again."

I felt her tongue on my neck and over my nipples and then her teeth biting and her tongue again and I felt her hot cunt sliding over my knee, and down my shin. She drew my legs apart and then she had my cock in her mouth not gradually, but all at once. She didn't move, just held me there deep. Then bit by bit rose and fell, then the same thing again and again and then with a furious rush she was up and pressing her cunt to my mouth. With one hand she yanked my hair hard. She pressed the other flat against the wall above me, her knees hard against the headboard. She was loud. A low moan and her fingers pulling at me beyond the point of pain and I could taste her. Was swallowing her. She was without shame. She was the most powerful person I'd ever known. I gave everything I could until she slid onto my cock fast and easy. She kissed me and licked my lips clean, my chin, and then her palms were firm on my chest, her sharp nails digging into my skin. She moved with an abandon and violence I'd never known. I came and somewhere in the midst of it she called out and as I softened inside her we fell asleep.

There is so much of me here that wishes my life had stopped there.

For that morning to have gone on and on. The two of us at peace, fitted together, stream of cold air cooling our skin.

But there is no stopping time.

The room brightened. She stirred and the next thing began.

When I opened my eyes she was sitting up with her legs crossed and the sheet gathered around her waist watching me.

I can see her as I sleep. Her lips slightly parted the way they are when she watches any object intently, as if she might speak to that thing. Animal or mineral.

"Good morning."

She extended her hand, "Tess."

Like that, all of the fragments brought together into a single syllable: Tess.

"It's nice to meet you," I said. "I'm—"

"Yes, I know. Joe. Joey. Joseph. I know."

We shook hands.

"Will you always call me by three names?"

"Always?" She smiled. "In our great future?"

"Yes. When we're old. When you're watching me die."

"Even then. Especially then." She smiled.

What did I learn of her that morning? That she'd just graduated from the University of Oregon. That she was sharing a house on the beach with her friends for the summer. That she was waiting tables at Bill's Tavern. Other things maybe. It doesn't much matter. Just that we began then, that I met Tess in this odd way, during that terrible summer.

Maybe some time went by. Maybe there was a night or two of her caution, or mine. A few days of that foolish game, but I don't remember it that way. We just leapt off the cliff without any hesitation. Or I did, anyway. I didn't play anything cool. She was all I wanted and pretending otherwise never occurred to me.

So either that very morning or a few days later, I said to her, "Come to London with me. Meet my sister. We'll go anywhere we want."

"All right," she said. "I'll do it. September. Don't change your mind, Joseph."

"No," I told her, "I will not."

And that was that. The beginning. Out of thin air, the way nothing happens.

I worked out a deal to keep the room and pay by the month. I could have found something else, but I liked the idea of living in a motel. And I liked the idea of keeping our first bed. We knew the housekeepers, and the people who worked the front desk and they all took care of us. They cleaned for us and included breakfast. It made our life simple and I thought there was something romantic about it, something tough, too. I kept a bottle of Jim Beam on top of a Gideon's bible. I admired the tableau and believed I was something wild. I was an idiot then. What a fool, what a faker, but my God I was happy.

Tess is in one of my work shirts. She is running barefoot down the hall toward the ice machine with a white bucket in her hand, flowers embossed on the sides. She is laughing, growling at me, baring her teeth, ripping wrappers off plastic cups.

And then later, once we'd settled in, the two of us sitting on the floor drinking bourbon out of glass tumblers she'd stolen from the restaurant. Her fingers digging up cubes of ice and dropping them one by one into our drinks.

I found a job tending bar a couple times a week at Driftwood, a steakhouse down by the beach, and she kept on cocktailing at Bill's. She had her room in the house with her friends, but even still we were making so much more money than we were spending, we both felt rich. She worked out a budget. We paid for rent and gas and insurance for the truck. That was about it. We mostly drank for free and ate for free, so the rest of the money we kept in a pair of folded jeans at the bottom of a drawer and that money was for September. For plane tickets and trains and all the rest.

We had our friends from the bar, from the restaurant, her roommates. There were dinners on the deck of their cottage looking out over the sand. People coming and going. Everyone sleeping with everyone else, everyone separating, everyone changing partners, while Tess and I were inseparable, playing wise, watching it all happen before us as if it were a film, as if we knew better. And while we were taken care of at the motel, we came to take care of all the others—dispensing advice, pretending to know something of the world.

Even then Tess had no patience for girlish silliness.

She is in the living room of the cottage, furious with one of her friends—a person whose name and face I have lost. Tess is standing in front of the open glass doors, which led out to their grey deck above the sand. A dark figure against the daylight. I can't see her friend, can't find her in that room.

Tess saying, "Why do you pretend you're so stupid? Why do you do that? Why play the idiot for these fuckers?"

It was the first time I'd seen her angry. Arms high, fingers gripping the doorframe, leaning forward. She was mesmerizing. That kind of fire. That kind of intelligence. Her absolute intolerance for bullshit. Her friend had no chance. Tess saying, "You are not a little girl. What kind of man wants that shit anyway? Put your tits away and speak for fuck's sake."

God, I can see her there. Coming off that frame with its peeling white paint, pacing the room. As if at any moment she would throw a punch.

Tess just seemed impossible. Her confidence appeared so true. Her constant and absolute belief in what was valuable and what was not. There was no tar in her, no bird, and nothing would stop her, whatever she was to do, whatever she would become.

Being near her made me happy. It was very simple. She made me believe I might too be constant. I thought perhaps she was an antidote. That I had been cured of whatever this strange thing was within me.

There may have been moments in those days when the weight would return, when some mornings I'd wake to find that bastard bird with its claws in my heart, but I don't remember them. In memory, we remove pain. I know this and I want to be truthful. I will try, but of those days, I recall only joy. All our friends were revolving around and around us. The beach and the fog at night and someone's dog running after a tennis ball and fires on the sand and the occasional storms coming in and Tess and her eyes and her naked body and the way she smelled and how everything I ate and drank tasted in some way of her. And how little else I wanted of my life. Just that. Just what we had. Our summer idyll.

14.

My parents would call on the motel phone, whose clanging bell always terrified Tess.

She is falling over laughing and clutching her heart. She's on the floor, spread out against the dirty blue carpet smiling up at me. I hand the receiver to her and she speaks so easily with them.

"I can't wait to meet you too, Mrs. March. It's beautiful here. Is it beautiful there? He's taking very good care of me, yes. He *can* be quite selfish, yes. You're right about that."

She is nodding. Grinning at me. She is so clear.

"What are you building, Mr. March? It sounds beautiful. Yes, I'd love to see your workshop one day."

We talked to Claire. We'd see her in London. Plenty of space in their *flat*. A guest room just for us. She was living with the banker now. Henry. She'd sent us a photograph care of the motel. We kept it propped against the flaking mirror frame. My smiling, radiant sister, our mother's blue eyes, our father's sandy hair, arms around a man in suit and tie. He is unremarkably handsome, balding, a tired, serious face.

"In their *flat*," Tess says jumping up and down on the bed. "A room *just* for us, *darling*," she sings in a terrible English accent.

And I watched her then, as I watch her now.

"September," she sang, her brown hair floating and falling.

15.

It turned very cold here in the night and when I woke this morning I could see my breath. I always sleep with the windows open. It's a habit I learned from Tess. She loves a warm bed in a cool room.

I found the pair of thick green socks she gave me for my forty-first birthday. They're made of cashmere. The kind of thing I'd have never bought for myself. She left them on my bedside table with a note that read, "For our winters."

It doesn't matter. They're just socks, but on a day like this they're a great luxury. I wear them with the ancient 501s she loves. The faded blue sweatshirt, once my father's. My uniform.

In the mornings after I get dressed, I like to look down on the clearing from our bedroom window. Today I watched a fox cut a neat black path through the frost.

These things still bring me some pleasure. Our warm bed, socks, my father's old sweatshirt, our animal neighbors.

I still open my eyes in the morning. I have not gone completely numb. I guess that's what I want to tell you. I wake up. I get out of bed. I get dressed. I look outside. I come downstairs and grind the coffee, and boil the water, and unfold the filter. I still make toast, cut up an apple. I still light the fire. Somehow it feels necessary to say it, to make clear to you that I also exist here in my present world.

16

A t the beginning of August my mother called the motel in the evening.

Tess was reading a book in a chair with her feet on the windowsill.

She is watching me, head turned to the side, light from the street crossing her face.

"Joey Boy," my mother said.

There was something wrong with her voice. I don't remember the conversation. Just the strangeness of it. I wanted to say, swallow, take a breath. She sounded thin. Incomplete. We talked for a while and then at the end:

"Are you all right?"

"Sure I am, sweetheart," she said. "Why wouldn't I be?"

"No reason," I said looking at Tess, who had closed her book. "I love you."

"I love you too."

That was the end of it. I put the phone back on the cradle. Tess sat across from me on the bed and raised her eyebrows.

"She sounded strange."

"Strange how?"

I shook my head. I let it stop there. I'd never told her about the bird. Never told her that I imagined sharing it with my mother. She knew sometimes I came up fast. And others I fell. In whatever way one person can know something like that about another.

"Like a lot of people," I'd told her. "Good days, bad days."

Maybe she believed it was that simple. Probably not. But we never talked about it then. And in those months we didn't need to.

"Maybe she wasn't feeling well."

"Maybe," I said. "Maybe that's all it is."

17

M y mother stands in the middle of the street. Her hair is blowing around her shoulders, across her face, twisting at her throat.

I am sitting on the curb. There is grass in my mouth, but I have forgotten it. I am no longer crying. I am watching her whipping hair, eyes wild and wide and the Carlson brothers in front of her, no older than ten, straddling their bikes.

She is screaming, "Look at me. Look at me, goddamn it."

She is moving toward them. There is a car behind her now. Chrome bumper.

"Look at me, goddamn it, you little shits."

She is leaning forward.

"If you ever," she says, "touch him again. Touch him again."

She is bent at the waist, her hands on their handlebars—a red fist on each—the wind is blowing harder. It is fall. Her black hair is snapping at their pink cheeks.

"So help me God. You touch him again. You touch him again. You touch him again."

Her eyes are unlike anything they've ever been. The driver blows his horn. Her hands come away from the bikes. She faces the car. The Carlson boys are pedaling hard now. They are gone and she is still standing in the street. The wind is at her back. Her hair is blowing toward the car. She does not speak. Only stares at the windshield, at whatever she can see through the shining leaves, the silver sky.

"Mom," I say, "Mom."

She turns and walks to me. The man rolls down his window.

"Crazy bitch," he says as he drives past. "Crazy fucking bitch," but it's as if she doesn't hear him, doesn't even flinch, and I know she is the stronger one.

She comes and lifts me from the curb and into her arms, even if I'm too old for it, too heavy for her. I don't want to be held. She draws her head back to get a better look at me. We're walking towards the house. I can see Claire so small on the front step watching as we pass.

"Joey," she says, and pinches a blade of grass from my lip. "Joey," she whispers as she carries me to the house. "Those little shits," she whispers, "those little assholes."

"Good for her," Tess says. "No one fucks with Joey."

I stand in the shower after she calls the motel and this is the memory that comes. My mother and her wild hair and those terrified brothers and the man leaning across the passenger seat to call her a crazy bitch.

It is the last in what I have come to believe was a series of premonitions. A series that began with the bird in February, and on to the restaurant in Los Angeles and all the others. Instantaneous recollections, momentary hallucinations, or that other thing: pure detached sensation. On the beach, or in the bar basement changing a keg, or on the highway, or in the shower. A radiating feeling of familiarity, a kind of haunting, which carried with it neither sound nor image. Only a vague vibrating. A chill. Cold mist along my spine. Something like what some music does to me. Something like that.

Or perhaps these premonitions were all imagined. My imagined imaginings. A warping of two levels of experience. My faithless memory of memory. As sharp and shining as the edges of this table.

My mother sings me to sleep in her softest voice, "If wishes were horses, Joey, beggars would ride. If turnips were watches, my sweet boy, I'd wear one by my side."

18.

My father taught me to feel the air for the suggestion of coming seasons. On short dark days we flew our hands out the window of his Wagoneer and felt for a balmy current flowing through the cold. A game I have always loved. Feel the air for a future season. Fall in summer, spring in winter. Warnings. Promises.

In Cannon Beach, in those last weeks of August I found fall everywhere. The light had begun to lengthen. The wind was more often cut with that sharp winter edge. The nights became colder. We stayed up later and later and tried to take the last of it. There were great bonfires on the beach. Ending parties. Everyone was preparing to leave. Tess and I were making plans. September we'd drive up to Seattle to see my parents. Spend a few days and then fly to London. We had plenty of money. Until then we'd work and walk the beach and watch the summer die away.

I became tense and irritable.

Tess watched me from her chair, over the top of her book, from bed.

"Joseph," she said. "Sad Joseph."

She smiled at me with tender sympathy, still charmed and intrigued by my ever-changing mind.

My fading summer joy was like the dilution of some wonderful and potent liquid. Drops of water dripping into the vial, weakening the solution bit by bit.

"It's everything all at once," I told Tess. "The end of summer, my mother's phone call, leaving."

"That's all it is?"

"Yes," I said.

On a night off, waiting for her to finish work, I sat at the bar watching a Mariners game. She was keeping an eye on me. The bartender was a friend of ours, a short guy with red hair.

I was okay. I liked being in that little corner. Things were all right, but then in the middle of the rush, I looked from the TV to see a group of guys watching Tess walk away. They were making a show of it and watching was what mattered to them. The display. It was nothing new and nothing she couldn't have handled herself. She was tougher than I was by a long, long way. But there was something about them, and then something about one of them. The way he sat slunk down in his chair. His leer. The way he collected his friends' grins.

Waited for them. Little gold coins. The sad prick.

I felt that twinge in my gut. Sharp irritation turned to rage.

They were nothing. They were the usual. They were the same old shit. The same thing Tess endured every hour of every shift.

Still.

The timing was wrong. The night was poisoned. Winter was coming. Too much bourbon. The night was rotten. I'm not sure. Something though. It was something.

The Mariners lost. Then it was the news on mute, so instead of looking at the television, I looked at the guy.

I wasn't that kind of person. I have never been that kind of person. Except for sometimes, right?

That's a funny thing. A funny idea. This kind of a person or that. I wasn't though. I wasn't until I was, until he snatched at her. Until he grabbed at her wrist.

When he did that I hit him and broke my hand.

19

When it was over, Tess and I sat on the floor of the motel room with our backs against the dresser. We were both looking at the small cast resting on my knee.

"Listen to me, Joe," she said. "Listen, I don't need you to defend my fucking honor. I'll do it myself. Do you understand me?"

She was shaking.

I couldn't look at her.

"I know," I said. "I'm sorry."

"Joseph," she said. "What's happened to you?"

"I don't know."

"But you have to tell me."

"But I don't know."

"You have to tell me anyway. You have to tell me anyway. Otherwise I'm going to leave. Do you understand? That I'm going to leave. It's enough, Joe."

"Enough?"

I could feel the slow creep.

"It can't go on like this. It can't continue."

I didn't know what she meant by that, by *continue,* but when I turned to look at her and I saw her eyes, I didn't argue. It wasn't what I had done that frightened me. It was the word.

I said, "What do you mean *continue?*"

"Joe, you've been like this for weeks."

"Like *this,*" I said. "Like what? Punching people? What are you talking about?"

I could feel the sweat on my forehead.

"Dark," she said. "Cold and remote. Like you were tonight. What do you think? Tonight was the first time?"

She was so angry. I watched her mouth. I thought of the last weeks, but I could not remember myself within them.

"Days and days go by, Joe. You're unreachable. You don't speak."

I looked at her and tried to remember, but I could not find a single image. There were only the generic symbols of our life—the beach, the house, the motel, the bars. I saw no instances of unhappiness, of tension, of my apparent darkness. Seeing her anger and frustration, it shook me. She was so insistent, so certain, and yet I could not see the person she was describing. As if I'd been thrashing and screaming in my sleep and now, in the morning, she was telling me how I'd kicked her, the phrases I'd called into the night.

"When?" I asked.

She must have seen it—my fear, my bewilderment. Her look turned from anger to worry, or worse, to pity.

"When I found you sitting alone out on the beach the other night? You don't remember?"

"I do."

"You were gone for hours. We were supposed to have dinner."

"I lost track of time."

"When I finally found you, Joe. You wouldn't look at me. You barely responded. It was like you were drugged. You don't remember that?"

"I remember us sitting together."

And that was all I could recall.

"I had to shake you, Joe. Just to have you look at me."

"Okay," I said. "Okay." I wanted her to stop talking.

"Okay?"

"I'll stop."

"Look, I can't tell you what to do. I don't want to. You have to decide. But something, Joe. You've got to do something."

"Sure," I said. "I understand."

But I didn't understand. Punching that guy, yes. But the other, the *continuing*. Not at all. I didn't know what couldn't go on any longer. I knew that I'd hit the guy hard. That now there was a piercing pain cutting from my elbow to my knuckles, a pain beating in rhythm with my heart.

"It can't go on, Joe, and either you tell me what's happening with you, or that's it. You see? Because I don't want that kind of thing."

She stood and walked out of the room leaving the door open. I listened to her moving through the hallway.

It was circling.

I felt it alight.

The pointed pressure. The constricting of my heart. The spreading weight.

Did it also take my memory? Did it black out time?

Had she gone for good?

Has she gone for good?

I wanted her never to come back. Part of me did. The coward. If she were gone, the investigation would end and I would wait with it in peace.

It was a kind of peace.

It is. You want nothing. Not food. Not language. Not sex. Not even to move. And if it blinds you to yourself, if it makes time vanish, then I'm sure you understand there's a frail peace in that too.

I sat slumped against the dresser until Tess returned with a bucket of ice. She poured us drinks and faced me. Legs crossed, elbows on her knees.

"Joey," she said, bringing her forehead against mine and forcing me to meet her eyes, "speak."

"Sometimes," I said, "sometimes I imagine a bird. I imagine

it circling. And there are times when it lands. When it lands right in the center of my body and I can feel its talons digging in. They're very sharp and very strong."

I was humiliated. She was listening to me.

"And then it changes. It's no longer a bird. It's something else. Tar. Tar that moves through me and pins me down and holds me there."

She never broke. Never looked frightened. Never looked much of anything. Just those lips parted, those eyes on me.

"I imagine tar. It could be anything, but I imagine tar. It's moving. It's in my veins, covering my heart, filling my lungs. Sometimes it feels like it's pulling my eyes, as if it's in my brain and wants to pull my eyes back through my head."

I looked up at her. I'd heard what I'd said. I could still hear it.

"I'm not crazy."

"No," she said.

"I'm just telling you what I imagine. How it feels. I know it's not tar. I know it's not a bird."

"I understand."

"I'm not crazy, Tess. I don't know why it comes. And I don't know why I can't remember."

She didn't answer. I'd told her what I could and for a while that seemed to be enough. We climbed into bed. I lay next to her, curled up with my head on her breast. She stroked my hair.

"It's recent," I said. "It's new."

"Like me," she said.

My broken hand was on her belly. I could hear her heart. Feel her breathing. Soon we were asleep.

20.

I gave up my job. I couldn't do it one-handed. And anyway, I didn't much want to work anymore. I went into Bill's a few times after that night. They said, "What's new, Tyson." They called me Holyfield, but I could tell they were unsettled. I didn't know what they'd seen me do exactly. I was famous in a way I didn't like.

The bartender, the redhead, was older and he didn't look at me with admiration or with fear. I was grateful for that. He had a bat beneath the bar and kept an eye on the door, but I didn't think they'd be back. They weren't those kind of guys.

I sat there those last few nights and drank my free bourbon and watched the Mariners. Those were the days of Ken Griffey, Junior. The last days when he played alongside Griffey, Senior.

My father and I always loved those two. We loved their whole story.

Tess and I walked for hours on the beach with the bartender's chocolate lab.

Tess in her big black turtleneck sweater and her hair blowing all over the place, throwing a chunk of driftwood for the dog. She had a dangerous, terrible arm. You had to keep your distance.

The dog had a ridiculous human name. Paul, I think. She loved that. "Paul, would you mind passing me the stick. Paul, can I trouble you to fetch the tennis ball for me."

I tried to get out from under it. She kept an eye on me,

forced me to speak. We were all right. Things were better. The weight slipped away as it always did. I ran and ran while the dog chased me, barking into the wind while Tess sprinted barefoot across the wet sand.

And beneath it all, beneath the images of Tess, the sunsets, and my throbbing hand in its dirty cast, was a premonitory sense of disaster.

What else?

Once, Tess threw the stick so badly that it hit poor Paul in the head.

Once, for an afternoon, the full warmth of summer came back to the air.

I told Tess that I believed I shared the bird with my mother. That it bound us together.

I was better, but increasingly I felt as if I were living without a layer of skin. That I could no longer filter the physical world. Nothing was processed, all the light and sound rolled through me and nothing was dulled, nothing was quiet or kept out.

I saw images in the air. I heard phrases in the wind.

These I did not mention.

Not less a layer of skin. That's wrong. It was more than that. As if there were no skin at all. The world was becoming sharper and sharper. I could not stop it.

The buzzing motel fridge woke me at night.

The sky in the early afternoon took on the texture of wool.

The wind on the beach made me hard.

Tess and I in a sheltered cove beneath the sun and sky, the swirling air tempered by the rocks and she is drawing her shirt up and off.

Her breasts in the sunlight.

The pleasure of it, of that warmth, of her body, of the sun, the wonderful privacy of that cove, the roughness of the dizzying blue sky, the way she moves on me, the heat of her, squeezing me in pulses that somehow seem coordinated with the gusting wind and her lips against my cheek, against my neck.

We're crying, the two of us afterwards holding on hard, staying as still as we can for as long as we can, because below the sand there is the doom, below is the chaos coming slow and sure and close. And I know it then. I am certain. I felt it there beating in my lungs, in the air, in the shortening days.

21

My father called on the motel phone. Tess was at work. "Joey," he said and already I could hear it in his voice. "Joey, you there?"

I cannot separate what he told me then from what I discovered later, so I'll tell you what I came to know—that evening, the next day, in the weeks to come. The truth by all accounts.

In the early evening of August 22, 1991, my mother, Anne-Marie March, drove to Hardwick and Sons Hardware. My father had asked her to pick up a few things on her way home from the hospital. As she was returning to the parking lot with her shopping bag, she noticed a man arguing with his wife in front of a silver Mercedes sedan.

She climbed into her car, a sun-faded blue Volvo station wagon. Before she fastened the seat belt, before she started the engine, she looked into the rearview. There were two young children with the couple and as their parents argued, they waited quiet and still.

The man was thirty-four years old, pale skin, fleshy face, thinning black hair, glasses. His name was Dustin Strauss.

My mother sat and watched the four of them in her mirror.

The children waited while the man raised the trunk and put his shopping bags inside. The boy, who was also carrying a bag, handed it to his father by one of the two handles so that the paper tore, and the contents spilled onto the asphalt.

My mother heard the sound of glass breaking. At this point she turned to watch directly through the back window. She saw the man slap the boy across the face hard enough to knock him into the door of an adjacent car. The woman, Strauss's wife, yelled at her husband, at which point he punched her in the jaw.

This is what she saw. This is what she remembers. Or it is, at least, the sum total of her testimony.

There is no argument about what happens next. There were other people in the parking lot, people who would become witnesses. There were the children. There is evidence. There were experts called. By all accounts what follows is the truth, even if the account missing is my mother's.

She says she has no memory of the time after the first blow. Still, I have read the papers, and I have seen the photographs.

My mother came out of the car holding a twenty-two-ounce Estwing framing hammer taken from one of my father's suede tool bags, which he'd left in the backseat. She crossed toward the Mercedes. The trunk remained open. Dustin Strauss was bent at the waist yelling at his wife while she knelt on the ground.

My mother swung the hammer and hit the back of his head. He fell forward onto his knees. She swung again. Then he was facedown next to his wife, who screamed at my mother to stop.

She did not.

She swung again and then again and then again and then again and then again. Seven blows in total. Seven blows according to the coroner.

When she was finished, the man lay dead in the parking lot, the Estwing on the warm asphalt beside his mouth.

She grabbed the children by their wrists, pulled them to the Volvo, and buckled them into the back. She returned to the driver's seat, laid her hands on the steering wheel and then, until the police came, did nothing more, while Mrs. Strauss went back and forth between banging on the glass, screaming for her children and weeping next to her husband's body.

Of course, when my father called he didn't tell me all of this. He only told me what he knew. That my mother had killed a man in front of Hardwick and Sons, where my father was well-known, where he had been taking me since I was an infant.

She was in jail.

I should come home.

He had to hang up now.

He needed to call Claire.

"It seems Mom has killed a man," he said.

That's a sentence you don't lose.

I waited on the bed looking at my hand in its cast until Tess came back from work.

"My mother murdered a man," I said and gestured to the phone as if the phone had something to do with it.

I can see her bright expression. She didn't touch me at first.

I was afraid she'd leave.

"With a hammer," I said.

She stood up from the bed and chained the door.

"Joey," she said and then, at last, touching me, lying down and pressing her head against my chest.

"Everyone will be shocked," I said. "Everyone will be surprised."

"Sure."

"But I'm not surprised."

"Joey."

"I'm not, Tess. Why is that?"

"I don't understand."

"No. Neither do I."

"But this is the first thing? There's no history of it?"

"No," I said. "No history of it."

"I don't understand."

"But what is the it, Tess?"

She didn't answer me and I didn't say anything else. She

walked her fingers over the dingy shell of my cast. And as we lay there with everything shifting beneath us, I tried to work out what it was exactly. This thing of which there was no history.

I knew it was the firing rise as I stood beneath the shower, the striding into that bar. It was the hallucinations and my vanishing skin and the night alone on the sand. It was what brought me to Tess and what broke my hand and what would finally make her leave.

The refrigerator was roaring, my mother had murdered a man, and I could feel Tess breathing against my neck and her fingers walking up and down, up and down, and I knew that it was the bird and it was the tar and it was the ecstasy.

22.

Claire called.
At first there was static on the line and then an echo. Everything we said, repeated.

"I don't understand," she kept saying.

Tess and I were looking at each other.

I said, "You should come home. You should just come home."

It had been nearly a week since my father called. Neither of us, not me, not Claire, had been to see him or our mother.

This was her third phone call, each the same.

"*You* haven't even been home."

"But I'm going," I said. "I'm going soon."

"So you say, Joey."

"Come back and we'll go together. We should be there."

There was a long silence. Tess was watching me. She'd been telling me the same all week, "You have to go see him, at least. You can't stay here."

But I was paralyzed by the prospect of leaving her, of seeing my father's face, and most of all, of visiting my mother in jail.

"Claire," I said. "Listen to me."

"I'm not," she said.

"You're not what?"

"Coming. I'm not coming home."

"Ever?"

"I'm getting married. We're getting married."

I imagined Henry smoking at a window. Henry studying my

sister the way Tess was studying me. My sister whose mother was now a killer. Henry's pink face, Henry so full of second thoughts.

"Claire, listen."

"I have to get off the phone now, Joey. I'll ring you," she said and hung up.

Tess raised her eyebrows.

"She'll ring me," I said.

Tess smiled. "She's not coming?"

"No. She's getting married instead."

Tess shook her head. "You two."

I looked away.

"Step up, Joey. You're going to have to step up."

I nodded.

"Are we invited to the wedding?"

Tess undressed and got into bed with me.

"She didn't say. She didn't mention it."

Tess saw Claire as a coward and a traitor.

That was that for her.

But not for me.

There is comfort, cold as it may be, in knowing that my sister remains alive. In many ways, despite her disappearance, she is what I have left. After all this time I have refused to condemn her, and even then, I was incapable of any true anger.

I hated seeing her leave for college, and then for England, and then to learn that she was being swallowed into some moneyed world none of us knew a thing about, rising in class, up and away from me, from us.

All during that time I was watching my mother. Through the phone calls. Through the sentencing. Through the haze of those weeks. Tess coming and going from work, the newspapers, the television.

Through those days of the thickening tar, I watched my mother. I listened for her at night. I saw her in the air.

In those first days, I wanted Claire with me more than I wanted Tess. More than anything. I wanted my sister home. I wanted her back to explain our parents, to take care of me the way she had when we were young, when our secrets were too great for mothers and fathers.

23

Unlike many of her friends who'd returned home from college posing as young anarchists with blue hair and pierced nipples, my sister came carrying a handbag, wearing expensive black clothes. Her last Christmas home from NYU before moving to London. I would have been sixteen, and she twenty. There was something damning about her presence even then. I think my parents felt like country slobs around her, which I'm sure is exactly what she wanted. They would have had a much easier time if she'd blown all her money at CBGB, but the idea of her spending it on clothes and haircuts baffled them both. It particularly irked my mother.

The four of us sitting around the kitchen table eating take-out Chinese, my mother exhausted, just home in her blue scrubs, and Claire wearing heavy dark eyeliner, dressed as if she were on her way to some chic gallery opening.

All of us in front of the tree, Claire giving my father a blue silk tie he'd never wear, my mother a kit of makeup she'd never use.

One night before she went back to New York, she took me to dinner at a nice restaurant downtown where some older guy she knew worked as a waiter.

I'm sure my mother saw Claire as mannered and ridiculous, but she seemed so elegant and sophisticated to me. The way she flirted with her friend, and so effortlessly ordered us wine.

"Hold the glass by its stem, Joey," she said.

I tried to make fun of her. There had been a time when I could have quickly embarrassed and provoked my sister. But now I was powerless.

She smiled at me with the tolerance some adults have for the innocent.

She wanted to know what I would do, not after high school, but after college, with my life.

Of course, I had no idea and told her so.

"You'll get out of here, though, right? You won't hang around and become a carpenter."

"I guess," I said.

I was sixteen. What did I care? But she was adamant about me leaving.

"Listen," she said. "Don't get stuck, Joe. There's so much better."

I tried to make fun of her again. I said, "A few months in New York, and suddenly you hate your home."

But she didn't laugh. "I don't hate it. But also, it's not all of a sudden. Anyway, there's more out there to have, that's all. Remember that. You can go anywhere you want."

"Okay," I said. "But I like it here."

She smiled at me. "Well, you are the baby."

"Fuck off. What do you want to do? What great thing do you want to do?"

"I don't know yet," she said, "but it won't be here. I won't end up a fucking nurse."

We'd taken my mom's Volvo to dinner and when we pulled up to the house, Claire didn't get out of the car. She turned off the engine and the lights, rolled down her window and lit a cigarette.

"So, now you smoke?"

"You want one?" She held out her pack of Camels.

I shook my head.

"Good boy, Joey." She leaned over and kissed my cheek.

I turned away from her even though it made me so happy when she did that. We looked at the house and through the window we could see my parents standing in the kitchen, clearing the table.

24.

Out toward the eastern edge of the clearing, a small stand of cottonwoods has appeared. Or I've just now noticed it. The trees obscure my view and their fluff blows all over the house. It gets stuck in the screens, between the deck planks. I went out there with a bow saw and cut them to the ground and then went below it and took them out at the roots. It felt good to do it. To be working all day in the sun. Cutting those trees away. Keeping things in order.

But then as I was coming back home I found a wide patch of Scotch Broom, one of those invasive species we're supposed to kill on sight. Despite its cute little flowers, it's an aggressive little fucker and swallows everything in its path. I hear it can kill horses, too. Tess rolled her eyes when we found the flyer in our mailbox. I admit, it was a little hysterical. All those exclamation points, language as if the weed were Satan himself. Beware the curse of Scotch Broom scourge!!!!!

But I keep an eye out all the same. This is farm country and people don't fuck around with these things.

I took the machete from the garage and just before sunset, I hacked those invaders to death.

25.

They sent my mother down to White Pine, one hundred and fifty some-odd miles southwest of Seattle. September seventeenth she traveled. She accepted all of it without contest. Despite my father's best efforts, she insisted on a public defender, who took a plea bargain.

Twenty-five years to life.

"I did what I did," she told the judge. "I am no more insane now than I was that day."

Meanwhile I did nothing at all.

I still hadn't spoken to her. I waited and I watched the news. Local. National.

Piece by piece, my father sold his workshop. Then he put our house up for sale, got into his Wagoneer and drove.

"Joey," he said when he called to tell me, his voice full of tin, "I rented a little place. Not far from the beach. I wish you'd come up. It's where I live now. Where we both do. Me and your mother."

I was looking at Tess's chair.

"Joey?"

"Yeah, I'm here," I told him. "I'm here."

"Come up?"

"I will, Dad. I'm on my way," I said. "I'm nearly there."

"Winter's coming." He was half-drunk.

"It's only just fall."

"I can feel it in the mornings," he said.

I left Tess in front of the motel. She was alone in the parking lot watching me go. A bright day. Cool. We'd made promises, but the farther along that highway I drove, the more certain I was that I'd never see her again. She must have been relieved to be rid of me. It was too much. All that weight. All the joy gone. I'd stolen it. Me and my family.

If I were Tess? I'd have been thrilled to watch Joey March drive away. Thank God. Good fucking riddance to you and your crazy, murderous family and your fucking bird. Your *bird*. Who *cares*? Stand up and live. Enough with your whining and your moping and all your boring sadness and your exquisite sensitivity and your lunatic mother and your selfish sister and your pathetic father all alone in his prison-town dump. Good riddance, asshole. I'd have been dancing on the bar.

No matter what she saw in me, or what she said, how could she not have thought, *Good riddance?*

26.

And if she didn't then, she certainly has since. Days and days when I have been inert, pinned to the floor, unable to see. Days throughout our years, throughout our homes—Cannon Beach, White Pine, Seattle, and at last, here, in our house on the coast of our clearing. Days when all Tess wanted was to play, to go wandering our beaches, our woods.

"Please, Joe."

When she wanted to laugh, when she wanted to fuck, when she wanted to wrestle, when she wanted to sing. Get up and do something about it, whatever *it* is, whatever people do.

But all I've ever known to do was run until my heart pounded it from my veins, or talk to Tess.

Or, in my way, to Claire.

It's the only medicine I've ever wanted.

Tess said, "Please, Joe."

This is Seattle, years after moving there from White Pine. Years after abandoning our war, after we'd become adults, bar owners, earners. It is morning and I have woken up so heavy that I can feel it in my lips. From bed I watch Tess singing to herself, naked, packing her bag.

It has been difficult lately. We are working too hard. We've gone a little numb, lost so much of our former selves. And Tess wants to be away. Everything is arranged. We have a cabin on Whidbey Island for the weekend.

It has been a long time since I've seen her so light.

I want nothing more than to make her happy. I want nothing more than to leave with her, to stand and pick her up and spin her around.

But I cannot.

I will not do what she asks. I do not want the advice or medicine of others.

And when she sees my face, she closes her eyes and takes a long breath. I know the expression. She is out of patience. She is out of sympathy.

"Please, Joe," she says, beginning to cry.

But I cannot.

And this time she goes anyway. Without me.

As well she should.

So I left Tess in that Cannon Beach parking lot and drove on with the image of her in torn jeans and that black sweater she loved.

And I was sorry to have done it to her. I was sorry to have drawn her down into our ugly muck. I was ashamed. I felt I had done her some kind of violence. So I drove on faster and faster, racing out of town, up the highway north toward White Pine.

I thought, the best thing, the kindest thing I can do at this moment in my life is to release Tess, free her of it all.

As if she were mine to release.

Whatever it did to my heart. No matter how that distance frightened me. I drove and I drove and I kept an eye on the mirror, on that unraveling spool of highway, that black path which ran from her big bare feet to the back wheels of my truck.

Against all instinct I never turned back.

Anyway, we weren't sentimental people.

There was only the future. For better or for worse. The past was dead. Sink or swim.

"Forward, Joey Boy, forward," she said. Calling to me from her prison cell.

"Toward the future, Joey, Joey, Joe, drive toward the future," she whispered.

Over the engine noise, my mother sang me all the way to White Pine.

It is a town tucked away twenty-five miles west of the 101 in a pocket of land where the highway breaks inland from the ocean. A protected cove, a natural harbor. Moored fishing boats, seafood restaurants. An aging wooden promenade. The Chowder Hound. Nick's Knacks selling postcards and disposable cameras. Wind chimes made of driftwood and oyster shells, spoons and sea glass. Carl's Clam Shack the only restaurant still open by the time I come to town red-eyed, miserable and starving.

In the afternoon sun, I sit at one of the red-varnished picnic benches and eat fried clams from a red plastic basket. It's the first thing I do. Drive into White Pine and have a late lunch while the gulls call and circle, their yellow eyes on my food.

My parents are in this town. I try to believe that. My father in his house. My mother in her cell. But it's a difficult thing to understand.

Somewhere here is a prison, and within it lives my mother. It seems impossible. As impossible as our house in Seattle emptied of all our things and a realtor sign stabbed in the front lawn. Or Claire refusing to come home, Claire marrying that pink-faced man in London.

Or Tess gone.

Or me gone from her.

Or my mother a killer.

I sit in the sun pushing the empty basket around the table trying to settle it all somehow.

I think of Tess. I wish for her. It does only harm. Still, I can't help myself wishing. And it's Tess that makes me saddest. Terrible as that sounds.

It takes all I have, but I stand up and I return to the truck and I go in search of my father.

The house is better than I expect. White with grey shutters on a street twelve blocks in from the beach. There's a picket fence and a short cement walkway to a red door. The front yard is scruffy and mostly dirt with a hardened pile of soil in one corner, a shovel stuck into it. This is not my father's abandoned project, I know. He doesn't leave things unfinished, wouldn't let soil go to waste. Would never leave a tool out to rust.

The paint is peeling on the door and on the pickets, but nothing serious, nothing he can't take care of. The Wagoneer is in the driveway and I'm parked in the street. It's a stranger's house, but it's not so bad. I expected maybe an apartment in one of those concrete and stucco blocks built around a half-drained swimming pool with some cheerful name painted next to the address—The Seaview, The Ocean Mist, The Dolphin Court. The kind of thing you see all over LA. I didn't want to find him in one of those places—bent over a hot plate, mattress on the floor, a folding chair at a card table. I'm relieved, but for too long I can't get out of the truck.

And when I do, pulling the handle, I can feel it start. This new life. What it means. The beginning of something else. I know that walking up the path and knocking on his red door is the next thing.

Behind it I'll see my father's eyes.

I'll find my mother in her cell.

I knocked and then there he was—tall and gaunt and brown eyes flat. He'd started to grow a beard again. The sandy scruff and blond hair falling around his face made him look pale and washed out.

"Joey," he said, his voice so full of relief I didn't know what to do but hug him.

He kept his arm around my shoulder as he gave me a tour. His bedroom, his bathroom. My bedroom, my bathroom. A kitchen that opened to a living room. TV on a stand, tinfoil antenna, a bookcase full of paperbacks. A couch, easy chair, coffee table, fireplace.

"I rented it furnished," he said.

"I can see that."

"Sorry about the single bed."

"It's great. You got lucky."

"*We* did," he said. "We did. Sit down."

I dropped into the chair. An overstuffed thing, soft and worn, covered in brown corduroy. I watched him in the kitchen opening beers, shaking chips from a bag into a bowl. His posture was weaker. He moved slowly, everything delayed. He seemed to forget what he'd set out to do. He came back and put it all on the table and sat on the couch.

"To you," he said with the clink of the bottles. "To my son."

I told him about driving up the coast. I told him about meeting Tess, how I saw her across a crowded bar, the way I swallowed my fear and went to her.

I made it simple. I made it clean. I didn't tell him that there had been no fear to swallow. I scrubbed it of the madness and ecstasy. I told him about bartending and living in the motel. About walking along the beach, about Paul the dog. I told him about the bonfires, and the house and Tess's friends. I gave him a summer without complication, a summer of independence and falling in love.

"Joey," he said. "What a time you had. It makes me happy to think of you there, doing all those things. Above all, in love. I'm sorry to make you leave it."

"You didn't make me leave it. Everyone was going home anyway. It was getting cold."

We talked around it and around it.

"Tell me about Tess," he said. "What's she like?" He was watching me with just the start of a smile on his face. His lips together, his eyes bright again. "When do we get to meet her?"

We.

I picked at the label.

He looked away. "Of course, she's welcome here."

"Thanks."

He shook his head, got up and walked into the dark kitchen. He was a ghost in that light. "I'm sorry, Joey."

"There's nothing to be sorry for, Dad."

"No?" He said it to the refrigerator shelves.

"What do you have to be sorry for?"

He came to the counter that separated the kitchen from the living room. He had a beer in each fist.

I knew he didn't understand. It was pure, incomprehensible mystery.

But I did. The shock I felt was brief. Like being punched in the head by a known enemy. Shock but no real surprise. No confusion. It was something like that. But my father, well, no layer of his being saw it coming. Not a molecule. Like being hit by a truck. One day you're walking down the street. One day, out of thin air, the phone rings.

I think it's what I understood that first night, in some stranger's corduroy chair, watching him in the kitchen. He was blind in his way. There were elements of himself he could not access. Or no. That's not right. Those elements were simply absent altogether. This, his great fortune. He was absent something his wife had in stores. Stores she shared with her son. My inheritance of fog. And my father in his new kitchen, his face turned to me, he had none of it.

I saw that then.

So I did not hurl my bottle through the front window.

Instead, I tried to subtract the acid from my voice, and I asked again, "What do you have to be sorry for?"

He came out to the couch, put our fresh beers on the coffee table and sat down. He leaned forward as if about to speak, but then said nothing. He looked just like a boy then, slumped against the cushions, deflated, frustrated.

"There's nothing to be sorry for," I told him.

"What's your plan?" He'd taken on the old voice again. Fatherly. Serious.

"I don't have a plan. I just got here."

"Well, maybe you *should* have one," he said.

I stared at him.

"I'm sorry."

Both of us waited.

"Have you been out there? Dad, have you seen her?"

He nodded.

The house was so quiet. I couldn't look at him any longer.

I shut my eyes and found Tess, and the motel bed. Her cool hand on my calf. The black highway. The Clam Shack, the red baskets, my father's ghost in the kitchen. And across the expanse of the coffee table, I could hear his breathing. My diminished father breathing as the two of us waited in the night.

Soon he will go out to the truck, collect my things and deliver them to my new room. He'll move quietly as I fade in and out of sleep. He will turn on a lamp and light a fire. I will fall deeper. I will dream. Some of this I will know by the sound, by the smell. Some I will only know later, when I find my clothes folded and stacked in the yellow dresser, my shoes neatly arranged on the floor of the closet, my jacket on a hook. Some I know in recollection, which is perhaps not to know at all.

But all of it happened.

In one way or another, it all happened: me, my mother,

Dustin Strauss, Tess, Claire, the small fire, the smell of smoke, that soft chair, my father taking so much care to be quiet, to put my clothes away, to keep me warm.

29

That first morning in my father's new house, I lay in bed and remembered him teaching me to swim. First waking after having slept deeply, then opening my eyes to an unfamiliar ceiling, and its coastline crack curving from wall to wall. Waking to that memory—the two of us in a public pool.

The hot concrete deck beneath my feet, the soft water, the lifeguards in their black sunglasses and red trunks, twirling their whistles, towering above me, my father's hand, my arms around his neck, skin that smelled so much of him and was so warm, us two descending, hanging on tight as he walked us step by step toward the menacing deep end, where the older boys dove for weighted rings, where he swung me around to his back and said, "Hang on, engine starting," as his feet came up and him breaststroking while I sputtered speedboat sounds, until we made it back to the shallows where I pretended to keep my eyes closed calling "Marco" and him gliding away saying "Polo" on and on until he let me catch him and climb his shoulders and crash into the water again.

I am walking alone to the concession stand, knowing he is watching me, pretending not to be afraid, standing on my toes now, reaching up to exchange the damp dollar bills for an ice cream sandwich and then returning, slaloming through the chairs, between towels, giddy for the achievement, and my father smiling at me as I walk-don't-run, walk-don't-run as quickly as I can. The folded paper, the Carnation rose, hospital corners, the delicate task of removing the wrapper without leaving any of it stuck to the cookies, the taste of it, the texture and always preferring the sandwich deep-frozen and stale.

The warmth of the towel around my shoulders as I fall asleep watching him read *Sports Illustrated*, wishing I had one more ice cream, knowing it would not be allowed.

This is what I woke to that morning in my father's new house, and because of the memory, when I came into the kitchen and found him at the stove frying eggs, I kissed the back of his head. He turned and smiled at me with such gratitude.

It wasn't our way. My kissing him like that, as if I were the caretaker, such a protective, paternal act. I don't know why I did it, but when he smiled I began to understand something that only years later would I be able to articulate.

Later while he was in the shower, I sat on the front step with a cup of coffee.

Now I lived in White Pine with my father, who had given up so much to live as close as he could to my mother, who had one day, with a hammer, without apparent warning, beaten a man to death.

My sister was in London.

Tess was in Cannon Beach.

I considered each of these things. I was not happy, but I was calm.

There was no circling bird. I was not burning with life. I was not pinned to the bed.

I was even. My brain had slowed to a gentle pace. I found a brief peace in the sun, on the front step. And while it lasted, in those hours, I tried as best I could to work out a plan.

I would see my mother. I would call Tess. I would take care of my father. I would find a job.

He sat next to me. He smelled of soap and, as always, of Royall Lyme, a bottle of which his first girlfriend had given him before he left for Vietnam.

"What do you do all day?" I asked him.

"I work on the house. I read. Go into town. I've been look-ing for a job."

I nodded.

"And I visit Mom."

"Every day?"

"Often as they let me," he said.

We sat for a while, neither of us talking.

"I think I'll come with you then."

He put his arm around my shoulder. "Sure," he said. "All right. If that's what you want to do."

30

Even today I hear sounds only my mother and those children would have heard.

And, maybe, at first, Strauss himself.

Two metallic clicks of the buckles.

Her shoes on the asphalt.

The solid steel making contact with Dustin Strauss's skull.

I have done experiments with bone. I have tapped a hammer against the back of my head.

I have tried to know.

I have been hearing these sounds now for nearly twenty years. Metal breaking bone. Metal moving through brain, the two textures. Hard and soft, a solid noise, a sucking noise. And those two children, four feet moving with my mother's two. The back door opening. The slight give of the brown fabric beneath them, side by side. Scrape and click, scrape and click of the two seat belts. Male into female. Male into female. The solid slam of my mother's door. Then the three of them waiting inside the sealed station wagon. Waiting while Mrs. Strauss cried over the body of her dead husband.

After all these years, it is the sound that never recedes. The images fluctuate in clarity, but the sound only becomes louder.

When I first arrived in White Pine, I did not ask questions. I did not read the papers. I did not watch the news. I didn't know the man's profession, or the names of his children. I had not yet seen the pictures. Not of my mother's mug shot. Not of her hospital ID. Not of laughing Dustin Strauss, arm around his wife, grinning children by their sides. Not of my father on a bench at the courthouse hanging his head. Nothing in those early days had been filled in, so that morning with my father, I possessed only what I had manufactured. I was lonely and terrified, but I was not yet haunted by those photographs, that videotape.

Tess though, she had seen all of it. I know that now. All of it. While I was lying blank in the motel room, she was out there reading about my mother and her crime. She came back to me each evening after work carrying all that information, all those images—victim, crime scene, father, mother, sister, me. The image of that bloodied hammer resting on the ground. For weeks she carried those images, those words—*brutal* and *horrific* and *senseless* and all the rest. And still she slid into our bed without hesitation, without fear, still she held me as we slept.

Imagine this young woman, twenty years old, coming home and not saying a word. Having seen the photographs of my mother's cold eyes, the way the papers added their dramatic shadows and sharp contrasts. Their cruel shading, doctoring the life from her face.

Still Tess came home to me. Even after all that, even after what I'd told her about the bird and the goddamned tar? After breaking my hand? After all the *I could die of you* nonsense?

Me, back then? I'd have run. Not a second thought.

31.

So for a long while I was numb in my oblivion, but abruptly, as my father started the truck, I was frightened. We drove east up Water Street to the top of the hill, which separated the valley from the ocean, and then north along Bay View, which everyone called the Spine. We followed that ridge road, with the town down to our left and the wide green valley to our right.

"There," he said after a while and pointed.

Nestled far away at the base of a steep yellowing hill was the prison. It could have been a factory or an electrical plant.

We began to descend toward it. Now I could see the walls, the fine lines of barbed wire, the guard towers at each corner. I made him pull over. I got out, walked into a sloping onion field and vomited. When I returned to the Wagoneer, I found my father sitting on the hood. I climbed up next to him and he handed me a gallon jug of water.

"They never turn them off," he said.

"What?"

"See the lights? Hard to tell in the day, but they never turn them off."

It was true. If you looked carefully, you could see that faint orange burn at the end of each post.

"At night it looks like a spaceship."

I glanced at the side of his face.

"And when the fog comes in, it all glows."

"You come here at night?"

He nodded. "She knows."

"What do you mean?"

"I've told her."

"She likes that? Knowing you're up here?"

He shrugged. "She doesn't talk much."

I see him there all those nights, boots on the front bumper, red Thermos at his side. Wearing his old Levis jacket, faded denim with the fake shearling lining, sitting in the cold, watching the prison, watching my mother, trying his best to look after her, to keep her company.

"Doesn't do much good," he said. "But it's something."

Soon we were down on the valley floor, on the prison road, and then pulling to a stop. It struck me as so odd that there would be a parking lot the same way you'd have one at a supermarket. Somehow it hadn't occurred to me that people came and went, that there were employees, that people came to work in the morning, and left at the end of the day. I'd never thought about it. Until then, prison had never been more than one awful thing—a foreign and far-off place of cruelty and terror.

I was frightened by the prospect of seeing my mother. By those doors and the light and the din of the place. The general, suffocating horror of it. It took a long time to get through, even though they all knew my father by then, there was still the signing in, the patting down, the processing, before we even got to the visit room with its yellow walls and fluorescent lights, the tables bolted to the floor and the bored guards giving the deadeye to everything that moved.

I'd imagined it packed with visitors, but not many people were there that day. We sat at the table my dad liked and we waited. Side by side, our hands on the blue fiberglass table, neither of us speaking, both of us facing the closed door, which was double-wide and painted the same sickly yellow as the walls.

And then there was my mother.

I was prepared for a wretched version of her. A woman wild-eyed and drawn, bruised, scarred, bloodied. But most shocking was how much she looked like my mother. How familiar she was. How much the same. She hadn't lost so much weight. She was still tall. Her hair the same black, her eyes the same blue.

There she stood before me. She was alive and she was whole. She wrapped her arms around me and whispered, "I love you," on and on and on while I cried like a child.

We all sat down and she leaned forward and laid her arms across the table. This is all that remains of our first visit. Us three, our hands joined.

Maybe we spoke, but I don't think so. They took her away. There's the sound of the door buzzing open and the sound of it closing.

Then my father and I were in the truck climbing out of the valley, moving across the ridge, while below in the darkening evening, the prison glowed, yes, just like a spaceship.

32

My dad took me to Lester's, a pizza place up the hill and well removed from the fading charm of the waterfront. Sawdust on the floors. Wooden booths. A jukebox. Two coin-operated pool tables. A long bar facing the front door, the requisite Bud mirrors and neon Pabst signs. It was one of those good places. Worn without being dirty. Something about the proportions, the lighting, the height of the stools. It's that golden combination. Certain bars have it, others don't. All the wood helped. That's one thing, so little plastic in that place.

We came in happy to be there and we took a booth we'd later claim as our own. The two of us turned a little sideways, watching the room, a pitcher of Olympia between us, the pizza in its metal pan landing on the table. Pepperoni, mushroom, onion, always. The two of us eating with such pleasure. The slice-shaped spatula. The indestructible white ceramic plates. Chili flake shaker.

"Good place," he said, so pleased to have me there, to show me this element of his new life.

"You come here a lot?"

He nodded.

"You know anybody?"

He shrugged. "Few familiar faces. Some of the waitresses. Bartenders. But no, not really."

"Takes a while, I guess."

He leaned back from the table.

"I don't like them much."

I looked over at him. "Why not?"

"This place? It's the prison here. Most of these people are guards."

He nodded at a table across from ours. A few burly guys. Some sturdy women.

"So what?"

He leaned toward me. "These fuckers have your mother in there, Joe. These are the people opening and closing her cell. They're the ones with the keys, the ones dragging her away every time I go to visit."

"So what are you doing here all the time? What are we doing here now?"

"You saw the papers, Joe. What they wrote about her."

"No," I said. "I didn't."

He looked at me for a long second. "No?"

I shook my head.

"There wasn't a lot of sympathy. Let's put it that way. Not a lot of sympathy."

"So what, you think there *should* have been?" I couldn't contain it. My adolescent tone. My generic contempt for him, for the bar, for the town.

"Hey, hey. Look at me. I've been there every minute from the beginning. I went to that jail. I slept on a bench. I went to the courthouse. Every single day. I sold all we owned to be here. I've given up everything to do this, while you and Claire did nothing. So don't give me that bullshit. Don't bore me with your bullshit. Every day I've been there. Meanwhile you and your sister? Who the hell knows where you were."

"I'm sorry," I said after a long time.

"Look at me," he said.

I did.

"I don't need you to be sorry. Just be an adult, okay?"

I nodded.

"They know who I am, Joey. You understand? I see the same guards here as I see there. And pretty soon they'll know who you are, too."

"So why come here then?"

He turned away from me.

"I want them to know. I want them to *know*, Joey. You understand?"

"No."

He sighed. I'd never seen such impatience and frustration in my father. I hated it as much as I hated my own insolence, that piercing sense of irritation.

"Look," he said, "These are the people who have your mother. They've got her in there, Joey. What do we know about what they're doing to her? Nothing. Are they beating her? Starving her? Is it worse? Half these guards are men. They think she's a goddamn animal."

"She was protecting those kids."

"One crack with the hammer, sure. But not seven, Joe. Seven changed everything. Seven, seven, seven, seven, that's all they talked about."

"They called her an animal?"

"Joey, listen to me. I'm here to protect her. Do you understand that? I want them to know I'm *around,* you see?"

There was no reason to it, no logic. I didn't like his desperation. None of it was like him.

"So I keep going out to the prison. And I keep coming back here. It's the only thing I can do. Force them to see me. Force them to look. Show them what else we are."

"I'm sorry," I said again.

"Sorry isn't the point. Just think, okay? Look around. I wish it hadn't, but the world's changed."

"I'm sorry I didn't come sooner. That's what I mean. I'm sorry you were all alone."

"It was better that way. Saved you some pain. The thing is,

you're here now. And I'll tell you, kiddo, goddamn am I happy about that."

He reached across the table and squeezed my shoulder. "I'm happy to have my son here. It makes me so happy to have my son here."

We were both a little drunk by then.

"You make me strong, Joe."

We listened to the jukebox for a while. I wanted to be strong too, but I wasn't sure what that would mean. Or how either of us could protect her. Or what good we could do for her or for anyone else.

That night in bed, on my back, listening to the sounds of the house, I tried not to imagine what might happen to my mother inside that place, or the things people do to each other.

33

I found a job pouring drinks at The Owl, a college bar down by the water. One of their guys had quit the day before I walked in, and they hired me on the spot. Three prime shifts a week—Thursday, Friday, and Saturday nights plus lunch on Wednesday.

What fortune I had in White Pine.

I was able to help with the rent, with the expenses, but there wasn't much left after that. Until the house sold, my father didn't have any money. And even afterwards, with the loss he took, and all the debt he carried, and my mother's income gone, things were tough.

Anyway, like that, I had a routine. Sunday through Tuesday nothing to do but work on the house, and go out to the prison. The rest of the time, I poured drinks.

All of it happened so easily. Moving. Finding work. I don't know why it always took me so long to fully understand that my life had changed.

One night in those early days, I came home from the bar, pulled the truck up to the house, turned off the lights and killed the engine. It was as if I'd never done anything else, or lived any other way.

Now I live here with my father. I am a bartender and my mother is in prison.

That was that. Nothing would ever change again. Now *this* world was immoveable, irrevocable. There was no future. I didn't know what else to do, but go to work, and wonder about Tess, and eat pizza with my dad out at Lester's and make believe we were protecting my mother.

Once I'd handled all the establishing details, those minor challenges—settling into a room, finding work, learning the streets—what then? All my life, there had been so much movement—one grade to another grade, one milestone after another milestone, and then the road north, and Tess and all our plans, and the two of us looking forward to a vague and expanding life composed entirely of romantic images. In that future we were always moving forward, passing through pretty villages, sunlight in our beer glasses, making love on beaches, racing in quiet trains through one countryside after another. In those days, nothing stopped, not the present, not the future. There would be no end to movement. Everything in our life aside from love would be external.

And then there in my silent truck out in the early morning dark, I believed I was watching all of it come to a stop.

How could I ask Tess to live in that town, under those conditions? Why would she want to come and live with two sad men in a prison town? What would she want of our fractured family? So again I convinced myself that the kindest thing, the best way to love her was to leave her alone. And so I did.

34.

I went to the prison with my father as often as I could and it was nearly always the same. It felt more like prayer than anything else. She didn't say much more than our names. Just smiled and stroked the tops of our hands with her thumbs. At first I was relieved by the absence of speech, but slowly it began to frustrate me. So on a Monday morning, I went alone. My father didn't argue, though I saw he was worried by it. He didn't like the idea of breaking routine, of giving up our new ritual.

I went anyway. Drove the Spine. Descended into the valley and parked my truck in the lot. I sat at the table, and waited for her. Soon they brought her out.

"You've come alone to visit the big bad witch of the west."

I nodded.

"Joey. Always the brave one weren't you."

"No," I said.

"Where's Dad?"

"Home."

The theater had ended. I saw it go out of her face. I watched her as if I were watching myself. And then I was certain we shared the tar.

"Are you all right in here?"

"Of course," she said.

"I'm not sure it's so obvious. You realize where you are, right? It's not some resort."

She removed her hand from mine, but was otherwise very still. She held my eyes, until I looked away.

"I do, Joseph, know where I am. Yes."

"I'm sorry," I said.

Her capacity for sudden cold formality had always frightened me as a child. The flipped switch when I was sarcastic with her, or whined, or, worst of all, had been cruel to someone weak.

Here it became something else, something worse. Trailing behind that anger, that quick shift, was now a history of violence. I could not ignore what she was capable of. I could not prevent myself from seeing her hammer.

"I'm sorry," I said again. "I just want to make sure you're all right. That they're treating you well."

"You said it yourself. Not a resort."

"No," I said.

"No."

"Mom. I'm here. Not for a little while. I'm here. I live here. I have a job."

"Why's that, Joey? Why would you do that? You can go anywhere in the world. Why would you stay here?"

I looked at her carefully. I was searching for something beyond the language.

"Why am I here?"

She leaned back and crossed her arms over her chest.

"Yes. Tell me," she said.

"For you. The same reason Dad is here."

"But your father is my husband."

"Yes. I understand that."

I knew she didn't like the sarcasm, but I couldn't help myself. It seemed my only defense. I was angry. I was terrified. I was young.

"Well, then, you also understand he has responsibilities that you do not."

I matched her posture. I wondered whether it was true. Whether my father had a responsibility to be here. Whether any of us did.

"For better or for worse. Death do us part, Joseph. Mine or his."

I'd begun to feel sick.

"You, on the other hand, may do as you like. Go where you wish. Look at your sister. Claire remains unchanged, it seems. So, what good is it for you to be here?"

"Dad says we can protect you."

She laughed and leaned forward and reached for my hands. "Listen, you have to go on, Joey."

Her skin was cool and dry.

Toward the future, I thought.

She gave a weak smile, and nodded. "Yes, Joey Boy. Yes."

The time was up then. The guards came for her. She hugged me and disappeared behind the closing door.

I met my dad at Lester's. He was at our booth with a pitcher and two glasses, back to the wall, rubbing his beard with one hand, caught in some thought, some worry.

"How'd it go?" He glanced up at me as he poured my beer.

I shook my head.

"She doesn't talk much," he said.

"She talked."

He looked hopeful. "Yeah? What'd she say?"

"She told me I could do anything I wanted with my life. She wanted to know what I was doing here, why I'd ever want to live in White Pine. She said you're different. You're her husband. 'Death do us part,' she said. 'For better or for worse.'"

He looked at me hard. And then nodded, conceding the point. "Yeah. Well, that's true. It really isn't the same. She's right, Joey. You know, you *don't* need to be here. Not the way I do. But I'll tell you, I'm *glad* you're here. Go anytime, but I'm happy you're here. I wouldn't want you to leave. I'd miss you. You're the only thing . . . but that's not the point, really. *She'd* miss you. She wants you here too."

"I don't think so."

God, I can see him there before me slowly becoming a child. Those eyes. That panic. As if the only thing worse than my mother murdering Dustin Strauss would be me packing up and leaving town.

"I don't think she cares. She made it clear. I don't think she cares. Actually I think she wants me to go. That's the feeling I get."

"I don't believe that," he said.

I shrugged.

"Well, it's not forever. It's not as if you're planning on staying forever." He turned away from me and brought his boots onto the bench.

A big table of guards was starting to fill up.

"How long is it, Dad?"

"As long as you want it to be. You can always leave."

"For you, I mean. How long are you going to stay?"

"Oh. Well, forever, Joey. I'll be here forever."

A wave of his hand. That was that. Life was life. Where else would he go?

"And you, Joey? What do you think? Hang around a while?"

35

Father was determined to find a job that might provide him health insurance, but after a while he gave up on that. He'd been called in for an interview at the college, and then at the hospital. Nothing came of either. Both were for janitorial jobs and they'd have made him miserable, but even still, those successive blows took their toll.

He went on about health insurance and I thought maybe he was suffering from some disease, something rotting him out from the inside. But he was healthy as anything—lean and muscular and solid. He wasn't a smoker. He ate pretty well. Kept weights and a bench on the little patio out back. He liked his walks. Maybe he drank too much, but who could blame him?

"It was just the idea," he said. "Some security. Your mother and I have always had it. It was a point of pride. We swore we'd always have a home, enough food, and health insurance. These were the things we'd never give up. Whatever it took. But now we're in the wind," he said. "At least your mother the killer is covered inside. But not us. This fucking country."

After a while he gave up on the idea and took a job at Arbus Lumber and Feed where he worked their yard, hauling wood and cutting planks to size.

In my memory, those first months are often distinguished and delineated by his minor dreams—health insurance, a garden, the protection of my mother, the possibility of her softening, of Claire returning. And then he became focused on Tess.

In the evenings we were both home he would ask about her. Over dinner, or sitting in front of the fire drinking beer I would tell him what I could. At first I was a begrudging reporter. She grew up in San Francisco. She was an only child. Green eyes, brown hair. Her mother died of breast cancer. Her father remarried quickly. He has two young children now.

I thought I'd appease him, and then after a while he'd leave me alone to forget her. But he wanted to make that impossible. For my father and me she was a symbol of hope, I guess. As if her presence might provide answers to the problems of our lives.

"Tell me about Tess," he'd say, but what he meant was, bring her here. He meant that she was the only thing that could save us. Not just me, but both of us. Bring her here, this woman I barely knew. This woman with whom I'd fallen so in love, who terrified me as much as my mother did, as much as the prison, as much as my awful new life, as much as the tar.

In those days I was constantly afraid. Of the specific and the general, the known and unknown.

I wouldn't want to return to that time, but I miss its sense of danger, of fragility. And I miss the fear as well.

After seeing my mother, I'd always leave exhausted and shaken. The sharp looks of the guards. The proximity to other prisoners. The awful sounds of those locks and doors. My mother herself. But I went anyway.

"I hear there's a girl," she said, though she knew full well there was. She'd twice spoken to Tess on the phone while we were in Cannon Beach.

"There was."

"Was?"

"Yes."

"You're not together anymore?"

"No. I came here. So, no."

"Well that was stupid," she said. "Why would you do that? Didn't you love her? I hear you did. I hear you do."

This was something new in her. The berating. The distance.

"Joey," she said, warmer now. "Don't do that. Don't walk away."

"Do you realize why I'm here? Why I left?"

"Yes, yes, yes, I know. You've said. For me, for me, you're here for me. But we've been over this. Why? Why would you leave the woman you love to be here with your mother? Why would you do that?"

I shook my head.

"You want me to be grateful? You want me to thank you for your loyalty? Would you be here if I weren't in prison?"

"No."

"No. No, you would not be. But because I am, you are. Because I'm here, you give up your life? Because I did this one thing? Because of a few minutes in a parking lot? Does that seem like a good idea?"

No, I thought. No, it does not.

"Joey," she said and took my hands. "You can't protect me. Go live. Go be with her."

I was so angry.

"What's her name? Tell me her name."

"Tess."

"Tell me about her."

"No," I said.

She smiled and leaned back, drawing her hands away.

"Okay. Either way, you need to answer that question. What are you doing here without this girl you love?"

I stood up and left and got into my truck and tore out of there.

The questions were only part of the problem. What disturbed me as I drove home that afternoon was her aspect, her detachment, the loveless way she looked at me not as her son, but as her patient, her subject.

Something had gone missing and that absence scared me

more than the prison, more than anything else. And so along with my sense (however misplaced, however wrongheaded) of duty, I suppose that's also why I stayed—the belief that somehow I might return this missing element to my mother. In being there, visiting her week after week, I might bring her some peace, give her back some warmth, staunch the flow of hot blood.

She seemed to be dying in there, all the softness vanishing and, reasonable or not, I wouldn't leave until I could change that.

Then I'd go.

Then I'd get on with my life.

I miss those days of fear and violence, days when love and desire always won out over reason.

36.

In White Pine in October it began to rain. Massive storms barreling in off the ocean. Weeks and weeks of wet sunless days. The wind blew straight onshore. Days it was difficult to distinguish between ocean and land.

Lodgepole pines forever gnarled and bent, defending their forests. The sun breaking through here and there, briefly returning color to the world. Great hunks of basalt standing guard, shifting with the sun from shining black to grey and back.

When the storms were particularly vicious we drove down to the beach and parked in the empty lot to watch them come. My dad with his red Thermos full of strong coffee, the pounding waves, a mix of salt and fresh water beating against the truck. The smell of Royall Lyme and coffee in the cab, the sound of the storm, the Wagoneer shuddering in time with the wind.

My father and I then were bound to each other the way we might have been had she died, had she been lying sick in a hospital bed. It was, at first anyway, an obligatory camaraderie. So it seemed to me.

Claire clearly felt no such obligation. Had my mother been dying of cancer, my sister would have been home. But not for this. This she took as an opportunity to remove herself from us. To excise us from her. Which she'd begun to do well before my mother had her little adventure with the hammer. Already in London. Already engaged. Already affecting her silly accent.

And here was an opportunity at long last, justification for a final severance.

Am I being uncharitable in suspecting that my sister was in some way relieved to discover my mother a maniac killer? To learn that she would be locked away for what would likely be the rest of her life? Certainly there are kinder ways to see Claire's behavior—she was in shock, could not accept what had happened, could find no way to reconcile mother and crime. Whatever her reasons, I don't begrudge her those choices. We are all looking for a chance to run. One might even see my mother's hammering Dustin Strauss to death in the same light. Here's a chance to escape. It didn't land her on a Mexican beach with a sack of cash, but she sure as hell got out.

So Claire dissolved into her new life. None of us was invited to her wedding. Claire March became Claire Lloyd and we never heard from her again. It is as simple as that. Her disappearance, her refusing to return my phone calls, drove me to feel an immediate loyalty to my father, and then, in turn, to my mother. It was no longer a responsibility that would be shared. It fell upon me to take care of our family, and I began to believe I was right to have come to White Pine. At least I had some rational reason for being where I was. If not me, who?

Those early days came to provide a vague sense of purpose. A slow incremental formation of an idea, the building of some kind of belief system. All the silent meals with my father in that little house with the fire going. Those afternoons the two of us sat in the cab watching the storms come. The red Thermos full of coffee. Him drinking from the cap, me from the chipped red Peanuts mug he kept in the glove box, the handle snapped off.

I believe now that here began my desire for a systematic life very far away. Some way to escape the disintegrating present. Whatever order I could muster would be an antidote to the all that madness. Internal and external, both.

But the result of too much order, I would come to find so much later, is a deadened mind, an insipid heart.

Just as with the medication they tell you to take.

But back then, and for so long after, I saw my only hope for happiness within a martial structure.

And anyway, happiness was irrelevant. My duty, I was certain, was to protect my parents, to be there in White Pine instead of flying across Galicia on a train with Tess.

This morning, Sunday, I dressed and went to town and had bacon and waffles at the diner. It's a nice walk along a country road, though you've got to be careful. There's not much of a shoulder and the logging trucks are speeding buildings driven by lunatics.

When we were kids, for a while Claire and I played a game she invented. She couldn't have been older than eleven.

She put me in her closet.

Her clothes fall around me. They brush against my cheeks and gather in folds across my shoulders. Soft dresses, a ratty green robe. I watch for her shadow to break the line of white light at my feet. Smell of laundry detergent, strawberry Bubble Yum and a sachet of my mother's cinnamon potpourri. In my throat I am making the growling noise of an eighteen-wheeler. From full throttle to downshift. The braking whine, the stuttering stop, which always makes her giggle.

I push the door open.

I roll down the window.

There's Claire, with her thumb out, wearing the giant sombrero my parents brought back from Tijuana.

I say, "Where to, ma'am?"

I've got my Mariners hat on low over my eyes the way she says a real trucker does.

"Where you headed?" Claire shields her eyes from the sun and gives me a wary look.

"Other side of the country."

"You're not some nut, are you?"

"No, ma'am," I say.

Then she's in the cab with me, the door closed, and we're sitting on the floor, while she goes on and on about what's out the window and where we're headed and all we'll do when we get there.

Do you remember that, Claire? You called it Hitch-a-Ride.

Sitting with our eyes closed, in the dark together, you going on and on, I saw everything you told me to see.

Tess and I liked Sunday mornings in town. We'd have breakfast and then do some shopping. I've tried to keep up that tradition, though needless to say, it's not as much fun. I'll smile and make small talk when it's necessary, but I try not to.

Tess draws people to her. No matter the room, she is always the center of energy. Hers is a beauty made of intelligence, of confidence and ease. Also, she's interested in other people. Truth be told, I rarely am. Unless I'm on the upswing, I get bored and irritated. Tess always wants to know how you are.

I loved to watch her talk to people, to watch them respond. Especially those we hardly knew. All the people in town, the farmers, the cashier at the diner, kids on their bikes. As long as I didn't have to talk much, I was happy to stand there all day. She was magical like that. No one was immune.

It's different now that I come in alone. The conversations are shorter and when they ask about Tess I tell them she's gone away for a while. It's the truest statement I can make. Well, perhaps it would be truer to say that she's gone away. But I don't have the heart for that. I can't help myself. I add a minor tag of hope.

Anyway, today I came in and ate my breakfast and read the paper—a thin, and very bad regional rag, but it's enough. It reduces the world to a few pages. It's all I want now. And sometimes, I don't want that. I've long given up, I'm afraid, trying to know everything, maintaining a constant state of outrage and fury. I'm embarrassed to admit that I've turned away.

We've lost a battle I was once so sure we might win.

After the diner I stopped by the farmers' market and bought a couple of steaks, a bag of red onions, a few heads of lettuce.

The woman selling pears and goat cheese was there. Often she's with an older man I take to be her father, but today she was alone. She had her hair piled on her head, a few black twists falling against her pale neck. I bought some pears and a small round of cheese.

She smiled at me in a way she wouldn't have if Tess had been there. It wasn't much, but I did like that quick chemical flash.

Here is something, I thought. Some possibility, some local promise. Perhaps I am not entirely doomed.

My father's truck amidst a terrible storm. A peculiar pressure in the air. Rain buffeting the back window.

He's pouring his coffee into our cups, the smell of it in the closed cab. The Thermos screwed closed and laid between us.

"Do you have an answer to her question?" He is scratching his beard. "What *are* you doing here without Tess?"

I'd not been back to see my mother. I was gathering courage, or preparing an answer, or trying to put language to this strange thing I was building.

"I don't know," I said.

"Well, whatever the answer, we can't stop visiting her because she's cruel from time to time."

"No?"

"Otherwise, why are we here? Otherwise, what's the point?"

I shrug.

"That's what she's asking you, Joey. That's what she's asking us both."

"And you have an answer?"

"I told you. I'm here to protect her. I'm here to love her."

"Till death do you part."

I can feel his eyes on me. "I'm sorry. I'm sorry," I say. Why can't I help myself?

"Doesn't matter, Joey, but that's right. Till death do us part."

I nod and sip my coffee and watch the waves march in one after the other and I think of Tess. I stare straight ahead and imagine her fingers tapping at the glass.

On cue, my father asks again, "You call Tess?"

He can't stop himself no matter how many times, and how many ways, I tell him to shut up.

I shake my head and laugh. He laughs too.

"Sorry," he says.

The March men, always apologizing.

I close my eyes.

I'm in our motel room in Cannon Beach. And here in the parking lot Tess is tapping on the glass, smiling at me through the fogged window, her hair all wet, but when I roll it down there's only surf and wind and rain.

"You're letting water in," he says and I roll it back up. We go on looking out at the storm and drinking our coffee and I return to constructing this thing. Because my mother is right, of course. Forget her demeanor. And anyway what am I to expect of a homicidal maniac? Deep sympathy and great tact? So forget her coldness. It fits her now. What she is. Killer. Prisoner. And hers is a good question. Really, it is the only question. White Pine or anywhere else. Incarcerated mother, or not.

What are you doing in this town without the girl you love? What are you doing here at all?

40.

My mother sitting in prison for murder, and my sister Claire having sworn off us, and I'm eating dinner with my father four times a week and seven nights a week I hear him snoring through the walls. He's pretending to take care of me, but mostly it seems the opposite. I worry about him especially at night, and wonder how I can prop him up a bit, how I might make him stronger while every day it seems his beard goes greyer, his eyes a little duller, sinking a little deeper into his skull.

So there's him in my head, and my mother locked up, but above all the one thing I really care about exists as a hole in my chest the size of a fat fist. So who gives a shit about the names of the guys I was working with or the sawdust on the floor or the smell of the places I went or the beauty of the beach in the early morning? But maybe all those things matter, too. I'm just trying to give you a sense of it. Or bring a sense of it back to myself. The strangeness. Always in my head trying to work out what the fuck I was doing there, just like she'd asked.

Say it's a Saturday in late October. 1991. It's busy. Two bartenders. Me and a tall guy with a beard. Maybe his name is Matt. Let's call him Matt. Half the guys I met back then were named Matt. Who cares? So two bartenders. Me and Matt and a barback. Call him Craig. The other half were called Craig. Matts and Craigs all over the place in White Pine. A senior from the college, let's say. So us three back there pouring Olympia and well drinks. The bottom-lit bottles behind us are mostly decoration. The occasional Cuervo shot, the occasional kid trying to impress her friends by ordering Frangelico on ice or some other bullshit.

Lester's is prison guards. The Owl is college kids. Two separate parts of town. Lester's up on the ridge. The Owl down by the beach. Both with sawdust on the floor. In this part of the world, you want a bar without sawdust on the floor? Go to Seattle.

This particular Saturday The Owl is jammed. They've got a band setup on the stage in the corner. Let's say they're playing Nirvana covers. Temple of the Dog. That kind of thing. Kids from the college doing their best Kurt Cobain. Matt and I, we've got a solid rhythm going. I'm a good bartender when I'm on and I'm on tonight. Everything makes sense. Everything logical. Here we are now, entertain us. Every now and then we've got to pack down the tip jar. Put a fist into all those ones and punch. Flying along. The place is jammed until close and when it's time, no one wants to go, but no one's an asshole.

The prison guard working the door is named Seymour Strout. Hand to God that's his name. Rock solid from the sternum up. Sternum down? Belly like you wouldn't believe. Seymour fucking Strout. He matters to me, to all of us, but for now, let's say Matt and I drink a few bourbons while we're scrubbing the bar down. And not the well junk either. The barback, too while he's doing inventory. Craig. The three waitresses are at a table doing the same, counting their tips.

Let's figure Matt's mixed them something special. He's working one of them. Julie? Cathy? Kerry? The girls there all had that long *e* at the end of their names. And at the end of every night what bartender wasn't mixing something special for some waitress somewhere? Maybe just the sad fuck whose mother is a murderer, the mopey kid who's lost the love of his life. So let's say Matt is working on Kerry and she and her friends are counting tips and drinking whatever it is out of rocks glasses at a sticky table over by the empty stage.

It's that end-of-shift feeling. Camaraderie and fatigue and fading adrenaline. Alcohol burn. All the noise sucked out of the room. Ushered out, really, by Seymour and his big belly. Maybe someone's got Paul Simon on the jukebox, because by the end of the night nobody wants to hear another moaning Seattle band. Let's say it's "The Obvious Child." Another song my mother loved. See her singing loudly, badly, fingers drumming the wheel. So it feels good. *I am remembering a girl when I was young. And we said these songs are true, these days are ours, these tears are free.* And it is one of those nights where I stuff two hundred bucks into my pocket, the paperwork all adds up, and I look around and smile at the new waitress with the red hair and think it's okay, it's all fine, this new life. *And some people say the sky is just the sky, but I say why deny the obvious child?*

So I take my drawer to the manager's office upstairs. Another name I can't remember. She's smart and fair and tough and keeps her distance and doesn't behave like she's the CEO of some multinational corporation the way a lot of them do. She doesn't sigh when your drawer is off ninety-seven cents as if you've just betrayed the fucking nation. Maybe we chat about something or other, because we like each other, but it's late and we're both tired and a little drunk, so have a good night and see you tomorrow and go easy on whatever it is you're drinking.

Then I'm coming down the stairs, not happy, but fine. I'm okay. I'm surviving. I'm alive. It's enough of a good night, enough goodness to smooth over the holes in my chest. Drywall over a bad frame. And downstairs, say I give the new waitress a smile just to piss off Craig and she smiles back, and I keep that, along with the two hundred in my pocket, and out I go past Seymour at the door who's waiting around hoping one of the girls will ask him to walk her home.

"Have a good one, Seymour," I say.

"Peace," Seymour says. "Peace," Seymour always says.

This is back before we knew each other at all, when I kept my distance, and hated him for no other reason than his being a guard.

This is back before I knew Seymour Strout was the gentlest bouncer ever born to bounce.

And here, right here, is my favorite part of the night. Stepping out into the fresh air. The parking lot all quiet. Only a few cars left. The smell of the ocean. The sound of the waves breaking across the wide beach. Sometimes the rain coming down hard, but not tonight. No reason to run for it tonight. So I take a minute before I pull on my coat. I let the air dry the sweat on my neck, under my arms. Let it cut away the dullness. Let it sharpen my eyes and light me up.

Then I see a flash of my mother in her cell. The cell I've never seen. Always there when I'm coming out of the bar. A quick stab, like's it's been thrust into my eyes. Always. Every time I step into the night, there she is, forehead against the bars, as with every prison cliché in the world. And holding on tight with her fists.

Then there is my father asleep in his single bed. On his back, snoring, lips parted, eyes fluttering, hair a mess.

So let's say that's how I'm feeling coming out of The Owl. I'm falling from a high like this one. I'm dreading climbing into the truck and pulling on my seat belt and above all the sound of the slamming door.

Let's say that.

But let's also say, because it is the absolute truth, that on this particular Saturday night in October of 1991 sitting on the hood of my truck beneath the single street light is Tess.

Is Tess.

Is Tess.

Is Tess.

I want to write those two words forever.

A long ribbon winding through these pages.

I wanted to wait. I wanted to draw it out for you. Build the suspense a bit, but here I am *now*, here in this room with the late sun falling the way I like across the clearing and I cannot wait any longer.

To hell with you.

The cross is in the ballpark.

I want Tess back.

I want her on my truck in the lamplight. Twenty years old. Dark brown hair a little longer now since summer, pushing out from beneath a black wool watch cap pulled down over her ears. Boots on the bumper, elbows on her knees, unlit cigarette between her fingers and those narrow green eyes and that half smile, with her head cocked to the side.

Oh, for a while you think you'll have unlimited moments like these. Soon you realize you're wrong. Not soon enough, but you figure it out.

I want this one back, goddamn it.

There is Tess.

Is Tess waiting for me in the cool, rainless night looking just like herself. More luminous than ever. Posing for me with her cigarette between the two middle fingers of her left hand the way she did back then so that she could cover her mouth when she smoked.

There she was.

Here she is.

And I cross the parking lot with all the symptoms. Thudding heart. Singular focus. I stop in front of her and neither of us speaks for a beat or two because we have to play this thing out for posterity, for the record books, for the film on which we imagined our lives were then recorded. And I think, Maybe she'll say, Got a light? Those days she's theatrical. But instead she raises her chin, squints and looks down her nose at me. She squints and I could kneel right there in the parking lot. Wrap my arms around her ankles.

Ecstasy is an inadequate word.

She does not ask me for a light. I stand before her, and she is so much like a queen up there. And I mean a real queen. Not some kind of ornamental royalty, but a woman who rules. The first Elizabeth, not the second, not the one Claire was so enamored with at the beginning of her teenage love affair with Britain.

Not that woman they've got in there now with the hats. The other one. The virgin queen. As if Tess was any kind of virgin.

Tess reaches back and presses her palms on the hood of the truck. Looks down upon me, her subject.

Says: "You never came to find me. You never called, Joseph. Why is that?"

Oh, of the moments in my life. Do you know what that was? Can you know? To see her without warning. As if she'd risen right out of the ocean. Without progression. Was born of fog. Appeared *in one fell swoop*, as my mother liked to say. In one *fail* swoop, as I heard it for so many years.

Tess, like an apparition.

The sudden appearance of the single person you've been waiting for.

Sometimes, I hear, you look up from your seat on a crosstown bus and she smiles at you.

Some of us can't be bothered, as Claire would say. Claire never the romantic. Claire with no use for the magical.

Sometimes I imagine her in London seated upon a great golden throne. Queen Claire the pragmatic. Regal and calculating beside her pink-faced king.

No waiting for Claire. Cut and run. Off with their heads.

But some of us are waiting all our lives.

In a different kingdom, we are waiting all our lives.

And here was Tess and what you want is what is next so

what is next is this: I did not answer her question. No quip. No clever line. She'd done her best, but I was no good. I did not sweep her into my arms. I did not pin her to the warm metal. Instead I took the remaining steps until I was between her legs, until I felt her knees bracing my ribs. And then with my face pressed against her stomach, I cried.

So much for the glamour.

Out of sadness, out of terror, and above all, out of relief, I wept beneath the streetlight, between Tess's knees, while from the door of The Owl, from across the dark parking lot, Seymour Strout looked on.

While I fell against my long lost love's breast and cried like a child, Seymour Strout looked on. A thick goatee—goatees as common in White Pine as Craigs. As Matts. As sawdust.

An audience of one. An audience of Strout. Off-duty correctional officer, Seymour Strout, smoking a Virginia Slim, watched us impassively from the orange-lit doorway of The Owl Bar and Grill. A man great of chest and belly both, smoked those delicate Virgina Slims. Lit each with a match, never a lighter, held it between stubby thumb and fat middle finger.

This Seymour Strout's single affectation.

And if asked? Those who dared? "Because I fucking like 'em."

"Who's that, Joseph?"

Tess's first words to me after so long as she moved her fingers through my hair. I looked up and followed her gaze to the orange doorway beneath the blue neon owl where he stood.

I said, "Seymour Strout."

And with that our reunion was witnessed. Notarized. It's a fact, which you'll see has poetry to it. Tess's return to me, Tess's arrival in White Pine presided over by gentle, lonely Seymour Strout.

"No one's named Seymour Strout," Tess said as she slid

down and dropped to her feet. "Joseph," she whispered, "I've missed you."

And enough then of the weeping, of Tess above me. Now she looked up into my face. I pushed her back against the grill of the truck and I kissed her as best I knew how. With as much tenderness and strength as I could muster. I did everything I could to translate all of it—the relief, the fear, the shame, the love, the lust, the regret, the rage, the bewilderment, the wildness.

I tried and I failed.

But goddamn if I didn't try. I was a kid, after all. A boy. Whatever I believed. And soon enough we were running onto the beach, running from the boardwalk lights, crossing the shadow edge, running into the dark. And then I was behind her pulling at her buttons. Behind her down on the sand, Tess raising her ass up and me yanking her jeans to her knees, her car to the sand and one hand digging handfuls of it, and another behind, groping for my cock, and she's saying "do it, do it, do it" until I was inside her fast and she's making those low noises she makes, and her skin so much softer, so much warmer than anything around us—the cold, wet sand and the pummeling surf, and the hard black rocks.

41

It was never enough with her. I was always doomed to failure. Whatever we did, it was never enough. No matter how close I held her. No matter how long I watched her sleep, no matter how long we looked at each other. No matter the fucking, the lovemaking. It was never enough. There was only so far. Only so deep we could dive until the air ran out. There was always a wall too high, too thick. For a while we tried with language. Long conversations. All the questions. All the answers. We tried with sex. Wrap your legs around me, hook your ankles, dig your nails, pull with all your strength, bring me in deeper. Turn this way, turn that. We filled and emptied each other in every way we could imagine. But that too, for all the rush and pleasure, that too was failure.

We tried and I like to believe, even now, that the trying counts for something. The trying in spite of doom. The trying to spite the doom. Isn't that what makes heroes of us? Isn't that the very nature of living? Isn't that the subject of all our stories?

I'm gliding upwards today. There are days when I'm weightless and sailing. I can't keep up with my feeble, burning mind. Days like this I'm flying. I see to the ocean. Not a rabbit moves in the forest without my noticing. On days like this I'm as sharp-eyed as the sharp-shinned hawks circling above us. Understand? Days when the world is clear?

All my mind's chaos and diversion. Its rhythms and languages. The updraft.

The deadfall plummet.

Today I have faith.

Today I have slaughtered the bird.

Today Tess is on her way home.

Today Tess has a fist full of sand and her breathing is slowing and I am softening inside her and motherfucker you think I'm flying now? Goddamn you should have seen us out there on the beach that night in a postcoital smolder.

You just can't imagine.

Let's say that if you'd followed us out to the boardwalk and squinted into the darkness, we would have been shining in the night.

42.

I drove us home to the little white house, which should have been dark save for the porch light, but the kitchen was lit too, and through the window we looked in on my father, who was reading a newspaper in his red-and-blue plaid bathrobe. Must have been well after three in the morning and there's my father as if it's time for breakfast.

So that's how Tess had found me at the bar. My father in on the plan, in on the surprise. My father waiting up to make sure all had gone as it should have.

There in the honey light of our little kitchen I put my hand on the hard small of her back and said, "Dad, this is Tess."

But what does any of this have to do with the good part? What does any of it have to do with my mother bashing that man's head in with a hammer. *With a hammer!* Where are the brains leaking onto the asphalt? Where's the blood? And the killer carefully buckling the victim's children into the backseat of her Volvo station wagon? What of crime? What of punishment? And what of her daughter's anger, humiliation and disappearance into the wilds of upper-crust London? What of the loyal husband who refused to leave his wife's side? What of the long-suffering son, your proud and erratic narrator?

What of his beautiful girlfriend? (How I hate that cold, ruined adjective.)

What of those strange games they played? Of the trouble they got into.

What I come to realize. As I go on. Battle on. The *good stuff* hasn't much to do with murder. Isn't to do with Dustin Strauss. That coward. That bully. Fuck that guy. Had it coming if you ask me. Truth is. I don't think about him.

So we are three. In a white house, in White Pine, in the dark morning, in the dim yellow light of the small kitchen amidst steam and vapor and the rich smell of coffee. We are three at three sides of the square table. One place empty.

Father, son, and holy Tess.

It is early, but we are not tired. My father, having been expecting her, has bought sticky buns, which he's laid out in the center of the table on a white plate.

Why is my father happy? Because he has, in a fashion, reassembled a family. Constructed one as if it were a cabinet. As if it were a sideboard. Because he believes our early morning meal is some kind of consecration. Because he sees it as forward movement. Because Tess replaces Claire in some way. Or because he loves Tess immediately. Because he's loved her since before she arrived. Loved her from the minute they first spoke on the phone. Which he did. We know this, because he's saying it now, between enthusiastic bites of warm, sweet pastry, he's saying: "I liked her from the start, Joey."

Tess is smiling at him.

She's laying into a second sticky bun as if she hasn't eaten in days.

"Ravenous," she'd say.

But it's not so much the satisfaction of hunger as it is happiness. Or are they the same thing?

I'm eating the same way, ignoring the fork, and shoveling the thing into my mouth by hand, by fist.

And why am I happy?

Because Tess is there.

Yes.

Mystery solved.

And Tess? Why is she happy? Why is she so full of appetite? So full of lightness and warmth? Why does she accept so easily my father's hand on the back of hers? Because she has been reunited with her love? Because she is touched by my father's eyes? His gentle warmth? His small kitchen, their knowing references to secret telephone conversations? Because she's missed me?

Well, whatever it is, we were happy. Chatting away, eating ourselves sick, the sky lightening outside and that good exhaustion slowly setting in.

We're leaning back from the table. The quiet has come now. The coffee is useless.

"Well," Joey March says, "we should sleep."

What he wants now is to slip into bed with Tess, to draw his knees behind hers, to take her breasts in his hands, to kiss her shoulder and fade away.

So he stands. He is lean and strong with thick curly hair messier and longer than he likes it, but just as Tess does. He stands without pain, with a fatigue that has nothing to do with age. He stands behind his father. He bends down and kisses him on the top of his head.

"Thank you, Dad," he says and says it again. "Thank you." All the while looking at Tess who rises now and follows him to bed.

The morning is coming faster. My father, who is as old then as I am now, will leave in a few hours for work. And our young heroes, in bed together for the first time in so long, will sleep deep into the afternoon.

And in that late afternoon, I whisper, "Good morning, Tess. My love, my love, my love."

I whisper straight into her skin, which smells of sweat and coffee and sex. Of the lemon oil she uses as perfume.

And what is the first thing she says?

"Joseph, I want to meet her."

Before she has opened her eyes.

And for no good reason I say, "Who? Who do you want to meet?"

She sighs. It's understood then. That's what we'll do.

Tess Wolff and Joey March. The two of us when we were young.

45.

I t couldn't have been the next day. You don't just show up at White Pine Penitentiary. The Pine, you learn to call it. You don't just show up there. You have to be on a list. There are rules.

So one day not long after Tess made her dramatic entrance, not stage right, not stage left, but there as the curtain opened, as the lights came up on a short-haired girl riding the hood of a Toyota truck, we went to see my mother.

Offstage, the wind whipped at the ocean and the waves crashed. Concussive sounds in the night. Unlit cigarette between her fingers.

Not too long after that we find this young woman in black combat boots, scuffed and unlaced. Torn jeans over long johns, waffled, color of cream, old-fashioned, five bucks at Army Navy. Tight Fruit of the Loom wifebeater. White, new, the term hers, not mine. And don't argue. She'll roll her eyes.

"Fuck *those* women," she'll say. Or did once. "Feminists in language only. I'm a fucking *feminist*." She laughs. "See? No bra."

Over which a wool shirt. The Pendleton classic. Red and black checked. Insulated. Satin lining. And the watch cap. Let's say black today. Sometimes navy. Sometimes white. This is the uniform now. A little tougher than in Cannon Beach. But it's not *that* tough. If you're following the chronology, keeping an eye on the years, you'll know she's in style. All of us dressing like half-assed lumberjacks back then.

God, do I see her. Unbuttoning the Pendleton, her nipples through the thin white fabric. Doc Martens on the dash the day we started out. The two of us driving up away from the beach, turning onto the ridge road. To our left, to the west, the town of White Pine, and the ocean. To our right, the prison of White Pine, and the vast valley and all its farmland beyond. Tess has turned to me and is beginning to speak. She's raised her hand to the back of my neck and is running her fingers through my hair.

"How is it, Joe? Is it better?"

I'm watching the valley, waiting for that moment when the road breaks slightly to the east and the spaceship comes into view.

"Is what better?" I ask not knowing what she means this time. Not pretending. Not delaying.

"The bird," she says.

"Ah," I say.

"Is it?"

"Yes," I say.

"Why?"

"Because it's the beginning. Because it doesn't come in the beginning. It only comes in the middle. And now you're here and no way it would dare now."

"If only," she says. "But those are lies."

"I'm glad you're here," I say, which is evidence of just how defunct language is.

She stops moving her fingers and instead cups the back of my head with a new firmness.

"What do you mean it's the beginning? What do you mean it only comes in the middle?"

"There," I say. "There." I point down into the valley. The prison slides out below us as if set in a slowly opening drawer.

I pull the truck off the road. It's about the same place where I stopped with my father. About the same place he comes to look over her as she sleeps. Or whatever she does in her eternally illuminated cell.

We have brought her earplugs. Balls of wax in a plastic box.

Tess will give them to her. Her first offering.

Tess doesn't run into the onion field to vomit. We lean against the grille.

"She's in there," I say, pointing for no reason.

"I hate it."

I nod.

"We should help her escape," she says.

I wrap my arm around her shoulder. We wait a while before climbing back into the truck and slipping into the valley, to the prison parking lot. The doors closing and our four feet moving across the asphalt.

Those two in love. Joey March young and afraid. His blood full of adrenaline. His heart full of dread. And Tess? What was her heart full of? Love? Perhaps. Fear? Maybe. But above all, fire and rage. No question about that. She is half a step ahead pulling Joey March's wrist slightly on the offbeat.

They are walking in the sunlight across the shining wet asphalt until they have become VISITORS, until they are swallowed by the double doors.

We stand in line. Wait our turn. Sign our names. We are scanned and frisked. We are ushered by a stocky woman with her long hair drawn up beneath her cap. Long hair I know is there because I've seen her drinking at Lester's. Seen her with the heel of a boot on the bench of a wooden booth. Seen her bent over a pool table, eye on the break, hair back in a loose ponytail. This woman in her civilian life.

I've seen her both ways.

All of us broken in half. Half at least. Most of us in quarters, or sixteenths, or thirty-seconds, or sixty-fourths. The woman at work, the woman at play, the woman in love, the woman at war, the woman at home, the woman alone and all combinations in between.

We're following her down the long cinder-block corridor, along the green linoleum. We can't hear our own footsteps. Or I can't now. Just the sound of those guard boots leading us along. Her broad back like a swimmer's. Back and boots showing us the visit room, with the benches and tables riveted to the floor, and the fluorescent lights and the vending machines. Cans of Dr. Pepper, bags of Combos, Funyons, Snickers, always Snickers. The boots gone, the door closes. And there we are, the two of us. Waiting.

Others, sure. Other visitors. Other prisoners. But they are vague color. They are general noise, general motion. The clarity, the clarity is in Tess. Hands on the table. Narrow eyes fixed on the PRISONERS door. The texture of the table. The rotten-fruit candy chemical smell. Bleach. Humming lights and human noise. Visitors and prisoners coughing and sniffling and throat-clearing. Shifting their weight on the creaking benches. Murmuring interspersed with sobbing, a raised voice quieted by the death look of a guard built like a squat furnace. One of Seymour Strout's colleagues.

And above it all, above the smell and sound, above even the hope and dread and rot exists something else, some other thing.

And it is this thing that holds the true authority.

And it is this thing that kills.

Tess in contrast. Her very existence, a kind of protest against it all. Her intelligence. Her warmth. Her smell. Her skin. Her rage. Her youth. All of it at war with the prison. Do you see the way this woman, just by her very presence in a place, challenges it and its terrorizing government? Is a menace to that sinister thing impossible to describe.

46

We waited sitting side by side. Holding hands. Tess in my father's place. Me in mine. All the people around us, the door opening and closing, all those prisoners ushered into the room. Blue for peaceful. Green for suicide watch.

Until at last, my mother appears in orange.

"That's her," Tess said, as if I might not recognize her. As if it had been Tess all that time coming to visit, and I'd just arrived in town. Right from the start it was that way. The instant my mother arrives in the room. Like that famous brand of love: an immediate and shattering thing.

She came to us moving in her new way. I'd noticed it the last few visits. A kind of imperious gliding. A dancer's affect—hands loose at her sides, chin high, a look of bemusement, the slightest smile. A joke she's still thinking about. A sweet story she's just recalled. The look she gave you: *Relent. I know all.* Her face so relaxed. Nothing tight, no lines, no furrows. She seemed to have become younger in prison, not older.

So, she came to us, moving through the room as if it were a stage, a ballroom. And this new quality about her grew more pronounced when she saw Tess. Her eyes lightened. The smile grew into something beyond what she reserved for her son and husband. It was something closer to an expression of pleasure.

"Joey," she said, kissing my cheek. "And you are Tess."

We have all seen some version of this. Two people meet and something is changed. In the air, in the room. Something is acknowledged. Around them we exchange knowing looks. Did you see that? Did you see? Often, it is someone's husband, someone's wife who catches it. That flicker. The terror it can cause. The implications. So often a signal that a marriage will shortly suffer great damage.

"You are Tess," my mother said again, but this time her tone meaning, *at long last*. The one I've been hearing about, the one who has captured my son's heart. The motherly mode, so different from the first.

"I am," Tess said with her fullest smile. No restraint. No caution.

My mother asked all the questions our time would allow. And in her new style consistent with the smile, the gliding, the hands at peace.

"Who are you, Tess? Where do you come from? What do you want from your life? Where will you go next? What are your intentions with my son?" This last with a laugh. "What are you doing *here*? A gorgeous young woman in a prison town? In a *prison*? Young lady, I don't approve."

She went on like that, Tess hypnotized. Enchanted, in the most literal sense. A spell had been cast. The straight-spined queen of The Pine has magical powers. Tess Wolff, our knight errant, is beguiled. The dutiful son sits silent and waits.

When our time ends, when our audience with her is nearly over, Tess slides her small rectangular box across the table. Six balls of wax rolled in white cotton.

"Thank you," she says. "The noise is awful. Thank you."

She presses her lips to the back of Tess's hand, leaving a red stain.

The queen has found lipstick in prison.

47.

This morning I dragged the ladder from the garage and pulled the satellite dish off the roof. I'd always hated the thing. That little billboard. Paying those people to advertise for them. Those white letters pronouncing to the world: We watch television!

I never liked the dish, and I didn't like drilling a hole into our house, and I didn't like their black wire worming in.

We'd lived with it for a long time, of course. Like most people do. We liked watching the Mariners. The news. Staying up late. Smoking a joint. Nowhere to go in the morning. Some college football too. Mostly, though, we watched a lot of movies. That was something we both loved. Good and bad. It didn't much matter.

But now that Tess is gone, I don't have the heart for them. And the news makes me want to kill someone. All that noise. All those chattering fools. And that kind of anger is no good for me.

Both my grandfathers died of heart attacks.

So did my father, as it happens.

I'm in the sludge today. There is no wide crystalline sky. No sharp edges, no florid poetry.

The fire does not appear cut from glass.

Today my eyes are smeared with Vaseline and I am thinking of my father's .45.

Anyway, the television. I couldn't stand to watch it. I wanted it out. That grey dish collecting all the trash of the universe and funneling it in through its insidious black wire. Something we'd paid for willingly. Eagerly. We'd invited the most hideous people into this house. All that cultivated outrage. All that ugliness. I should have put a bullet through our expensive screen, but instead I just wrapped it in an old blanket and propped it against the back wall of the garage.

Since then, I've started listening to more music. I don't know a thing about it, just that I like some of it a lot. And I mean with an upsetting intensity. It could be anything, too. No particular genre. I treat music like paintings. I walk through a museum until I'm hit in the chest. I guess that doesn't make me very sophisticated, but it suits me well. What do you expect from a guy with a subpar education?

Anyway, it's the way I like to live when I like to live.

48

Y ou should have seen her. The expression. The eyes. Walking to the truck you'd have thought we'd been to see the pope.

Tess's eyes shone. With what? With ideas? No. With plans. With plans.

And I suppose that kind of sparkling look isn't quite calm, is it? Isn't quite peace. As we walked, Tess squeezing my hand tight, I couldn't have imagined what she was planning. I'm not sure she knew herself. Not yet, not really. But that's when it began. The seminal moment.

"I love her," she said as I drove us up the prison road.

And this is what we want, is it not? The woman we love to love the first woman who ever loved us? Test passed. We may proceed. We may go on without difficulty. Or that kind of difficulty. So, why did it concern me? Why was I frightened by it?

This instant and severe consonance.

I think of Tess who had the future in her eyes as we rose out of the valley.

"I love her," she said before the road cut the prison away.

It wasn't peace. Peace wasn't what she was after.

When we pulled up to the house and the engine was off, she said, "We should find our own place."

Which meant many things. That she was staying, and so we were staying. That we would walk into my father's house, and tell him so. And he would look at us with such happiness, and the three of us would get drunk together on a bottle of Smirnoff from his freezer.

It meant that Lester's would deliver a pizza and we'd eat it together in celebration and Tess would tell the story of meeting my mother for the first time in the visitors' room of the prison at White Pine.

What she would not do is tell either of us what she was constructing. Because she did not yet know. Or because she did not have language for it yet. Or perhaps, unlike my father and very much like my mother, she demanded her secrets.

49

A two-bedroom house ten minutes' walk up the hill from my father's. Salt-blasted, storm-struck, weather-beaten, peeling navy well on its way to grey. Two white-trimmed windows facing the street. Two windows side by side beneath a pitched roof, cedar-shingled. A child's drawing of a house. Redbrick chimney. A nice wide porch out front, and three steps down, a dead lawn and six cracked concrete pavers to the sidewalk, a sidewalk which takes you along a quiet street.

Ours was Mott. Named for who the fuck cares. Mott Street. 232. The house worse for wear, but not a dump. Room for improvement, which is what you want in a house. That's what houses are for. What arrives finished is for people without souls, without imagination. I trust nothing finished. Nothing that doesn't leave me some room for work.

Two bedrooms upstairs, windows on the street, and a bathroom in between. Downstairs a living room with a brick fireplace and brick mantle painted coats and coats of white, darts of char shooting up from within. A dining room. An old porcelain light fixture pointing at the floor, a white warhead at the end of a brass rod. Radiators that spoke in tongues. Beat-up wooden floors everywhere, except the kitchen, which was all yellow linoleum. White Formica counters edged in aluminum straight out of a 50s diner. Wood cabinetry painted yellow, a gas range—oven and burners, splintered enamel both, and a clock in the console, the old saw, telling perfect time twice a day. An angry fridge.

There was a yellow yard out back, home to two good apple trees, both behind a tall pine fence many years newer than the house itself.

All to say, we were happy.

The two of us at the Salvation Army, at Goodwill.

See Tess moving backwards up our porch steps? See the expression on her face? *You* ask her if she wants to trade places, if she wants a rest. I've learned my lesson. She takes no shortcuts. She takes no shit. She will not be helped. She is the bravest, toughest, fiercest. Strongest. Look at her face. Watch while that horrible green corduroy (the people's fabric of White Pine) couch slowly slips out of her hands. While she loses her grip, inch by inch. The sharp end of a wayward staple cuts the soft skin of the inside of her right arm. See the blood there? You tell her to drop it. You tell her to take a break. It's a single minute in a life, Tess. But she will not let go until the couch is inside and facing the fireplace.

It fits just right, just so. Like it was bench built for our new little world. The front door wide open and, outside, the tailgate down. Our brand-new plastic-wrapped mattress is piled with boxes of the cheapest shit the great town of White Pine has to offer. Tess's jacket left on the lawn, flung off in frustration. How dare it inhibit her. How dare it keep her warm when she wants to be cool.

The middle of the afternoon. Warm despite the season. All the windows open. All the doors. House and truck. Our lives exposed to the world. And Tess, sitting on our corduroy, has me on my knees. One leg in her jeans, one leg out. One side bare, one side not. Her hands on the back of my head, she holds on tight. My fingers curling inside her—ring and middle—with my tongue pressed hard against her, no soft flicking, no light touch today. Today it's hard pressure, and her fingers tightening, tightening, she comes quickly the way she does. She comes hard. And after, she pulls me up, pulls me to her and kisses my mouth and says my name the way she did then, more than once and in all its variations. Sometimes Joey, sometimes Joseph, sometimes Joe.

"We're home, my love," she says. "You and me."

She laughs and returns her slender naked leg back to her jeans and runs into the sunlight singing to me one song or another.

And I am happy. The two of us, day after day filling that place, making it ours. Making it fortress and nest, stronghold and citadel.

50

After we finished our work that first week, when nearly everything was in place, my father came for dinner. He arrived with a bottle of champagne and a half-cord of firewood in the back of his Wagoneer. Tess made chili.

"To your mother," she said to me. "To your wife," she said to him. "May she come home soon."

We all raised our glasses and drank.

So it was like old times. Like the beginning in Cannon Beach. Me behind the bar, Tess out on the floor.

She picked up shifts at The Owl. Kerry, or Julie, or Amy, got pregnant, or flunked Marine Biology, or got arrested for selling Ecstasy, or just pitched it in and left town, or whatever happened, and like that, the way things go in the past, with such simplicity and ease, Tess was working right there alongside me just like in the good old days.

In that time of joy, we woke in our new bed, upon our new mattress, in our new sheets, in our new home, with sunlight in the trees. In my memory, in those mornings we made love always. And after, always, one of us would go downstairs to our new kitchen and make coffee. I can feel it. Standing still, looking out the kitchen window at our scruffy yard, waiting for the machine to do its work, listening to the ranting refrigerator, my feet against the cool linoleum.

Reaching through the cold air for the *White Pine Witness.* Red rubber band. Cardinal in the tree.

Paper under my arm, a mug in each hand as I climb the

stairs. Our stairs. Those mornings, those days, that house, the seed of a dream perhaps only I maintained. Tess in bed sleepy and naked. The two of us reading that terrible paper, the crime blotter our favorite page. Tossing it and turning to the books we collected, which were everywhere. Which grew up from the floor in stacks, and extended along the shelves we built with cinder blocks and planks of pine my father cut for free. What else did we have to do those mornings but read, and make love, and drink coffee and fall back to sleep?

My father came by some afternoons to help with one project or another. In the evenings we went down to The Owl in my truck to provide alcohol to those who wanted it. To pay for our new life together, to earn our living.

Perform some task in return for currency, use that currency to wrap ourselves in clean white sheets, to keep ourselves warm and sheltered and fed. All we had to do was show up on time, pour alcohol into glasses, distribute those glasses. Do it fast. Keep things clean. Keep things organized.

In return, you may have this life. You may have your time of joy.

The problem is that we want other things. Some of us more than others, and after a while, after the castle has been built, fortified, and polished, we begin to look out the windows. We are restless. There are holes. There are desires we may only sense, a humming, a chill, a sensation impossible to understand, impossible to disregard.

Then there are two choices: bury it or change.

And it should be clear by now that Tess would bury nothing. So as those days passed, glorious in memory, glorious despite my mother, mornings in bed, nights at The Owl, dinners with my father, walks on the cold beach, all the desperate, savage, tender sex, through all those early days (infinite as they feel, how many were there really? Twenty? Thirty?), Tess had an eye to the window. And perhaps I did as well, knowing that the tar would return. Winter coming, days shortening, Tess drifting, nothing left to do with the house until spring, but sit and work and wait. With everything in its place there was nothing left to do but look outside. And we found that outside it was not like Cannon Beach.

In Cannon Beach there were no wars, no winter storms.

There my mother was not in prison.

After the home has been built, the firewood stacked, the bed made, the animal dressed, regardless of place and culture, whatever the quality of our food and shelter, in the quietest moments of our minds, relative as they may be, do we all look elsewhere?

51.

In the beginning, on nights we didn't work, Tess and I stayed home. We lit a fire, we made dinner. And then on one of those nights, after we'd eaten, Tess poured us glasses of bourbon, and we went out onto the porch. This simple change, this was the beginning, the true beginning. The simplest thing. Tess carried the drinks, and I brought the blanket we kept on the couch. Some generic Navajo pattern. Green diamonds inside of diamonds inside of diamonds on white wool. A gift from my father, which we loved and which was part of our early life in the way that stuffed animals are in the lives of children.

I followed Tess out the front door, turned off the porch light, sat next to her and pulled the blanket around our shoulders.

"Cheers," she said and held her glass out not to me, but to the street, to the neighborhood, to the night. And I did the same, both of us facing forward. There may or may not have been a clink, but we certainly committed a drinking sin. No meeting of the eyes. I suppose it will come as no surprise that I am superstitious. What's stranger? The sense that I am inhabited by a long-taloned bird, that black tar spreads through my veins, or that I knock three times on wood whenever it occurs to me that Tess will never return home?

There was a streetlight on the corner, yellowing the sidewalk. There were all our neighbors' houses, each small like ours, and most in better states of repair. Across the street was a white house set farther back on the property than all the others on Mott. What space it lost in the backyard, it gained in the front. And in that space was a neat garden. Perfectly staked and rowed, flower beds framed with redwood planks. Paths made of wood chips. Nearly all of it was dead or dying that time of year on the north coast of Washington State, but it was clean and cared for, and held such promise for the spring.

As we sat beneath the blanket, we watched a tall man appear. Or perhaps the better word here is *materialize*, because there was no arrival, no door opening and closing, no light coming on, no footsteps. He was just, all at once, present. He carried a plastic bucket, and walked the rows stopping here and there, kneeling to break a stem, or pull a weed. He was slightly stooped, with dark hair that fell into his face. Even Tess, who never hesitated to speak to strangers, said nothing. And the longer we were silent, the more it felt as if we were watching something we shouldn't have been. Observing some intimate ritual. As if we were spies, peering into the man's house, watching him bathe, or pray, or masturbate. Having not announced ourselves, having not called to him, *Hello, neighbor*, a simple courtesy, a warning: beware, you are not alone. A cough, even. Some gesture.

But we kept quiet. And after walking each row and filling his bucket, he upturned it onto a compost pile and disappeared around the side of the house.

So what? A man comes out to do a bit of gardening at night. Stranger things have happened. Yes, that's true. But Tess was thrilled by it, and so I was too. You should have seen her eyes when she turned to me.

"The night gardener," she whispered.

She loved mystery. And so she made him a character. Even if he was no one to us, and, really, makes no difference here.

It's the most fundamental thing I know about being alive: Everything that lasts is invention followed by tenacious faith.

52.

What do you know so far? You have a man alone in a pretty house of glass and wood, an isolated house at the end of a long, unpaved, spruce-lined driveway. Occasionally he walks to a town he refuses to name, but mostly he stays at home. At one time he lived here with a woman named Tess Wolff, but she is gone now.

Where has she gone?

Will she return?

Why did she leave?

All good questions, to which I do not have answers.

What else? This man we know in turns as Joe, Joey, Joseph March, when he was twenty-two years old, fell madly in love with Tess Wolff. I do not know a truer phrase than *fell madly in love*. To fall madly. To fall madly into love. It has been over-used and corrupted by a world that destroys good phrases with overuse and commerce. A lazy, stupid, regressive world that beats the meaning from words, beats them to death, until they are only noise, only filler. And I know I sound like a crank, I know. Still, I'm saying take a second and consider the phrase, is all. Nowhere have I read a better description of what happened to me. I fell madly in. Pronoun, verb, adverb, preposition. Flawless. A mad falling. See what happens to me? Derailed again. My whole life derailed. The updraft, the downdraft. The drugs kick in, but there are no drugs. Without warning they come, these wild highs, this, the good madness, comes on like fast fire. And how do you expect me to stay on track when I'm alive like I am now? That's the point. I am always derailed. Forgive me, for today I am discursive. What a word that one, too, what sound, what meaning. Discursive, digressive and meandering. And baroque too. And absurd. But what can I do? It comes on and I am changed. Never believe in solidity of self.

They are so clear to me. The present, the past, Tess, and Seymour Strout, you, the Night Gardener, the Trampoline Girl, my murdering mother, my struggling father. Days like this I see all the threads, each square-knotted to a different finger, the whole story, my whole life, each a red thread.

But do you follow me?

Tess would tell me if she were here.

You would tell me if I knew who you were.

I will try to get back to it. I will try to return through the muck of today's construction to some kind of sense. It's so difficult with my brain firing like this. You've seen what happens.

Half my life cycling the tar, the light, the bird, the upswing.

Can you imagine how Tess felt?

It's no wonder she left.

In 1991, a young man, a boy really, falls madly in love with a young woman. Summertime on the Oregon Coast. Straight out of college. Sunsets and sex. Joy and light. And then the shattering, inconceivable news. The boy's mother has committed a brutal, bloody, spectacular, incomprehensible crime. Anne-Marie March, mother of two, homemaker, nurse at Harborview Medical Center, takes a hammer to Dustin Strauss's skull. In front of his children. In broad daylight. In a parking lot. She has no criminal record. No recorded history of mental illness. The summer has ended. His mother is in the news. Local, then national. His mother is in jail. His mother is in prison. And all along, from the first hammer blow, it seems, there are those who make her a hero. The strong defending the weak from the bullies of the world. From a man who beat his children, who beat his wife. Did the despicable coward deserve his fate?

This woman, this supposed monster, underpaid and over-worked, a nurse of twenty years, treated countless women and children for terrible injuries sustained at the hands of hus-bands and fathers and brothers. Women who returned to the hospital, time after time, often holding those very hands. Women who would later turn up dead. A State *reluctant to get involved in family affairs.* Anne-Marie March had had enough. There is a limit and these things do not happen in a vacuum. In myriad ways we grant these men permission. This same cul-ture that destroys language, destroys women. And yet the jury of her peers, composed of three women and nine men, could not see beyond the number of blows. Once, yes. Twice, or even three times. But seven times? No, seven times suggests some thing else. Cruelty, malice, or worst of all, intent. No one, ladies and gentlemen, deserves seven blows. And so Anne-Marie March will spend her days in the White Pine Penitentiary. While men go on beating their wives and chil-dren, while the State keeps on keeping out of it. For some a hero, for others a monster, a shrew. The lazy world, which insists with Christian zeal on the solidity of self, stamped my mother evil, and Anne-Marie March faded from the news.

53.

On the porch one evening. The two of us watching the Night Gardener gardening. Tess saying, "I want to see her alone." We had been out to The Pine together, the two of us, and sometimes the three of us, a number of times and in various combinations. Me alone, my father alone, but never Tess alone. My mother was always better, and she was always the same. Physically, she was stronger. She seemed to glow. Her spine had straightened. Still, her eyes remained flat. The coldness deepened, the distance more profound.

It was her old toughness without the warmth.

What happens exactly? Physiologically, what happens? To the eyes, I mean. How do they brighten? How do they dull? Whatever it is, hers were awful. And combined with the way she held herself away from me, her questioning, as if I were some stranger, one of her many acolytes seeking advice, come for an audience with Empress Anne-Marie.

I often had the impression she was preparing to leave. Even if that's the one thing she wasn't doing. And yet every visit the same feeling. Talking to her I saw the light of interest go out. Click, and off it goes. Like one of those old TV sets. The picture drawing in from all sides to a pinpoint of light.

When we were kids, Claire used to blow at the last instant like it was a candle.

My mother drawing away just like that. But in the slowest motion. Visit after visit, an incremental contraction.

No one else saw it. The others, my father, Tess, they talked about her health. It drew them closer. An intimacy built around a shared love for my mother. Love is the wrong word. I loved her too. So what's right? An enthusiasm? A belief? A faith? Yes. And me? No, not quite. I didn't buy it. I didn't buy the routine. The silent sage. The found-truth-and-God-in-prison routine. Not if the God she found had stolen all her warmth. Had stolen her from me.

What I saw when we came to visit was the slow disappearance of my mother. She was being replaced by something else, something foreign.

Anyway, we weren't the only visitors. Right away she had fans. She showed us the letters. The small gifts. Dream catchers, and coasters and poems mounted on cardboard. Mostly women. Men too though, which, while he'd have never said it, troubled my father.

Dear Mrs. March, you are a hero. Dear Mrs. March, It's about time. Dear Mrs. March, There is a limit to what we will accept, is there not? Ma'am, I have no pity for that man, whose name I will not write. My pity is for his widow, and for his children. And now they are free, while you are not. Dear Mrs. March, Without you, I would not have found the courage to leave. Dear Mrs. March, Every night I dream of leaving, and each morning I find myself here in the same bed, with the same man, and I cannot find the courage to do anything but make him breakfast. Dear Anne-Marie, I'm fifteen. I read about you in the paper. My father is a rich man. Last year he broke my collarbone. He is in the living room. You are in jail. Mrs. March, when I was a boy my father killed my mother. I saw your photo in the paper and I am glad for what you did. Dear Mrs. March, Should I kill my boyfriend? Dear Ms. March, We are a group of women. Dear Ms. March, We have run out of patience.

The letters came and came and came.

My mother turned from nurse to killer to heroine.

Tess and I on Mott Street, the two of us working together at The Owl.

My father our neighbor.

Claire gone.

We say it all the time, but it's true, isn't it? How quickly things change, how quickly the foreign becomes familiar.

Often I forgot where my mother was and what she'd done.

One can't always imagine the hammer. One can't always imagine the cell. Times she was just my neighbor over the hill.

On the porch that evening. The two of us watching. Night Gardener gardening. Tess saying, "I want to see her alone."

"Sure," I say.

"It doesn't bother you?"

"Of course it doesn't. Why would it bother me?"

She shrugs.

Of course it does. Someone else has taken her attention. My love is looking out the window.

But I say, "Sure, Tess. Go see her. She'd like that. With Claire gone."

"With Claire gone?"

"You know what I mean."

"I'm not trying to replace anyone, Joe."

The rest may be approximate, but I'm sure of that line. I hear it so clearly.

She hangs her arm around my neck the way she did, the way I loved. She presses her mouth to my ear. "Maybe I'm going to ask permission to marry you. Maybe I'm going to make my intentions clear."

And I thought, *she has not come here for me.*

54.

When Tess returned from her first visit alone, she said, "That woman is extraordinary."

We were at the bar and I was getting ready for the rush, filling the reach-in, cutting limes, moving buckets of ice. She had her elbows on the service end. She was bouncing on her toes. So young, so giddy.

I kept at it. Marrying vodka bottles, arranging glasses. I couldn't look at her. I didn't know why it worried me so much. Why it made me unhappy. It should have been the opposite, right? But it frightened me.

Tess is dressed for work. Either tight jeans and a black tank top, or a black miniskirt and a white tank top. One of those two combinations. A little owl over her right breast. Lots of dark makeup around her eyes. Her hair all mussed the way she did it then. She could have climbed out of bed, put on a bathrobe and made a killing. But she truly was something those nights. And as happy as she was, it only made it worse. Or better. Depending on your point of view.

"How is she?"

"She's great, Joey. She's fucking great. She's incredible."

"What'd you talk about?"

"Everything. You and me. What we're going to do. My life. My family. The letters she gets, her visitors."

I looked over at her. "What *are* we going to do, Tess?"

She laughed. "That's between me and your mother."

I'm slicing limes. Plastic handle. Riveted. Blue. Serrated

edge. White cutting board. Each lime is six pieces in five moves. I'm fast with the knife. I was a good bartender. Excellent, really.

What else? I'm five foot eleven. And I was a little over six feet with the work boots. And then the thick rubber mats gave me another two inches. I'd been a solid high-school athlete. Shortstop and guard. I kept in shape. Running on the beach. Carrying kegs. Some dumbbells and a bench in the garage. A pull-up bar. I was sturdy like my dad. I still have his shoulders. The point is that back then I was at the height of my power. Behind the bar I was tall and I was strong and next to Seymour Strout I looked like a child.

This night I'm thinking of, he's walking toward us. I'm back there cutting those limes and Tess has a plastic sword pinched between thumb and pointer and she's stabbing cherries, which drives me crazy. I don't like anyone messing with my bar. Not even Tess, but I let her do it.

At the time, I don't know why I'm so irritated. I've got that tight, cold feeling in my spine, which moves upwards into the back of my neck. My vertebrae are compressing, a long and narrow accordion closing, tightening. When that happens, I want to take a hammer to the Pabst mirrors. But I keep it down. I keep quiet. I go about my work. I don't know if Tess notices. When she's happy, I don't think she notices much of anything. She loves to jump on me when she's like this. And usually that's what I want more than anything. To have her climbing all over me like an orangutan. But tonight I wish she'd just shut up. I'm nervous. I don't like that she's gone to see my mother alone. I don't like that she's so happy about it. That she's so enamored with her. I don't know why that is, other than to say I felt betrayed somehow.

Then Seymour Strout walked in.

A little about Seymour. He'd played on the defensive line for the U of O.

"Nearly went pro," he liked to say.

Seymour was one of those guys, the biggest dude I'd ever stood next to in my life. The biggest I've ever known. Six-six, two-eighty. People asked all the time.

"Six-six, two-eighty."

Said it quick as radio code.

He was always hot and always sweating, so he wore a white towel around his neck. He bought packs of them out at Kmart. He kept them clean. Never frayed. If he found a run, or a hole, or a stain, he'd say, mother*fucker,* and replace it. Man he loved that word. After Oregon, he joined the Army and got out two years before George Senior stormed the desert. He kept his head shaved and was always mopping at it with the towel. He liked to smoke outside even if back then you could smoke wherever the hell you wanted. Like most people who work in that world, he too had a thing for ritual. Plus he was ex-military.

You should have seen him on winter nights standing out front beneath that neon owl. Cold as hell and he's sweating in his black T-shirt and towel, a Virginia Slim between his lips, smoke and vapor coming off him like some kind of swamp creature. As my dad used to say, he was something else, that guy.

When Seymour worked, he worked the door. He kept the peace, that's for sure. Anyone got out of line, got loud, gave us shit, started a fight, he ended it fast. And usually just by giving the problem his attention, taking a few steps in the appropriate direction. He was polite. That was his threat. "Excuse me, sir," he'd say to some sophomore English major, "would you mind lowering your voice?" You've never seen anyone shut up so fast. Or, if he happened to be at the bar at the right time, "Excuse me, sir, you seem to have forgotten to include a gratuity."

I really came to love that guy. We both did.

I tried so hard not to. I tried so hard to hate him, my

mother's keeper, but he was too gentle, too serene, too funny, too kind.

Tonight Tess says, "Hey, Strout," and gives him a big smile and they slap hands. It's a thing they started doing. A high five before work. I pour him a shot of Smirnoff and a tall Coke chaser. Same start to every shift.

He'd usually come straight from the prison and I'd ask, "How is she?" And he'd say something like, "She's great, J," or, "Better than ever, brother." And we'd leave it at that. But today, Tess being in the mood she's in, having had a few already, she says, "Why don't you let her out, Strout? How do you sleep at night?"

The accordion compresses. Seymour looks at me from behind his Coke. Big fist around the glass, the glass in front of his mouth, his brown eyes turned down at me, that tender expression of sympathy and sadness.

"I wish I could, Tess," he whispers. "You know how much I wish I could."

I loved him even if I was frightened by what he knew of my mother and their secret world.

He wasn't like most of the men who run a door. Washed-up football players, or wrestlers, or off-duty cops, or local fighters. Even if Seymour *was* a washed-up football player. He may have been sad, but he wasn't bitter. And he wasn't like those guys who are in it for the authority, who are more often looking for someone to punch than they are to stop a fight. He wasn't one of those *give me a reason* guys. He liked looking after people.

I worked bars from the time I was eighteen years old. From back to owner. From LA to Cannon Beach, to White Pine, and on to Seattle. And in all those years I never met anyone like Seymour. People outside never see these things. They're blind to it. The skill it requires, the combination of physical strength and intelligence, intuition and style. Artistry. You know how rare it is to find a good waitress? A good bartender? A good bouncer? How difficult it is to *be* one of those things? And yes, I know I'm supposed to say *server*, but I don't like the word. Anyway, I'd rather wait than serve. And fuck if I'm going to say waitperson. Or associate. Or *team member*. Or any of the other bullshit those drones insist we use.

People walk into a place and sit down and order a drink like they're talking to a machine. They don't even glance up at you.

Anyway, Seymour wasn't looking to break anyone's jaw. Not at the bar, not at the prison. Everyone liked him. Me and Tess. The other waitresses. The manager. The regulars. He did the thing he was supposed to do. He made The Owl feel safe. He knew names. He smiled. He didn't do that raised chin, arms crossed thing. He didn't wear sunglasses. He didn't need any of that shit. He was calm and he was tough and he didn't have to pretend. He was gallant too. Those frat boys got away with nothing. I liked him for all those reasons.

And because he was a little lonely. I could see that right away, something familiar in the eyes.

We liked him and he liked us. As a couple. Gravitated, as they say. At the start I thought he had a thing for her, but soon I realized it wasn't that. He liked us together. Not me, not her: us.

Strange families are born in bars.

What else about Seymour? Mostly he worked days at the prison. He was a guard and had been for a while. He said The Owl was to make extra cash, but I don't think that had much to do with it. He lived alone in a little apartment down by the beach. He didn't have much to pay for. The prison was a union job. Gave him a pension, health insurance, a good salary. He wasn't in debt. There's so much freedom in living like that. It was the same for Tess and me. Just like it had been in Cannon Beach.

On the other hand, too much freedom will get you into trouble. You start thinking about what you want. What's next.

What's right and wrong. And what you might change. If you're working three jobs, taking care of your kids, and paying off a mortgage, there's no time for that juvenile nonsense.

Anyway, Seymour liked to get away from the prisoners, the other guards. And I think he liked the warmth of the bar. The spirit of it. The nightly celebration to counter the miserable gloom of The Pine. He didn't go to Lester's much. He said being with civilians kept him even.

When people asked about the prison, he always made the same bad joke: Difference between The Owl and The Pine? Fewer assholes out there.

The other thing about Seymour is that he rarely talked about my mother. Even with all the shit we gave each other in the course of a shift, he never brought her up. So when Tess suddenly said what she did that evening, it was like something had been broken, changed. A Breach.

55

T hat night an hour before closing, after Seymour went out for a smoke, Tess said, "What's wrong with you? Don't you want to hear about it?"

"No."

"Baby," she said, "petulant little Joey," and walked away.

The last drinkers came. Tess worked the floor. I worked the bar. Seymour on the door. I kept away from her. We didn't play our mid-shift games. But later, when it was over, after I'd cashed out and delivered my drawer, I came down to find Tess and Seymour sitting at a corner table, a bottle between them.

I brought a glass of ice.

"Strout doesn't want to hear it either," Tess said. "Nobody wants to hear it."

Seymour shrugged. "Your girl here's been drinking."

"I think you should both know that something important is happening out there. I think you should both know that your mother who *you* don't want to see, who spends her life in a prison, isn't just anyone. She's your mother and something important has happened. Not that either of you gives a fuck."

Seymour smiled at me. "You see?"

"Neither of you *sees*," Tess said. "Why would you? Boys. Everywhere I go, little boys." She poured herself another bourbon. "Why don't you tell him what's happening, Strouty? Maybe he'll listen to you."

He laughed. "And what's happening?"

"What's *happening* is that Anne-Marie March is a hero. And

even if neither of you wants to hear it, a lot of people are saying it, and a lot more believe it and that's what's going on."

Seymour stirred the ice in his glass with his finger. I watched because I couldn't look at Tess.

"Nothing? Neither of you boys has anything to say? She gets letters. Hundreds of them. And the other women in there think it too. Isn't that right, Strout? Ain't that right?"

I looked at Seymour who was watching his finger chase a shard of ice.

"Tell him," Tess said.

"Not my place."

"Go on, Seymour," I said. "Tell me."

"She gets a lot of letters."

"And the women?" Tess knocked her knuckles on the table like some kind of belligerent lawyer.

"She gets along well in there," he said. "People seem to look up to her."

"Go on, tell him. She's a hero to them, Joseph."

"She's not Christ, Tess."

"Goddamn right she's not." Tess pounded the table again. Seymour caught the bottle before it fell. "She's Joan of Arc, you assholes."

She stood up and headed to the bathroom.

Seymour shook his head. "I'm sorry," he said. "I know you don't want to talk about it."

"Is it true?"

"Well, she's popular in there, yes. She's a smart lady who killed a man. A man who was a piece of shit. That's a pretty good combination for prison cred."

"So, they like her?"

"They do."

Neither of us spoke for a bit. Just drank and studied the table.

"What do you think?" I asked him.

"Of what?"

"What she did."

Seymour wiped his face with the towel and looked up at the ceiling.

"What do I think? You know, Joey, I spend a lot of time around those women. Maybe I'm not the best person to ask."

"Why not?"

"Things get fucked up. They get distorted. It's hard to remember who did what. Why someone's there. You react to the way they are now, not to what they did. If someone's a pain in the ass, then you don't like her. Someone's nice, she lets you do your job, then you like her. That's the way it works for me anyway. Other guards it's the opposite. They don't give a shit about the way you are now. They forgive nothing. That's not the way I live, but maybe that makes more sense, maybe that's better because sometimes the ones who did the worst shit, they're the easiest to handle. And the biggest assholes, they're the ones who probably shouldn't be in there in the first place. So everything goes all upside down."

"You didn't answer my question."

"Well, your mom, she's polite. She's not a pain in the ass."

"So you like her."

"I do."

"Even if she did the worst shit?"

"I didn't say that. And believe me, there are women in there who make your mom look like a nun."

"Like what?"

"You don't want to hear about it."

"I do," I said.

Seymour took a mouthful of bourbon and looked at me carefully. It was like my father trying to decide if I was ready to hear about sex. There were times Seymour seemed a lot like my father. Not like my dad, the guy who lived down the street, but like my father. Another father. A different kind. A father with a little more violence in him, a few more secrets, a man with a darker heart. And then other times it felt more like I was his. Or that me and Tess were his parents and that he was our enormous son.

Seymour swallowed his bourbon, crunched the ice between his teeth.

"A woman in there set her children on fire. Another beat her son half to death for forgetting to turn the lights off. There's one who chained her twelve-year-old daughter to a bed and sold her for sex to neighborhood men. It goes on and it gets worse and worse. Much worse. There are things in this world you just don't want to know about. Things you want never to have heard."

"And you like some of these people?"

He shrugged. "I'm glad they're locked up. If you've fucked with a kid like that, you get treated pretty rough inside. By the guards, by the other inmates. You get beat up, you don't always get fed, privileges disappear. You're always in danger. You can never rest, you can never stop worrying. Being inside is supposed to be the punishment. It's being locked up that's supposed to be the torture. So what am I going to do? Torture them more? No. As long as they're inside, I'll treat them the way they treat me."

"As long as they're inside?"

"It's different out here. If I saw something like that. Came across it on the street." He shook his head.

"You didn't answer my question."

"What do I think of what she did? Did that man need to die? I don't know. Probably not. But a coward like him? I think about what I'd have done. If I'd been walking by and saw it. Shit, Joey. I'd have done the same. It's just the kind of thing that sets me off. And who knows? Would I have hit him only once? Would I have stopped? When the string breaks and you lose your mind, who knows how long it takes to remember the rules? To remember you're a person."

I'd never heard Seymour talk so much.

"You ever been in a fight?"

I nodded.

"You ever won?"

I laughed and nodded.

"Then you know what I mean," he said. "Look, I know she's your mom, Joey. I know it must be hard to think of it."

Tess came back from the bathroom, put her arm on Seymour's shoulder.

"What did I miss?"

"Just us, Tess," Seymour said, and smiled at me.

"With an aching in my heart," she said and sat down. "So what's next, kids? What's the next thing?"

Seymour said, "I think you should go to bed. That's what I think is next."

"I don't mean now, you fucker. I mean bigger. I mean in the days, boys. The days to come."

"What do you want to happen?" I asked. "Now that we live here in fucking White Pine, Washington. What do *you* want to happen?"

She slid her chair forward, inching it along the floor, making as much noise as possible. Then she put an arm around my shoulder, and an arm around Seymour's.

"What I want, boys. Lean in here. Huddle up."

Can you see us there late at night? Me and Tess and Seymour, the only people in that bar, the three of us leaning forward over a little cocktail table. Tess drunk as hell. Maybe start from outside. One of those gliding shots where you can't figure out the way the camera moves so seamlessly through the walls. You start way out across the road. Maybe you start with the roaring ocean and then swing over to the nearly empty parking lot, and then that sinister owl smoldering above the dark door. And then you're inside with the beer, and sawdust and cigarettes. The music's on low and there at a corner table in this empty bar is our trio, our strange family. A young and very drunk woman sitting between two men, one of them massive, one of them me, and she's brought her voice down and she's saying in a stage whisper, "What I want is for something to happen. What I want is to *do* something. Can you understand that? Before I fucking die, I want to *do* something."

And if you insist on the existence of beginnings. If you believe in that kind of thing. Then this is that.

56

Nothing has changed in the morning. This hangover, as with all her hangovers, was insignificant. I brought her a glass of water. Coffee. Aspirin. Cooked her two fried eggs, bacon, toast. She took a long walk on the beach and by the time she was back she was fine. Me, even then, even in the heart of my youth, when I drank like that, it took me a full day to recover.

Tess hated it. She had such little tolerance for frailty.

So after the breakfast, and the walk on the beach, she returned home and she was fine. She was fine and nothing had changed. The night was not forgotten. None of it was non-sense. She returned home and after a shower she came downstairs. It had turned very cold. We had a fire going. I'd stake my life on this memory: her hair a mess, barefoot, wearing the one dress shirt I owned, white, which had once been my father's. The shirt I'd worn for my interview at The Spruce, The Owl, and every job before that. A cherry stain on the sleeve. Frayed buttonholes.

She seemed impossible—her skin, her eyes, her knees. I don't know how else to say it. Impossible that such a woman existed. That she was there in my house, in my shirt. No make-up. No bra. Hair a little longer, a little wilder.

It caused me such joy to see her.

And such pain.

And such fear.

What combination has more power? And what combination more unusual?

Through the course of my life, no other person, no other thing has ever given me all of it at once.

I suspect that a child might.

It's what I have often imagined holding my newborn daughter might be.

I don't know. I suppose I'll never know.

All of it can mean only so much.

Just like language.

The stories of our great lovers are always stories of failure.

I may be a man alone in the woods singing to the invisible and the invented, but it matters that when Tess comes down those stairs she is unlike anything I have ever known.

57

The streets were full of fog. Smoke rose from the chimney of our little house on Mott Street. Tess was pacing. "There is a group," she said. Here she crossed the room and sat next to me. "Out at the college. They've been writing. They visit her. They want to organize. They have run out of patience. That's what they say. How they sign their letters. *We have run out of patience.*"

"With what?"

"With all of it, Joey. But most of all with the violence."

"Funny," I said. "Funny that these women who've run out of patience with violence have chosen my mother as their hero."

She looked at me with such irritation and disappointment. Why did I provoke her? I hardly needed the explanation. I resisted because it was my mother. Because of Tess, because there was something in her that frightened me, a thing I didn't want and wasn't ready for. Not for the change, nor for the disruption, nor the inevitable complication of our lives. Not even in the name of revolution. I didn't want my mother to be a hero, to become a symbol of some ill-conceived and miniature revolt. I resisted for those, and for a thousand other reasons.

But mostly I just wanted things to stay as they were. Because I was my father's son.

"Not funny at all," she said. "They think what she did is what should have been done. And what should *be* done. That she was defending another woman, defending two children who could not defend themselves. They think she should be released from prison."

"So they want to change the laws."

"They think the laws should change, yes. But that's not what they're primarily interested in."

"What are they primarily interested in, Tess?"

"Action."

"Action. So a bunch of girls from the college, all of whom have run out of patience, will roam White Pine with hammers dangling from their belts?"

She despised me when I spoke to her like this.

"They don't know yet, Joey. They don't know what they'll do."

"I see. And they go to visit my mother for what? Advice? Leadership? Inspiration?"

"I don't know. She told me about them yesterday. And now I'm telling you."

"And now what?"

"She wants me to meet with them."

"Meet with them."

"Go out to the college, yes."

"Why?"

"I'm not sure. To see what can be done."

"As her emissary."

"I don't know exactly."

"And will you go?"

"Yes. With you. We'll go together."

"Is that the word from on high?"

She nodded.

"Why? Why would I do that? Why would you?"

She sighed her exasperated sigh and looked out at the trees while I watched her and waited.

"Because I don't want to spend the rest of my life in a fucking bar. Neither do you. And because, Joey, I am angry.

Because I am angry in a way you can't possibly imagine. You can try, but you cannot understand it. Just like I try to understand you or what has happened to your family. I try but I can't. It is the kind of anger that comes from too much fear. Do you understand me? Just like your mother. And just like her, I don't want to ignore it. I won't. I would rather fucking die."

"I don't know," I said. "What is the it, Tess?"

She walked over to the fire. "The things they do," she said. "The things they're allowed to do. What we accept. What we endorse. What we celebrate."

I watched her.

"Accept, endorse, celebrate. Is that some kind of a slogan? Something the women without patience stamp on their T-shirts?"

"Fuck you. It's not them. It's your mother. *She* said it."

So, the master, the guru in chains, was at work on her proverbs.

"She says it?"

"Yes."

"What does it mean?"

"That we're complicit."

"In what?"

"Violence, Joe."

"Violence."

"Against women."

"We accept, and endorse, and celebrate it."

"Yes," she said. "Yes. And please stop with the sarcasm. Please. I know I don't have to explain this. I know you agree."

"Of course," I said.

"So then what?"

"The idea of her in there inventing herself as some kind of prophet."

"Not a prophet. But so what? You'd rather she goes soft in there watching Jenny Jones?"

"I'd rather she's not in there at all."

"Well, she is. So if this is what she's doing, so what? Why does it make you so angry? Why do you hate it, Joey? You should be proud."

"Proud?"

"Yes. To have a mother like her. To know you come from someone so strong."

That expression on her face, the one I loved most. All that life, all that determination. I was tired of arguing. I didn't know why I was angry. Not then, not precisely. Or why I was resisting. I fell back into the couch, gave it up and closed my eyes.

"Now what?" I asked. "What happens now?"

"I've seen it, Joey. Don't forget that. I watched you break your hand. I know what's in you."

"That was different," I said.

"What's the difference?"

"That was for you."

"So is this," she said.

58.

Yesterday, late afternoon, the electric rise. An hour before the sun falls through the trees and I'm sprinting hard through the clearing chasing an elk into the woods. I'd pulled all the pots up onto the counter and was scrubbing them as if they weren't clean already, sweating from the work and the steam, when I saw it feeding. And then I was out there in the cold, in my jeans, barefoot, shirtless, not feeling anything but my own liquid body gliding through the thickening purple air. If you'd seen me from the window, you'd have thought I was after blood, but all I wanted was to be next to the animal or part of it somehow. If I'd had any idea at all what I was after, which I probably didn't then. I was just running, so happy and full of sky, certain I could catch the thing and put my arm over its thick, hot neck, or maybe ride it, wrap myself around its back, feel its warm belly against my thighs, push my face against its fur. I ran off the trails, deeper and deeper into the tangle of branches and shadows. The animal was long gone, but I ran on until I had no more breath and the full night had come. But still the rising and I lay down in the underbrush and buried myself in damp leaves until I was nothing but a pair of eyes pointed upwards. The ground was as warm and soft as our bed and I stayed there writhing, shivering with all the power I felt, my fingers slowly clawing at the earth, my hands opening and closing like cats' paws and I thought, Fuck Tess, who needs her, I'll go find the woman with black hair and blue eyes where nothing is hidden, her plain, pale face, rosy farmer cheeks, the sweet green pears, hard pucks of cheese, and I will carry her home over my shoulder and show what I have within me.

When I made it home I was cold. My feet were bleeding. Long, deep scratches across my chest. Leaves in my hair. I went to bed and stained the sheets and now I can hear them turning in the wash.

There's sunlight in the clearing and I am alone again, waiting for whatever I will do next.

59

W ill you go again eventually?" Tess asked.
"Of course, I will."
"May as well go now then."

So up the hill, along the Spine, down the valley, onto
Prison Way, into the parking lot, through the check-in, the
metal detector, the hallway, to the visit room, to my place at the
table.

You think memory is enough. But then you're there and see
how wrong you are. It's something else entirely. Intensity of
sound, rush of color. Smell. Sometimes it's too much for me.

It seems I'm missing most of the filters. Or they work only
half the time. The older I get the brighter the light, the louder
the sound. It is worse now, but it has always been this way. As
long as I can remember. A shirt tag like a tack in my neck. A
seat belt edge like a blade across my shoulder. Paralyzing jack-
ets. Everything irritating. Nights when the sounds get louder
and louder. Angry pipes. Complaining trees. Pine needles hissing in the dark. Baying coyotes. Mice in the eaves. The tawny
owls calling, Joe, Joey, Joseph, Joe, Joey, Joseph. Come home,
come home, come home.

Cities terrify me. All the motion, all the people, all the talk.
Chattering and chattering and chattering. The saturation. The
grime. How do you stay still? How do you keep it out? How
do you keep from drowning? Interior, exterior, the light, the
color, the noise, the smell, every moving part, the intuition, the
animals, the cars, the fear, the trees, the glass, the desire, the

food, the smoke, searing meat, need, elbows, hideous people, vulgar, shuffling, lurching people.

All of it comes in one liquid mixture pouring through me fast. A wide and steady stream in ever-changing colors blasting from a toppled hydrant. When it comes, I cannot stop it. On the bus it pours into my mouth. Subways are worst of all. I have terrible dreams of those subterranean trains, in the tunnels where there is no escape, no natural light. Locked inside where there is no relief, no sky, no air, no exit. The adrenaline comes. The sweat follows. My body vibrating the way it does on dark corners, in bad alleys, footsteps behind me, when a fight is inevitable. It is the adrenaline of war. And soon my whole face is gone. I am left with a dark oval, a void, the stream flowing in.

And even here, so far from any city, before the quiet woods, where no cars can be heard, no neighbors can be seen, still the noise rises. The needles, relentless birds, the rain, buckets of shattered glass against the windows, against the roof, the pipes like choking old men.

When it happens now, when the filters fail and I'm afraid I may die, I go into the guest bathroom and I draw the blinds. I close the door and push a towel along the bottom crack to block the light, to block the air the way Claire and I once did in the bathroom we shared in Capitol Hill, when we were kids and she wanted to smoke our mother's Marlboros.

I turn the lights off and lie on my back and I stay there in the cold dark until it passes. Until the noise has vanished, and the sense that it might kill me has gone.

These days, it's the only thing I know to do.

I stay there in the stillness with my sister Claire and I wait.

60.

I'd driven out to The Pine and was waiting for my mother at one of those tables, its legs riveted to the floor.

"Everything's a weapon," Seymour told me more than once.

And then there she was, Seymour escorting her in. Which was a shock. Though it shouldn't have been. The odds were good, I guess. He nodded. Gave me that look of his—all at once tender and contrite and apologetic and wise. It was strange to see them together. Or strange to see them come in from somewhere else. It suggested a life without me. Not really a suggestion, I guess. Because that's just what they had, isn't it? The two of them inside. Me out. I imagined them entering a dinner party. Bustling in from a cold night, pulling off their coats, their scarves. Sorry, everyone, for being late, traffic was terrible. That kind of thing. A happy couple. They were no couple, of course, but the intimacy was undeniable. They shared a world that I did not. The routines, the food, the gossip, the texture of the place.

I don't know why it surprised me. Why I hadn't considered any of that before. It takes me time with these things.

I'm slow to see the obvious.

Seymour left her at the door. The first time I'd seen her in a month, maybe more. She looked healthy. Strong. Her hair was longer, parted in the middle and pulled back into a ponytail, the way she'd worn it when I was younger, the way she'd worn it in all the photographs of her life with my father before us. Her posture had changed again. She had always been a graceful woman, but now she moved with what seemed to me an affected slowness. Her chin slightly cocked, a subtle, condescending smile. A dancer walking onstage, not yet dancing, just finding her mark, preparing, but even in the preparation there was theater. She'd lost color in her face, but she wasn't sickly the way she'd been in those first visits. The whiteness of her skin making her eyes appear bluer.

She held me.

"Joey," she whispered, "Joey," as if we were anywhere, as if I were her child home from school. I liked the normalcy of her voice, the strength of her arms. I think I had been afraid that she was dying in there, that she would be withered and emaciated, that a woman like her could do nothing but die in a place like that.

"You look good," I said.

We both sat.

She touched my face. "I am, Joey."

"I'm glad. I hear you've become a revolutionary."

She laughed. "Is that what you hear?"

To see her like that, flashes of the other person, of the other time, it made me happy. As simple as that. The way that only relief makes me happy.

"Tess," she said. "She's lovely, Joe."

"I know."

"Do you?"

"I do."

"Don't fuck it up."

I laughed. "So you no longer think I'm wasting my life living here in White Pine?"

She shrugged. "That depends."

"On what?"

"On your life here in White Pine."

"What does that mean?"

"I think you know what it means."

"Tell me. I'd like you to tell me," I said.

She sighed. "Joey. Do you want to be a bartender the rest of your life? Do you want to stay here? Never go anywhere else, never do anything."

"I'm happy. Bartending, living with Tess. We're happy."

"Is she?"

There was the cold edge.

"You seem to think you know. Why don't you tell me about Tess. Now that you know her so well."

I couldn't stop myself.

"Don't be a child, Joey."

"Tell me about her."

She held my eyes for a long moment. "All right. No. No she's not happy. She is restless. And if you try to stop her, you will lose her."

I kept my mouth shut.

"I know you want to stay still. Keep things as they are. But you have to resist it, do you understand me? Don't get stuck, Joe."

I leaned forward. "Whereas you," I said, "*you* like to shake things up."

She drew back as if I'd shoved her.

"Whatever the case. Whatever I've inherited from Dad, I have your instincts as well. There are the things I've inherited from you as well."

"And what are those, Joey?"

"A temper, for one."

We both smiled. We both relaxed.

"What else?"

"It's hard to say, exactly."

"Why don't you try?"

"I will," I said. "One day, I will."

She looked at me with focus unusual even for her.

I imagined that she understood. That she saw it in me, this fundamental and frightening element. This thing, which was herself. I imagined I wouldn't have to say it, that it was simply understood. Through that long speechless exchange. But perhaps we were both just waiting for some explanation. Hoping for some understanding that didn't exist. And again, I wonder what difference it would have made.

She tapped her fingernails against the tabletop. They were painted red. Just like her lips.

"You know, Joey, Tess's mother died."

"Yes," I said. "Of course I know that."

"Of breast cancer."

"Yes. Did you think I wouldn't know?"

I felt the anger surging again.

"Of course you know. And you know, too, that you're lucky. To have both of your parents alive. Parents who love you. Who care about your life, about the way you live."

"Yes," I said.

She was so strange, speaking in these platitudes. So inconsistent. Foreign and familiar, foreign and familiar.

I see her fingers, the way they wrapped around my hand, the varnished fingernails shining, reflecting four times that terrible fluorescent light.

"We love you, Joey. Your father and I."

Her face had become flushed. Her eyes were shining as if she might cry.

"We love you very much," she said. "We're fortunate to have what we do. And fortunate to have Tess. All of us are. This family of ours. And I want for us to give Tess." She stopped. She wiped her eyes with the heel of her free hand. "I want for us to give her the family she's missing, the family we have. Can we do that, Joey?"

I don't know if I'd ever seen my mother cry out of sadness. Out of joy, yes. On some Christmas mornings, with all of us home, eating breakfast together. Yes, I'd seen her cry then. That way. Or in recounting some good story from the hospital, some life saved, or disaster averted. But not like this. Not with such pain and desperation. And yet beneath it all something was not quite right. I couldn't shake the sense I was being played. That this woman, at that moment wasn't her, wasn't the person I'd known as my mother.

Still I said, "Yes, Mom. I will do everything I can."

"We all will," she said. "All of us will."

"Okay," I said. "We all will."

Even if I wasn't sure what she meant, I agreed and squeezed her hand until it was time to go. I held her tightly and kissed her cheek and watched as she was taken away, this time by a guard I didn't recognize, a heavyset woman with red hair who didn't look at me once as she walked my mother from the room.

61

Emerson College was named not for the Transcendentalist, but for and by Henry Emerson, a ruthless Presbyterian missionary responsible for delivering a measles epidemic to the White Pine Valley, which effectively eradicated the indigenous Chinook. Half the adult population died, and not a single child survived. The college, however, does. A former seminary, it is now a much expanded but still small campus of brick buildings and creeping ivy. At the entrance there are two large plaques, one in memory of Henry Emerson, the other of his wife, Lucy. There's a charming clock tower, and green lawns and sandy paths, which meander over the barrier dunes down to the ocean. In a struggling working-class town populated by farmers, fishermen, and prison guards, it is an oasis of liberalism and academic luxury twelve miles south of White Pine.

Between two pillars a long and well-paved road slopes down a gentle hill. One way in, one way out. It's something like The Pine—the drive, the suspense and drama of the long approach, the parking lot, the administrative buildings, the insular world.

It was there the women without patience were encamped. And so there we went to meet them. Even if it wasn't exactly clear to either of us why. We traveled on orders, emissaries of the cause. Whatever that was, whatever it would become, here we were crossing the great quad, passing kids not much younger than ourselves, who seemed to us so much like children.

A cold day. Fog and sun. Everything just as you imagine it. Backpacks and hustling students. Leisure and panic. Frisbees. The theater of permanence and safety. Tess and I searching for some building. Asking directions from an out-of-breath boy, hacky sack in hand.

Somehow I'd expected one of those raked lecture halls, but it was instead an upper level seminar room. Pine chairs around a pine table. The door was open and when we arrived they all hushed. There was a lot of ceremony. Showing us where we should sit. Presenting us with Styrofoam cups of coffee. Thanking us for being there. They had us at one end, and they were all gathered at the other making jokes about which was the foot, and which was the head. Then an uncomfortable silence as Tess and I sipped our coffee, while the women looked on as if we'd arrived by helicopter from the Pentagon. The only black person in the room, the only person who wasn't white, cleared her throat and introduced herself. Marcy Harper. The only one I remember.

Marcy Harper who said to Tess, "We weren't expecting a man. Ms. March didn't say anything about a man in her letter."

Tess nodded and smiled and both gestures were unfamiliar. The pace of the nod, the restraint of her smile. Now she was tolerant and wise. She'd changed. Without warning me, she had shifted just the way a great actor does. Transformation instantaneous and absolute.

I could never do it. Not on purpose. Not like that. I've never had the control. My transformations have so little to do with will. My changes originate elsewhere.

This was something she had been preparing for. All those weeks and here was a fleck of her secret life. This is what she saw out the windows at night. On the ceiling when she went vacant after sex. This is what she saw: herself in this room, her spine a little straighter, her hands interlaced, resting on the table.

"I understand," she said turning and smiling at me, her colleague. "This is Joseph March. Anne-Marie March's son."

There was a shift then. Those women turning their attention to me with a new focus, relaxing, their expressions altered. No longer cold, they looked on in anticipation. My turn to speak.

"*Mrs.* March," I said.

They squinted. They soured.

"She's married to my father."

And then someone said, "*Ms.*"

This person, who once appeared so sharply defined, exists now only as part of that blurry mass of memory, like the waitresses at The Owl, like those friends on the beach in Big Sur, those friends I loved so much, who I could never leave, who I would never lose. Like so many people who've been taken by death, or by distance, or by time. Even those you're not ever meant to forget, those you're expected to keep forever clear and definite, even they blur.

She said, "*Ms.* We use the neutral *Ms.* Regardless of marital status."

And another person said, or something like it, "We choose not to be defined by our partners."

"Well—" I said quietly.

Quietly, though what I wanted was to chuck my chair through a window.

"Anne-Marie March is my mother. I am her son. I am here because she asked me to be."

"And we are pleased to be here," Tess said in her new politician's voice.

"We are all very happy to have you," Marcy Harper said, smiling at me.

All of us just children.

There was a small scar. That's when I first noticed it. Right then when she smiled. A small scar running up and around the outside of her eye, a soft C turned inward.

"We're certainly not here to lecture you," she said glancing about the room.

The others chastened.

Her eyes were deadly. She was like Tess. She was like my mother. An intelligence and confidence to kill.

I smiled at her.

Someone asked politely, with caution, "Why does she want you to meet with us? Why are you here?"

Tess, who had been sitting quietly, looked up. "We are here because Ms. March cannot be. Because you wrote to her. Because she asked us to see what can be done. What this small group might do. We came to listen."

Marcy leaned back in her chair, while the rest of them began to speak.

You can imagine, no? Maybe you've been in those under-graduate classrooms with the freshly politicized. You've known the thrill of having outrage articulated. The thrill of finding others smarter, and angrier, than you are. Of believing, however briefly, that you might change *things*. That you might—and here phrases like corpses—*make a difference, change the world*. With knowledge, with awareness, with letter-writing, with dis-cussion, with art, with marching, and placards, and editorials, and leaflets. With pure fury. You remember the way that felt. Whatever the injustice. The energy you had to fight it, the ways you would take back the night. What you'd do before you had to work, before you had to pay your rent, chip away at your debt, take care of other people, before the exhaustion came, and all that lovely fury turned bitter and cold.

You remember the way that new language sounded, the repeated phrases, how you adopted them, and briefly believed they were your own. The novelty of that rage.

And later how you ran up against its limits.

They said, We are tired of the way women are treated. We are angry. We want to effect change. We want to act. They said, culture of violence and objectifying and sexualizing and demeaning. The rape. The abuse. They said, traditions, hypocrisy, double standards. Systemic, they said, and patriarchy. We must exit the patriarchy.

They said, *We admire your mother. Because your mother fought back. Because your mother refused to walk away. Because she did what we wish we had the courage to do. We will no longer grant permission. We too will fight back*, they said.

They talked until they ran out of language.

Marcy spoke then. "I think the question finally is this: What are we willing to do about it?"

She met my eyes.

"Yes," Tess said. "That's right. That's certainly the question."

"When you say you want to fight back, does that mean you believe in what my mother has done? Do you believe in fighting with hammers?" I asked.

I carried the gravity of my mother's violence. It was unearned.

And then, "Your mother acted in self-defense."

"No, she was defending someone else," I said.

"And in that case, she's justified. Self-defense or the defense of someone else," someone said.

"Why then is she in prison?"

"The patriarchy," they said.

"No," I said. "No, it's the seven blows. She wouldn't be there if it had been one, or even two. But there were seven. So the question is whether or not you believe in what she did. Do you believe Dustin Strauss deserved to die for his sins?"

I don't know where all that talking had come from. Or the affect, the courtroom register. The new momentum, the enthusiasm for my vague position. Tess made some move to speak. A breath or a cough. I knew she'd imagined the meeting otherwise, that she was to be the leader, but I went on anyway.

"My question is real," I said. "Not rhetorical. I wonder what you think. Does violence call for violence? Does a man deserve to die for beating a woman?"

"No," someone said, of course not. And someone else, "No one deserves to die. No."

"And yet, you have made my mother your hero."

"It wasn't intentional. She lost control. She couldn't take it any longer. It was the last straw. She snapped. It could have been any of us. Any of us could snap. There is always a limit."

"Yes," I said. "It could have been any of us."

Marcy spoke again. "Could it have been you?"

"Yes," I said.

"But you are not as angry as we are, Mr. March."

"No?"

"No. That would be impossible."

"Why is that?"

"Because you're not a woman," she said. "And no matter whose son you are, you can't know the anger, because you can't know the fear."

"I don't claim to."

"And yet you're here. Another man at the front of another room. Self-satisfied and superior. Another man illuminating the world for us silly girls."

And even as arrogant and as stupid as I was in those days, I knew enough to keep my mouth shut. Because she was right. Because I was precisely what she described.

"Another man running the room, while a woman sits at his side with her mouth shut." Marcy flashed her eyes at Tess, a look that contained no sympathy, and then she turned back to me. "You are here as a guest, Mr. March. You can spare us the lectures."

"Yes," I said. "Okay."

And because I was humiliated, because I was a graceless fool, I stood up and left the room without apologizing. I walked out onto that wide lawn and bought a cup of coffee from a cart and sat with it on a bench.

My shame made me angry.

Tess would be furious.

And yet I was surprised to find that I hadn't been deadened by the experience. The wounds were superficial. In the fresh air, my adrenaline diluting, I felt oddly energized, thrilled by what had happened, surprised by a sense of pleasure.

Soon the door swung open and Tess crossed the lawn. She narrowed her eyes at me, mocking, scolding, but she *wasn't* angry. And the relief of that only brought me higher. She sat at my side and ran her hand through my hair.

"Joey, Joey, Joey," she said, teasing. No more admonition than that. Just the two of us side by side on a bench in the salt air.

62

I had no true conviction. There was nothing beneath my sad performance in that Emerson seminar room. What I wanted then were orders. What I wanted then was the freedom of being someone's soldier. And Tess must have known. Whatever the reason for my stubborn resistance—fear, the state of being young and male—it had passed as quickly as the time it had taken Marcy Harper to dispatch me from her table.

"We're going to do it, Joey," Tess said, her fingers still moving through my hair. "With these people or without them."

"What is the *it*, Tess?"

"I'm not sure. But I think we have an idea, don't we? I think we have some idea."

I shrugged.

"Anyway, fuck these women. I'll tell your mother."

I smiled. "I like Marcy Harper," I said.

She laughed and turned to me with her sharp, murderous eyes.

"Yes, so do I," she said, though I didn't believe her.

We were quiet for a long time. In the weak sun, Tess stroking the back of my head, coffee turning cold in our cups, we watched the mundane drama of Emerson quad on an early winter's day.

After a while, Tess began to talk.

"In Portland once," she said. "My first year in college. I was what? Eighteen? I was downtown at a café, at a little outdoor table. A few of us had come up for the weekend, just to get away from school, to be somewhere else for a change. My friends had gone off somewhere and I was alone, reading by myself. There were people everywhere. I was caught up, completely lost in whatever the book was. And then all at once I could sense someone behind me. I thought at first maybe it was the guy who was working there, so I started to turn my head, but just as I did there was a low voice in my left ear. I could feel breath on my neck. I froze. It said, 'What are you reading?' I didn't respond. I stared at the pages, praying he'd go away, but he stayed there breathing on me. He smelled like toothpaste and sweat. I kept my eyes on the page. I couldn't move for some reason. Then he whispered right into my ear, 'You fucking bitch, you fucking whore, I'm going to follow you home and rape you.' I made a noise then, a little cry of fear or surprise or outrage, but still, even after that, I couldn't move. And he mocked me. He imitated my sound and he did it perfectly, too. Then he kissed me on the cheek, Joe. It was so vile. I closed my eyes and when I opened them I couldn't feel him there anymore. It took all my will to turn, but by then he was gone. There were people everywhere and they all seemed like they were walking away from me. I looked at the others sitting around tables, but none seemed to have noticed anything. I'm sure they thought he was just my boyfriend stopping by to say hello."

Throughout this whole story, Tess had kept her hand on the back of my head. Eyes dead forward as if she were speaking to the passing students, or to herself. Now she turned to me. She slipped her left foot beneath her right thigh the way she liked to sit on the couch at home when we were talking, or when I was reading and she suddenly wanted to play.

She is leaning toward me, the incredulous expression, part pain, part disbelief.

"We drove back to Eugene. I looked out the window and

said nothing to my friends about it. But that man was every-where. His breath. His lips on my cheek. His hissing voice. I was only terrified. And disgusted. I wasn't even angry yet. And when I got home I went to a phone booth and called my mother. This was a little less than a year before she died. She still hadn't told me she was sick. I called her and told her what had happened. It was a Sunday night and everything was so quiet and dark. The phone booth was outside our dorm. I wanted the privacy of it. I remember every detail of making that call. Walking out into the night in sweats and an old T-shirt, barefoot. My hair still wet from the long shower. The fear I felt crossing the dark walkway. The fear I felt standing alone. A frightened little girl all lit up in a glass box. Determined to stay there. I told her my story and when I was finished she said, 'Well, Tess, you know, it's always the goddamn same. There's nothing you can do, but put your head down and protect your-self. It's the way of the world, I'm afraid.'

"And I said, 'Of course there's something you can do. Of course there is.'

"She may have begun to talk, might have said, 'once . . .' or 'when I was your age . . .' but in the end all she told me was, 'You're lucky, sweetheart. They do a lot worse.'

"'What do you mean?' I asked, not because I didn't know, but because I hoped she would tell me her own stories, because for a moment it sounded like she would, but she didn't. All she said was, 'You know exactly what I mean, Tess.'

"I waited for a moment. I remember there was a long pause, and how badly I wanted to ask about her life, but just couldn't get myself to speak. And then she said, softer, 'You have to be careful, honey. That's all. You have to protect yourself. It's the most important thing.'

"I remember it so well, Joe: standing in that cold phone booth, the quiet world outside, listening to my mom's voice. I can see her and I can see me. Me. Myself a thousand years ago.

That girl missing her mother, her mother so afraid for her daughter. Just the two of them talking across those lines."

That was the story Tess told me one afternoon. Or as well as I can render it. It can't be accuracy that matters. It can't be accuracy that honors. It must be desire. It must be purity of intention. It must be love itself. And now, here I return through all the layers. Through my memory, my desire, Tess's memory, what she withheld and did not, knowingly and unknowingly, her mother's memory, what she withheld and did not, knowingly and unknowingly, and so on until we are returned to the bench at Emerson College.

From which we wandered out along a campus path to the ocean.

We walked and walked and then, when the wind came up, hid out high in the dunes. There she told me that after her trip to Portland, after the call to her mother, she had joined groups like Marcy Harper's. That she'd marched and protested. She'd spent years doing it. Writing letters and organizing concerts and stapling flyers to telephone poles.

Shameful as this is to admit, child that I was, until then I'd never thought of the way women live. Even after my mother did what she did. It wasn't until that day out in those dunes. Sitting with her, listening to her stories. A litany of minor and major violence. That stark difference in daily experience. The normalcy and constancy of fear. I'd never thought about it. Not really until Tess came along.

She told me the way they had all slowly given up. The way they had lost the energy for the fight. Kept their heads down. The older ones ahead of her graduated, went off to work. They went on about their lives. Took it all for the way of the world. Just as her mother had said to do. Awful but unchangeable. Like so many other things. And if I want to have a job, and if I don't want to be alone the rest of my life, and if I want to have children. So keep your head down, don't make eye contact, keep walking.

But Tess wouldn't do that now. "Something has changed," she said.

First when we fell in love. Then when she'd learned about my mother. After she'd gone to see her. Now she was energized. Now she was on fire again. For the second time in her young life.

We loved those vast Washington beaches. Their dark mirrors, water sliding across the wet sand, the doubled pipers hunting crabs. We stayed pressed together, side by side, facing the sunset. Just our heads above the edge of dune, looking out over the giant beach.

We were up there on our bellies, in our sniper's nest, protected from the wind blowing hard and cold, straight on shore, me with my binoculars, Tess with her rifle.

63.

I went for a run this morning. It wasn't even light out. Not that it gets very light lately with the weather we've been having. Rain and fog, rain and fog. But I woke up this morning and ran, slicing through the grey, straight on into the trees. I was loose and light. I could have kept going too, but I wanted to be back here before I lost it. You can't always have me gloomy. You can't always have me scratching around in the weeds. It gets tiresome, I know. Believe me I know.

No bird, no tar today. You see how it's arbitrary? How yesterday's brain would tell it another way? And tomorrow's will another? There's no logic to it. It's just the way it comes. One day, fire, the next day, black swamp, and that's the way it will always go for me.

Isn't it strange that I've given darkness its objects? Made it the tar and the bird. Given it weight and talons, substance and movement. But the other thing, the burning rise, the upswing, the brightness, the clarity, the elevation, and sure vision—all of it is abstraction. The language of religions, of revelation and epiphany.

None of which is right.

It is not God I see. It is not God I feel.

I can't imagine what you think at this point, but trust me that I have no illusions. Not now. Not any longer and certainly not of that kind. It's not God I felt. It is only supreme and wild pleasure. It is only illogical assurance and conviction. What is *that* exuberance called? What fits in that empty space? What animal? What substance?

I can't find it.

It is neither beast nor object.

And maybe it's better this way.

Maybe that's the real beauty, the true magic: the dark dying exists in me as a tangible thing, while the other is beyond the realm of language.

Tess and I were out on the Olympic Peninsula hiking the Cape Alava loop. It was early spring in one of our first Seattle years.

We'd come around a point and found a doe giving birth to a fawn. Not fifty feet from where we stood, its little legs dangling from its mother, and Tess grabbed my arm, dug her nails into my skin. As I watched the fawn fall to the pebbled beach, the doe nosing it up to its feet, there was a splitting in my chest. I pulled Tess away as quietly as my heart would allow. I shook her and said, "Did you see it, Tess? Did you? Come on, we have to swim," and I began taking off my clothes.

"It's too cold, Joe. It's going to rain again." She had her arms around me. "Slow down, Joey, slow down," but there was nothing she could do. I was naked and running across the slick rocks, through the wind, toward the ocean. I slipped and fell and felt nothing. Soon I was at the very edge and I dove headlong into the water. I tore open the back wall of a wave and called out and laughed at the soaring gulls and swam pulsing with elation, brimming rapture, qualities of pleasure I'd never known, while Tess stood alone, so far away on the shore calling to me, words impossible to hear, but I could see her as if she were there above me balancing on the surface of the water. I swam and swam and drank the salt water as if it flowed from a spring and felt none of the cold, none of the rain, not my broken thumb, nor swelling ankle, nor bleeding knee, only pleasure, only water and air and whatever it is that sends me into the world like that.

When I made it back to the beach the rise was fading from my blood and I staggered across the rocks, my thumb blue, blood falling down my shin, so cold I was barely able to stand. There was Tess with a red towel, furious. We were a full day in. Alone out there. Rain coming and I was, again, her invalid.

She made us a camp beneath the trees, dressed my wounds, splinted my thumb, taped my ankle. Said again some variation of the same thing: one way or another, the high or the low, enough is enough. "Otherwise, one day I'll be gone. And then what, Joe?"

Still. I would not do what she asked.

But to the point. The point is that it's arbitrary. Just no telling. No logic here, no system. No rhyme. No reason. There's just the waking up and the going on. The waking up and the going on. Though my father would disagree.

That's it. My father. That's what I was getting to. I've left him out too long. He was in our new house. When Tess and I first moved in. He'd come over with a bottle of champagne. One of his gestures. One of his rituals. A housewarming. What an odd celebration. Saying come and see. Saying, look, friends and family: We have arranged our furniture in new rooms, we have hung our clothes in different closets, now we sleep in this new bed. Odd. All that moving and rearranging of objects, of ourselves. Acts of hope. Hope that from this new place, we will become better. Is it more than that? Happier maybe? That in this new place we will make things we've never made before? Become people we have never been? Or that we will come to know one another in ways we didn't before? Perhaps all of those things. Mostly, though, I think, it is another prayer: if we have everything just so, if we arrange ourselves behind these walls, let us remain unaffected by ruin.

But not my father.

He didn't see any of it this way. His was another vision of the world. One of order and meaning. My father, more than anyone I've ever known, refused the idea of grey ruin. He wanted light and hope. Demanded it. And so gave himself to ritual. For as long as I can remember. And I still see deep into my childhood. There was my father always arranging rituals, insisting on them. So much ceremony. Our dinners around his fine table. Gifts for each occasion, the celebration of each moment, the notes he wrote to us. Look at this, he said, see what good thing you've done? Stop for a moment and be grateful for it, be proud of yourself, look what you have built, look what you have made, what you've accomplished, my son, my daughter.

"We are lucky," he said all through our childhood. "Never forget that we are lucky."

And then in White Pine he began to say, "We are blessed."

It was the next step. The logical extension. Where better to find order? Where better to find meaning than within St. Andrew's-by-the-Sea, that simple stone church turned Quaker meetinghouse? Andrew, patron saint of sailors and fishermen. First disciple of Christ. Killed on the cross. Tied, not nailed, and left to die. That is what I know of St. Andrew.

We were not a religious family. There was no church in my childhood.

My latterday father's church-cum-meetinghouse was set on a flat stone outcropping at the north end of the main beach. Weather-beaten and twice rebuilt. A point of great pride for those parishioners. A symbol of unbreakable faith. Father, son and holy ghost. Body and blood of Christ. I couldn't ever understand it. I still can't. My mind goes still. Nothing breaks me faster than code and a long list of characters. But my father, he liked to believe, and he liked to pray in that simple room while the waves fell against the rocks below.

64

Some time had passed, perhaps more than usual, since we'd last seen my father and one night not long after our driving out to Emerson, Tess and I went to his house for dinner. He was cooking from his favorite cookbook. He loved it because it included photographs of each ingredient the way it should be prepared for a given dish. All of it was laid out for him. He'd opened some good wine from one of those Washington wineries that now sells a single bottle for eighty bucks. Then, those places were practically unknown and he loved showing us what he'd found. Wine, another realm of ritual and order, just like the church, just like carpentry.

They were easy together, Tess and my father, affectionate and playful. That evening I sat in the living room in the corduroy easy chair and watched them in the kitchen. It drove him crazy when anyone tried to help, but Tess wouldn't leave him alone until he gave her a job. He took his preparation seriously—each ingredient arranged in a neat pile, or in a small ceramic ramekin. He followed recipes as if they were sacred commandments, and he was tortured by vague instructions like "to taste" or "a pinch." Tess made fun of him relentlessly, and when he asked her to read them aloud, was always hiding things, or editing the recipes to include ridiculous additions and outsized measurements.

I loved to watch them without me, playing in their world together. Tess laughing and my father pretending to be angry and Tess consoling him by jumping on his back and kissing his head, or tickling him when he was chopping carrots with one of his deadly Japanese knives.

"What have you done to those peppers? That's not a perfect square. It's ruined, it's all ruined."

He'd threaten to cut off her hand.

This night I'm thinking of, Tess had nearly convinced him that the recipe called for some enormous amount of chili flakes. He'd measured them out and was holding the metal scoop above the simmering sauce. I was holding my breath. Tess sitting on the counter, her hands on her knees, watching, bottom lip between her teeth. He turned and narrowed his eyes at her. She broke then into her weird squeaking laugh— half gasping, half giggling. My father chased her into the living room where they squared off in front of me.

Tess liked to box with him and she brought her fists up trying her best to keep a serious face. He took slow openhanded swings at her head and she ducked them the way he'd showed her.

"Drop, don't bend, drop, don't bend."

Before it ended he let her punch him in the stomach.

"Go on little girl, let's see what you got."

She hit him with all her strength. Gave everything. Tess so determined.

When she landed it, he laughed and said, "Like marble. Don't break your hand, little girl."

They liked each other so much.

Those evenings with my father, the three of us eating dinner in his warm house, the fire going, getting a little drunk, laughing, seeing the two of them together, that kind of affection, I wanted nothing more in my life.

But then my mother was out there locked away in the cold. And no matter what joy we felt, what softness, what comfort, she was always there—a counterweight, a reminder of what existed in the world beyond our fortune.

65.

Tess and my father were boxing. They played their game. I sat in front of the fire and watched. We were drunk on wine. It was a nice night. We were all happy for a few hours. My mother had murdered a man. She was in prison for it. My sister Claire was in London. We hadn't heard from her. It had been months. It was winter now. December or January. Short days. Massive storms. It was probably raining that night. The heat was out. The furnace was dead. That old monster in the basement had gone cold and still. We ate in front of the fire. We drank more wine. Then there was some kind of downturn. One of those shifts in pressure. A disturbance in the atmosphere. Laughter turns to quiet. A lull. And then my father started talking about the meetinghouse.

We were having dinner. Three people in front of a fire. Rain outside.

"I've been going to church." He said it to the wall. "The stone one."

"That's nice," Tess said. "The one on the rock? What kind of church is that?"

"It's a meetinghouse, really. Quaker. It used to be Catholic."

"Why?" I asked. "Why are you going to church now? All of a sudden."

Tess gave me her laser look.

"I like going," he said. "I like sitting there."

"Are you a Quaker now?"

He shrugged. "I don't know. Maybe I am."

"I think it's nice," Tess said.

"It is. You two should come with me sometime. It's very peaceful."

"No thanks," I said.

"I'd love to." Tess smiled at my father.

Why I went sullen, why it irritated me so much that my father, who had never been even vaguely interested in religion, was now, maybe, a Quaker, I'm not sure. Because I was like him and I did not want anything else to change. Because I thought it was a weakness. Or a symbol of weakness. Or worse, madness. And one mad parent was enough. Because I wanted him the same, wanted him to be still. I was the one who would change, and I would measure that change against his constancy. That was the way of the world, its natural order. Not the other way. No version of the opposite. It was a sign of chaos, and I'd had enough of that.

I wanted his house and the truck out front, the light on in the kitchen, him reading in the fat corduroy chair. His routine, our dinners together, all that was left of permanence, of the solidity of home.

Everything else had been obliterated. Nothing else was steady—not Tess, not my mother, not my mind. And now my father had found God. Now my father had begun to pray. It was the last straw and the final nail. It was the piece that blew me open.

Even now I think of it the same:

I'm hanging onto scaffolding.

There's a hurricane wind.

My body is blowing like a flag.

My father says, "I've started going to church," and I'm torn away, flung into the air, thrown into space.

Maybe I was looking for an excuse. Maybe it could have been anything. Yoga. Veganism. Kung fu. But it was God, so God sent me spinning.

That's why I've chosen this scene, this night among so many others. Because it was when something broke in me, when I gave up on staying still, when I tried to give up on order.

Tess and I walked home.

Maybe the rain had stopped.

She punched me on the shoulder. "Why are you cruel to him?"

I didn't answer. I didn't know.

"Joey."

I shook my head.

"He loves you," she said.

"I know that."

"So stop it. Let him be."

"I'm sorry," I said.

"Don't apologize to me." She leaned the side of her head against my shoulder. It was one of her gestures that no matter what else happened always gave me a shot of joy. "Let him be," she said again, this time with her softer voice.

"I will," I said.

"Tell him."

"I will."

We walked the rest of the way home without talking.

When we came to the house Tess sat on the porch. I went in and got the glasses of ice, our bottle of Jim Beam. I brought them out and sat next to her.

It was a ritual I loved.

But I had given up on ritual.

I poured the bourbon.

"Cheers," she said.

There was the sound of glass on glass, that eerie clink.

"I'll do whatever you want to do, Tess."

She looked at me.

"What do I want to do?"

"I don't know. But whatever it is, I'll do it."

She kissed me. Her fingers through my hair. She drew back just enough to speak. She touched the side of my face.

"Joe, Joey, Joseph," she whispered. "I want to go to war."

66

It won't be a surprise to you that Tess, secretive as she was, had been searching well before my father found God. Her reconnaissance had begun alone. But being stubborn and frightened and therefore blind, it was a surprise to me. I would never learn. No matter how many times Tess revealed to me her secret lives, I would always be astonished by them.

"Come with me," she said.

This was one night after dinner. My father had been over, and I, having sworn to be better, was not impatient with him. When he left I was proud of myself.

And for that pride, Tess, she said, "You're a stupid prick."

She masked it as exasperated teasing, but it was something she'd never called me before, and it wasn't really a joke. I think of it as a measure of her building rage.

"You're a stupid prick, Joey. You think you deserve some kind of reward." She patted me on the head. "Good job, Joe. You weren't a total asshole to your sweet father. Extra cake for you."

She left me washing the dishes.

"Let's go," she said twenty minutes later coming down the stairs in her shiny black raincoat.

"Come with me," Tess said and I followed her into the streets where there were living rooms flickering blue, smokers on their porches. Little orange embers ominous in the dark. See the couple on a stroll, the dog on a leash. I don't know about now, but then when we neighbors passed each other, we said, hello, we said, nice night, lovely evening. It was that kind of town. Small enough for it.

Yet it was an isolated and fractured place divided by distinct loyalties. A prison guard earned more than a waitress, a Walmart manager, a bartender, a secretary, or a fisherman. And the guards had the keys, meted out punishment, gave and withheld pleasure and privilege to the wives and husbands of their neighbors. That's a different kind of currency in a town like ours. A different measure of class. And often what we gave of ourselves outside was returned inside. You want your husband to have peace, you learn the code, you go to Lester's where you offer what you will.

There are no pure systems.

We went on up the hill, me and Tess, moving in and out of light—porch light, headlight, streetlight—and turned onto Vista Street where she slowed her walk and took my hand, a gesture more protective than romantic.

A little more than halfway down the block we came to a white two-story house behind a white picket fence. A wide porch wrapped around both sides of it and seemed to continue around to the back. I say *seemed* because at the time we didn't know. But I should tell you that it did do that. It continued on around to become a deck wide enough for a long table, six chairs, and a barbeque.

It was a house like the other houses—in style and size. Perhaps a bit more polished, fresher paint, well-pruned trees. It occupied a double lot. That's what made it distinct. The picket fence contained both the house and the lawn next to it, and on both sides those rows of pickets turned away from the street and continued on into the dark, surrounding the property where the streetlights did not reach.

There was the house on one lot, and on the other, thick green grass, a triangle of mature oak trees and between those, a large round trampoline.

We stopped here. Tess released my hand, and knelt to tie her boot. She took her time, but nothing moved. She stood and we walked on to the end of the street and back again. What she was waiting for, what I was meant to see, was not there.

"I would rather show you," she said.

67

It still makes me laugh to think that the romantics among us compared our neighborhood in White Pine to North Beach. Still, it had its charm. There were streetlights on the corners. Some houses were well-kept, others less so, but nothing was derelict.

There were student apartment blocks out by the college, a row of pretty houses up on the ridge, a few ramshackle beach cottages as well, the farms out in the valley, but aside from those places, most of us lived in The Hill.

The oldest houses, built by missionaries and fishermen, were set back a few hundred yards from the oceanfront, just where Water Street began to rise. The neighborhood rose from there into a compact grid, block by block of small single-family homes—a combination of Victorian and Craftsman—now occupied by prison guards, and professors, fishermen, and the families of prisoners who had a little money, and a little luck. Like us.

There was, in those days, an unusual intermingling of the classes. Strangest of all was that the guards so often lived next door to the families of their charges. I've heard that it is no longer this way. They've started writing about the town for reasons other than reporting executions. A thing in the *New York Times* travel section, no less. The death knell of any good scruffy place.

White Pine has become a resort town, where food is no longer farmed but sourced. The Owl was replaced by a wine bar serving not pizza, but flatbread. Lester's though is still around, or was last I checked. Still serving Olympia, pizza, and PBR. Still a guard bar, I hope.

I'd like to get back there one day. I'd like to sit with my dad in our booth and listen to the guards complain about all the newcomers and their green lawns.

Go up there and sit in our booth, share a pitcher and a pizza. Onion, mushroom, pepperoni. Just the two of us.

I miss him.

It's the simplest thing in the world isn't it? Missing someone. It is the purest form of sadness, I think. A person gone. A person absent from you.

Once a person, now an abstraction, now a ghost. Nothing to do about it. Not with the dead anyway. The dead are gone. Funny how true that is. How deeply true. The dead and the missing.

I'd like to go up there with him and share a pizza. That's all.

And somehow knowing that it's impossible, that I'll never listen to him talk, it makes all of this more urgent.

I want this to work.

I want Tess to come home.

I know there's no logic to it.

I can feel you pitying me. I can hear your sorry heart.

But I believe. If I can just finish this, whatever it is, I believe Tess will be there on the other side. You must have faith in something. Isn't that true?

I wish you'd answer me.

68

L ast night I was waiting to fall asleep. It was very dark, no moon, and I was lying in the center of our bed with my arms and legs spread out wide.

The windows were open and the air was coming in nice and cold, and I was huddled down beneath the comforter.

I was lost within that bed, that room.

I mean that I couldn't find myself in time.

People say, I didn't know where I was.

But last night, the air moving over my face, I didn't know *when* I was.

I kept thinking, *When am I? When am I?*

I couldn't answer it. I didn't know when I was. Or who was still alive.

I don't want to lose my mind. I don't want to leave this present life.

When my father said, "The purest expression of love is truth," or "The purest expression of truth is love," he was drunk on his new religion. In love with his bromides. Full of faith in some cosmic reconciliation. Faith in the idea that goodness and truth and love and kindness and purity, whatever those things were, would somehow heal him. Would heal us all.

"I'll object with kindness," he said, "will her into peace. Do nothing unkind. Abandon anger. I will only love. I will construct, I will not destroy."

And he did those things, you know.

He wasn't one of those awful people proselytizing and

pious and seething. He really was a kind and gentle man. So much like a wide-eyed child who arrives in adolescence and finds a way to reject all its implications. My father looked around at all the violence and horror of adulthood and he shook his head.

"No," I imagine my father saying, his wife in prison, his children having abandoned him in their respective ways, "No, I will remain as I am."

Then he turned and walked in the other direction.

69

We went to work, hung around with Seymour. Seymour, whom you must miss by now. How could you not? Who wouldn't miss a man like that? I'll return to him. I will.

But for now imagine us at The Owl.

Imagine Tess running that room, threading those drunks.

Imagine me pouring drinks for the college kids crowding the bar.

Imagine my father out at Arbus Lumber, working his station, dispensing good advice from behind his green apron.

Imagine Tess wound around me in the early morning, the two of us a pulsing knot.

Imagine time passing.

What do you see? Calendar pages blown into space? A spinning hour hand? A speeding sun rising and falling? A turning earth, tracing stars, a wheeling sky going dark and light, dark and light?

Tess and me on a cold night, both of us in our wool beanies pulled low. Now we are on Vista again. And even from the corner we can hear a distant, rhythmic sound—two bass notes, the first slightly lower than the second, and underlying those, a double high note. The same repeated phrase.

Thump-thump, squeak-squeak. Silence. Thump-thump, squeak-squeak. Silence.

We are walking.

The sound is louder.

Bass drum, bad violin.

There is a girl flying through the oaks. Vista bends slightly. We see her before we see the house. Her long hair rising as she falls, falling as she rises.

Bass drum, violin, and she floats, her pale face flashing through the branches.

Tess squeezes my hand. She speeds up and I follow until we come to the fence. The girl keeps bouncing. A joyless face. Until her eyes find Tess.

Then there is life. She takes a last great leap, turns an easy backflip, little white shoes arcing through the air. She lands, climbs down, and comes to the pickets.

"Hi Tess," she says.

"Hi Anna. Nice flip."

The girl smiles.

"This is Joey."

"Hi," she says. "Are you her boyfriend?"

"Yes. I guess I am."

"Okay," Anna says and shrugs as if granting permission. "But are you nice?"

"Sometimes," I say.

"He is."

"Okay." She looks at me a long moment. "Okay," she says. "So do you want to see a flip?"

I say that I do and she returns to the trampoline. Drum and violin. Anna going higher and higher. Front flip, back flip.

"Gumdrop," she sings, landing on her butt, "jellybean," flopping on her back. "Indian," landing cross-legged. "Gumdrop, jellybean, Indian."

Thump-thump, squeak-squeak.

"Gumdrop, jellybean, Indian."

She chants in rhythm with the drums, altering her skinny body midair while we look on.

Tess is quiet. I watch. I don't ask the questions. I know they'll be answered. I'm in no hurry.

It is late and it is cold for a child to be alone on a trampoline. The girl is charming but she is strange.

The sound of the bouncing rises inside me. It is in my ears, thudding behind my eyes. The street is otherwise so quiet. She must drive the neighbors mad. Or maybe it's only my failing filters. Maybe it's not so loud. Maybe, but in memory we are inside a kettledrum. The violins are screaming. On and on she goes. The music changes slightly here and there, extending or shortening the time between beats, but mostly it is the same.

Though then it was not music. Then, in that present, there was just the sound of a girl on a trampoline. The music, the drum and violin, they come only in recollection.

The present doesn't need comparison.

Only the past is made of metaphor.

"Gumdrop, jellybean, Indian."

The girl goes on bouncing, goes on chanting, goes on flopping like a fish, while Tess and I watch. Her audience of two.

And still I don't ask the questions, which come to the sum of one: What exists inside that house?

Tess loves her flourishes of drama, her suspense, her intrigue, and I would give her those. I would go along. I would stay her second, her soldier. I would follow orders.

"If you go looking for something, you will find it," my father told me deep in his season of platitudes.

Ask Tess and you know what she'd say? She'd say, the problem is what most people call looking. That's what Tess would tell you.

And she'd be right.

Most of us haven't got the heart for it.

Most of us stay where we are and instead of searching, we pray.

Tess on the other hand. I think by now you know. Tess had the heart.

There is the click and slam of a door. A man strides across

the lawn. He comes barefoot through the cold grass in jeans and a white T-shirt, white vapor blasting from his nose and mouth.

He pauses at the trampoline and presses a palm against the blue protective padding.

"Gumdrop, jellybean, Indian," the girl chants.

"Anna," he says with surprising evenness. Surprising for a snorting bull. "We don't say Indian."

"Gumdrop, jellybean, *seated man*," she says without breaking routine. Or, used to the correction, as part of routine.

The bull comes to us. He says, "Seated man. Same number of syllables. Better to break those habits early." He smiles and extends his hand. "Sam Young."

I take it. I say, "Joe March. This is Tess."

"Tess Wolff," Tess Wolff says.

They shake.

"Gumdrop, jellybean, seated man," Anna repeats a last time, falling back flat, arms and legs outstretched.

"I am a starfish," she says.

"Out for a walk?" Sam Young asks.

He has a flat nose, which seems to draw the corners of his eyes downward, making him appear a little sad. He is amiable, and well spoken. His eyes are indecipherable in the dark.

I imagine them colorless.

Then.

Now, I know their color.

"Stopped to watch the acrobat," Tess says.

"She's a good one. You two live on Vista?"

"Mott," I say.

"Out for an evening constitutional?" He laughs. Chuckles. A chuckle the only thing to accompany that question.

Sam Young is a professor at Emerson. Of History. I do not know which. Or whose.

The trampoline a birthday gift for their only child. Anna the acrobat. Anna the starfish. The jellybean, the gumdrop, the Indian, the seated man.

On we went. Speaking the double language.

And us? We work down at The Owl. My father lives here. We came to visit and we liked it. Cheap enough. Pretty town. Good beaches. Good place to stop for a while, et cetera.

"What's your father do?" he wants to know.

"Works out at Arbus Lumber," Tess says. A tone of challenge only I can detect. What of it?

"Ah," Sam Young says. He relaxes. "Honest work."

Tess and I stand silent.

"Anyway. Better get this one to bed. Say good night, Anna."

She remains a starfish. "I'm dead," she says. "I can't speak, I can't sleep."

"Anna," Sam Young says now with a point of impatience.

"I'm dead."

"And I'm not going to ask again."

Anna takes her time. She climbs from the shining surface of the trampoline. A little animal dragging itself from water onto land.

"Good night, Tess," she says. "Good night, boyfriend."

Sam Young smiles an apology at me.

"Nice to meet you both," he says. "Have a nice walk."

We watch as he catches up with his daughter, and ushers her inside. The sidelight goes off. Pop. Gone with all their sound.

"Honest work," Tess says.

And then our footsteps replace the beat of the Trampoline Girl.

70

T hat night on our porch, the night we came home from meeting Professor Sam Young, Tess spoke for a long time. She said, "I go after work, or on nights I can't sleep and you're dead to the world. You can't know everything, Joe. What fun would that be? Walking by myself is different than walking with you. I know you understand. You must feel it too sometimes, the desire for a little quiet, to be alone. So I walk. I love to look in on those houses. People watching television, eating dinner, a naked man. I like to see them fucking, too. I love that. I wait for it. I don't hide in the bushes. I'm not that nuts. I just walk slowly and I hope for it. It turns me on, but there's something else too. I'm not sure what. There's something about being alone at night, outside, all that black space around me, watching from within it. So that's why I started going. Or it's half the reason. The other half is that I was looking for something. Waiting for it because I knew that it was there. I knew what every cop alive has always known. If you listen, if you walk slowly enough and long enough, you will hear someone scream. If you wait. And that's what I was waiting for. Everywhere in the world, mostly it's the women who scream. And in a neighborhood like The Hill, it's not mostly but only. And I did hear them. Crashing plates and crying and yelling. I stopped in the street and waited. I don't know what for. Or I didn't when I started out. Or didn't know that I knew. Sometimes the sound stopped and then it was impossible to find the house. Or it didn't stop and I still couldn't tell where it came from. A couple fighting, something falling, a woman screaming, but I couldn't trace the sound to the act. Was it the backyard of one house, or the bedroom of another? And what had I heard anyway? Then one night when you were fast asleep, drooling on yourself, I got out of bed and went out. I was off. A Sunday maybe. Around midnight. I was walking up Water, so quiet, not a car on the road, and then I heard that trampoline. The same sound over and over. So that after a few wrong turns, I tracked it to Vista and came to the fence where I found Anna. She wasn't doing her flips. Just jumping up and down like a little machine. It was frightening, Joe. The vacant look. I don't know how long I watched, or when it was she saw me, but even after she did, after I registered in her robot eyes, she went on jumping. She went on despite the noise in the house. A woman yelled, 'Stop it. Stop it. What did I do? What did I do?' Something fell, something broke. They were the sounds of a kitchen fight. The woman screamed. It went on like that and all the while I stood behind the fence with the girl looking at me and me looking back at her. 'Leave me alone,' the woman said. She sounded exhausted now. Exasperated. 'Please,' she said. Then there were heavy footsteps going off somewhere. The girl stopped bouncing. She sat on the edge of the trampoline and dangled her legs. She was less a robot then. She told me her name. I told her mine. 'I have to go to bed,' she said as if I should have known, scolding. Me the child. She walked around the back. That tiny little girl alone. So determined. I heard the door open and close. I heard some footsteps. The woman's voice, but not the words. A light came on. A light went off. I waited and then I walked home to you. That was the first time."

71

Tess and I fell in love one summer in Cannon Beach. My mother killed a man and went to prison for the difference between one and seven. My father sold our house, gave up his business, moved to White Pine, and took a job at Arbus Lumber. Out of duty, yes. But he would say there's no difference. Duty is born of love. There are no other factors, he would say. And my sister Claire stayed in England where she married a man named Henry Lloyd who had a red face and thinning hair and a lot of money. He was twelve years her senior and she would never come home. And me, I moved to White Pine too. I took a job as a bartender at a place called The Owl, where a massive man named Seymour Strout worked the door with a towel around his neck, and a pack of Virginia Slims in his pocket. Me, I had come out of duty, but I do not know if that duty was born of love, or if there were other factors, or if those factors add up to love or one of its derivatives. And then Tess Wolff appeared on the hood of my truck, beneath an orange streetlight with her heels on the bumper. Tess whose mother died of breast cancer, whose father had remarried nine months after that, not enough for a year, but enough to have a child. Two of them. Girls. Fraternal twins. She came to White Pine to worship my mother with the passion and devotion of an acolyte.

Tess saying, "You can't know everything, Joey. There's something about being alone at night, outside, saying nothing, looking in, all that black space around me, watching from the dark. In the dark, alone on the street, it was me the threat, me the watcher."

And I will tell you about Tess. And you will take me as an authority, as someone with real knowledge. As someone who *knows* her. But I do not. I have my memory, muted and warped, but that doesn't mean knowing.

It means nothing, really.

Tess is gone.

No matter how often or how hard I try, I am always fooled. It is like the eternal. I know it does not exist, and yet I keep falling for its illusion. Even now. Here within the lulling routine of days. This life will last forever, I think. No matter how many times I'm proven wrong.

In the wisdom of her early twenties, Tess said, "Love is not possession, Joe Joey Joseph."

And that took a long time for me to learn. Long out of my own twenties and even now I struggle. I like ownership. I like control. I am, after all, my father's son.

I know the two things are connected. My faith in permanence and my desire to possess.

These are not instincts easy to break.

I worry that Tess remains nebulous. And that cannot be. You must see her for any of this to matter. It is not the story, it is *her*. It is Tess I'm trying to translate.

The story is vehicle and frame. To have and to hold.

But she must be palpable. Her courage, her intelligence, her independence, the force of her lust. Her rage. How all of it seemed alive in her body.

These are the facts you must understand.

These are the truths you must receive.

Listen: she moved as if nothing embarrassed her. She favored no angle, hid no part of herself. Her mother said, "Stand up straight, what are you trying to hide? What are you trying to protect? Nothing." So, she stood up straight.

She didn't bite her fingernails or pick at her lip. She didn't twirl her hair or barricade herself behind folded arms.

But she was always in motion. Once I thought this was how she hid. Taking an ankle in her hand and pulling her heel to her ass. Bending at the waist. Interlacing her fingers and reaching above her head. But now I believe she was giving relief to a body that needed to move, to muscles that ached for something I'd never entirely understand and could not see.

"Harder," she said when I rubbed her shoulders. "Dig your fingers in. Yes."

"Push harder," she said.

"Fuck me harder," she said, her voice, the same low growl.

Tess, she wanted more of everything.

72

This morning I collected the telephones. We've had them since we moved in here. Cordless with their bases strewn about. Upstairs and down. In the bedroom, in the kitchen, in the guest room. At the time, all those years ago, we were seduced by their sleekness, by their power, their features, their capacity for megahertz.

If you could have seen Tess laughing that day about the megahertz of these phones. She loved the word. Look at all the *megahertz,* Joe.

One of those things. You understand.

Anyway, it had taken three years to build the house and by the time we bought the telephones we were into the finishing touches. Everything just so. The end of so much motion, and change. The sale of our bars in Seattle, traveling back and forth between there and here. Building this place with all the usual problems and delays—materials arriving without workers, workers arriving without materials, disappearing electricians. So by the time we bought the cordless phones and plugged them in, we were in a state of relief and celebration. At last, everything as we wanted it to be. It was, I thought, what we had been working for all our lives. Or our lives together. Our life together. It was the realization of a fantasy. The proper culmination of things. A house in the country. The great domestic dream come to life. Apple trees, a garden, a deck, a clearing. Deer and elk. Foxes. The sound of the wind. Hawks and owls. Bright cardinals. A wide white bed. Cool air at night through the windows. So many places to sit, to read, to look out upon our land, our kingdom.

There were other things, of course. Other finishing touches, other details. Photographs. Paintings we'd bought over the years. Stones we'd kept from as far back as Cannon Beach. Other objects gathered through time. Even remnants of our lives before each other.

But today I'm telling you of the telephones because this morning I went around disconnecting their bases, removing their clear wires from our walls. Dropping each receiver, base and power cord into an old brown paper shopping bag.

How long had it been since that satisfying click? A feeling, a noise I've always loved—the sure connection between wire and wall.

No one calls the landline anyway.

Now people are devoted to cell phones, but I prefer the larger receiver in my hand, the fullness of sound, voices so close and pure and uninterrupted.

Or I did.

I've become tired of spoken language. Of the constant talking. No one shuts up. I can't stand it any longer. Not my own voice, not the voice of most anyone.

I've removed the satellite dish.

Now the phones are gone.

What's left?

The people in town.

And I don't mind them usually. Or the village small talk. I don't go in all that often anyway. Just for breakfast and the paper sometimes when I feel my mind begin to slide away from me. When it's pushing so hard against the bars I'm afraid they'll break. When the bird comes, when the tar is thickest in my veins. Then it soothes me to be there.

Except for when they play the wrong music. Then I have to leave immediately.

Maybe I've become a curmudgeon, but I don't think it's that. Not only. It's just the noise is too much. I look around and see the people nodding their heads, and reading their newspapers, and meanwhile my brain is burning and I have to leave.

The music.

Which is a language I wish I could speak. Or at least fully understand. I don't mean the incessant shit they play in the diner. I mean what I've been listening to here. The good radio. Our CDs. The records, which were once my parents'. I have sorted them all. Not so much the good from the bad, but the brutal from the rest. There are sounds now I can't endure. Just as with certain light. Fluorescent, flashing neon, the naked bulb.

It's to do with the holes in my system. There are cracks. There are gaps.

The modem.

Sending its invisible signal into the house. Its round blue light providing hope. Stamped into the plastic are three crescents widening from a single point and these are what I imagine pulsing through the air—delicate little half-moons passing through the walls, through my body. And maybe riding on one of those will come a message from the dark. Will come word. Maybe, but I think the modem is the next to go.

The computer.

It rests bulky and outmoded in our office defiling my father's redwood desk. Even in our most glorious days, I hated the thing. All its wires and plastic and heat. Ugly and threatening. I'll get rid of the thing today. Maybe I'll go to the garage and find my father's .45. Take it out to the clearing and murder that horrible machine. Maybe I'll take a hammer to it.

The mailbox.

White half-oval riding a sturdy wooden post. A red metal flag, which when there's mail the mailman continues to raise. How many men like that left in the world? Our little mailbox at the end of our little road. I go out once a day anyway. Flag up or down. Just in case he makes a mistake. Paul Thomas, the mailman, never makes a mistake. The box is always empty when the flag is lowered. I go anyway to make sure. We've never met, but we leave him a bottle of Jameson and a hundred bucks in the box every Christmas. And always before the New Year he replaces it with a whiskey cake wrapped in foil and red ribbon along with a card saying, *Thank You! Merry Christmas!* It's signed, Paul and Sally, who I take to be his wife, though I don't know for certain. Could be his nurse, his lover, his sister, or his daughter. Could very well be his dog.

I don't know which of them makes it, but the cake is invariably foul. Tess and I look forward to it. To learning how bad a cake can be. Just to evaluate the heights of its vileness, to see if it was possible to make a worse cake than the cake of Christmas past. Christmas Eve we slice two slivers. A sacrament we deliver to each other's mouths. I love that. The absolute wretchedness of something causing such joy. My theory is that Paul and Sally (human or canine) are teetotalers, that they are simply returning our whiskey to us in a different vessel—a dense disk of sugar and flour and fruit.

Tess, on the other hand, believes they hate us. That their delivery is an annual gesture of violence.

Whatever the case, each year, that single mouthful of cake, which we are honor-bound to swallow, makes Tess laugh with an uninhibited recklessness that I love as much as anything in my life. The wildness of her laughter. The spectacle of her falling sideways, laughing the air from her body.

It's obnoxious. Unoriginal too. A young couple from the city thrilling at the kindness and poor taste of their country neighbors. You see what your wild revolutionaries have become? Bourgeois snobs, insipid invaders.

What else is left?

The cell phone.

Speaking of hope. This I cannot give up. I leave it on the edge of the table where the signal is strongest. I keep it charged. I keep an eye on it.

People used to say, send word. Send word when you get there, send word when you land. Send word when there's time. Send word when you're settled.

I love this phrase, and I will admit that what I hope more than anything is that. Tess sends hers through the mail. That I will walk up our long drive to see the red flag raised, and there on the cool floor of the metal box will lie a letter.

But Tess sends no word.

And instead I go on sending you mine.

73

Something about crawling around beneath his table today, about collecting the telephones, the weight of them in the shopping bag, made me think of my father.

My father who found calm within the Quaker meeting-house out on the point at the end of the bay where he practiced *waiting worship* with a small congregation of Friends.

A democratic faith devoted to peace and without hierarchy.

My father listening to God in all the ways a body can listen.

"I'm just puttering around the house," he'd say when I called.

"What are you doing, Dad?"

"Not much, Joe. Just puttering."

Which could have meant gluing a chipped mug, or installing crown molding in the living room.

And then, as I do now, I would see him in White Pine. The same living room, the same kitchen, the same front door, same front yard. The pile of soil was gone, replaced by a crabapple tree. The whole place refreshed as if he owned it himself. Refaced cabinetry, new furniture, which he'd made over the years using the Arbus workshop. A new fence out front. Fresh paint.

The landlord couldn't believe her luck.

My father wanted nothing in return—not an option to buy, not a reduction in rent, no reimbursement for improvements made. He only wanted a home he could afford to stay in, to work on, to putter around, a home not far from his wife.

By then, Tess and I were in Seattle living in a shitty apartment down by the water in Belltown. A damp and grungy fourth-floor walk-up full of windows. We looked out on the bay, and the fishing boats coming and going, and the tankers out further, and beneath us a mad carnival of crime and general degradation. All that heroin, all those people rampaging below our windows at night. None of it bothered us then.

We'd just ridden into town from White Pine. We arrived believing we were cool to violence, immune somehow to its reach and power. We were not its victims, but its perpetrators.

We had done what we had done.

I was my mother's son.

We were made of violence, Tess and I. Formed and drawn and bound by it. Woven through our creation myth.

Tess and I. We. The single object I believed us to be.

And were it not for my mother and her hammer, would Tess have ever followed me to White Pine? And was she following me at all? Was she not also following my father? My mother? All of us at once? We her surrogates.

And who was surrogate to whom? It wasn't one for one. Father for father. Mother for mother. It's not so simple with Tess.

And what was I? Proxy for whom?

Well, whatever the answers, I think of Tess and me in our apartment above the bay, the two of us on the run from White Pine, pretending to be invincible and unscathed.

We came determined to start again. Two frightened and arrogant kids sailing into the big city from their fishingtown-collegetownprisontown.

"Sink or swim, Joey March," Tess said when I stopped the truck in front of our new home. "Begin again. Round two. Shake it off. Nothing to regret. What's done is done. One, two, three, go."

We were young, but we were so tired, so ground down.

Still, I knew we'd swim.

Now that it was out of our system.

But the truth is that *it* was never in mine. Not that. Not what Tess had in hers.

I tell you this as someone whose system is fractured. Is coursing with venom and pollution, a system of disconnected gears and failing filters.

Not only.

There are other things in me, yes, but still, I tell you this as someone who knows something about the dark. As someone with talons sunk in his lungs and cold tar in his veins.

But who also knows the blazing rise, the ecstatic clarity.

And each its respective violence.

But neither is what Tess had.

What Tess had was never in my system. I go on telling myself.

Maybe I am not so much my mother's son.

74

It was 1992. Very cold, very clear. A Sunday morning. At last, we'd accepted my father's invitation to worship and now we walked from our house to his, and then down to the water, past the tourist bureau, Nick's Knacks, the harbor with most of the slips empty, the fishing boats already out to sea.

A couple of guys smoking outside The Clam Shack. Wool beanies, Mariners caps, Carhartt coats. It was blowing hard and we leaned into it just slightly as we went. Any word we spoke was whipped away. He'd explained the rules.

"You sit. You wait. You listen for God. And if you feel compelled, you may speak. But it is unnecessary, and most of us don't."

We walked the gravel path to the meetinghouse door and I remember the relief of stepping inside—the warmth, the sudden stillness, the protection from the wind, which strained hard against the unstained glass.

"God is in the wind above all," my father said. "Invisible. Delivering all things."

So he believed. So he claimed.

There was that far-off howling and the water moving against the rocks. It was a single room. Modest. Unadorned. Wooden pews. A single silver cross.

"Peace is in God and in his world," my father the new Quaker told us before he opened the door.

I liked being with Tess on one side and him on the other. I

liked the sounds of the water, and the panes bending, and the stillness of all those other people.

I liked the winter light carving into the room.

That day they were rioting in Los Angeles. The city was on fire, while the three of us sat together in the quiet meeting-house—Tess on one side, my father on the other.

We sat and we listened and we were waiting for God. That was the edict.

Near the end, I turned and looked at my father. He sat upright, his long torso very straight. Eyes closed. His hands were folded in his lap, like a debutante's. I saw him then in some new way and felt an abrupt surge of love. He was a man who fought, who refused everything he abhorred—violence, indifference. He would let none of it seep in. And whatever we call it—honor, character, integrity—was what I saw in his new posture, with his thick, scarred old hands resting there so delicately.

There is nothing much else to recall.

We sat and we waited and when an hour had passed we rose and we left.

We were quiet and calm on the walk home along the water and when we said goodbye in front of my father's open door, I hugged him with an uncharacteristic strength and intensity.

He said, "I love you, Joe."

And I said, "I love you, too."

Tess kissed him on the cheek.

"And *I* love you, Richard."

She laughed as if it were an obvious and unnecessary thing to say, took my hand and we walked away from him, turning the corner and heading up the hill.

We were going to Lester's for a pizza and a pitcher. I could feel the swelling brightness, but it had not, for a change, arrived from nowhere and without explanation. It came from Tess, and from my father, from the stillness of that hour, from the light and the gulls, from the peace of our stroll along the waterfront. Perhaps it also came from love. Or *was* love, that sharpness, that general, nameless pleasure. But there was also in that admixture of causes, relief.

I believed that something had changed in Tess. That the joy I felt—and yes, maybe joy is the right word for these rushes, these swells of confidence and clarity—was in part to do with the belief that Tess had changed, that she might have abandoned her plans.

That I'd been freed from the duties of revolt, the duties of war.

But at Lester's sitting in my father's booth, a pitcher of Olympia between us, waiting for our pizza, Tess said, "Do you think a woman should live like that?"

And then my nameless pleasure was replaced by disappointment.

I did not know her plans precisely. And perhaps Tess didn't know them herself.

Even so they were inevitable.

I don't know if we continued speaking. We must have. But what I remember is her gaze on me and her question and that feeling of defeat, that rise of fear.

75.

The winter light carving into the room.
This line has been humming in my mind now for days and I realize suddenly it is not mine.

I have stolen it from a poem Tess loved, which she found at Left Bank Books, a little place around the corner from our first apartment in Seattle. It was a shop she adored, her favorite in the city.

The book she found by accident. Something about its title. Something about its cover of red volcanoes. She brought it home and fell for its longest poem. For months she read pieces of it to me.

Tess in bed facing the bay, and me with my back to the windows listening, watching her full of daylight.

I haven't thought of it for a long time, but those words, *light carving into the room*, I see that they've infiltrated me:

Well there are many ways of being held prisoner,
I am thinking as I stride over the moor.
As a rule after lunch mother has a nap

and I go out to walk.
The bare blue trees and bleached wooden sky of April
carve into me with knives of light.

I only remembered the last two lines. I had to search out the rest. There it was on our wide bookcase—a slim file of time.

On the title page she's written, *Tess Wolff. Seattle, Washington. November, 1995.*

The same year they murdered Yitzhak Rabin.

The same year the Mariners lost the pennant to the Seated Men. The year three American soldiers kidnapped, beat, and raped a twelve-year-old Okinawan school girl.

It's the same year they blew up the federal building in Oklahoma City.

These things were on her mind in 1995. They are in her notes in the book's back pages, pages soft with use.

I'll keep it on the table, and maybe read it all later. I can't now. Her asterisks, her lines are like the light. They carve into me, and I don't have the heart for it today.

I don't have the strength to feel the softness of those pages, which somehow are the softness of Tess Wolff in 1995.

Not only, of course.

That wasn't all she had.

Not all softness.

And looking at that stanza in front of me now I think I should have paid more attention.

Well there are many ways of being held prisoner.

Beneath which she's drawn a long black line. Thick and steady.

We were autodidacts in our way. Both of us having squandered our educations in a safe haze of disinterest, going along, half-reading, half-listening, skipping classes. Almost from the moment we met, we regretted it together. Our shared experience of wasted opportunity. Even in Cannon Beach that summer we were reading, listening to music, trying make up for the shame of laziness, of wasting those four years in our respective colleges.

Loving Tess made me hungry for everything and I want to believe that it was the same for her.

That what we were together was a single insatiable beast.

What do you think? Can two people become one voracious animal?

Well, I'll tell you this: For a long time, we were so hungry.

Speak of the drifting mind.

It's that to see this book twenty years worn, to remember Tess reading it in our fresh new bed with the bay outside and us exhausted and frightened and on fire, how can you expect me not to drift?

Just think of us then as a single insatiable beast.

There is no courage without fear.

And us two, we were a brave animal.

There was nothing we would not eat.

The bare blue trees and bleached wooden sky of April/carve into me with knives of light.

As does the rest of the world. Sometimes I think that's the advantage of these failing filters. They prevent me from dying. These broken parts are weapons against numbness, against anesthesia.

I won't ever go cold.

I will die the other way.

I will die with fire, goddamn it.

76.

Tess can go to hell. I cleaned up a bit. Showered and shaved for the first time in weeks. I can't remember the last time. Last year, she bought me one of those ridiculous razors with twenty-seven blades per cartridge, each designed by the defense department and coated with liquid diamonds or some bullshit. Still, the thing cuts tight and then there was my face, slowly reappearing, stroke by stroke. Gliding again, I had the high concentration, and dissolved the beard, nearly all hard white, quadrant by quadrant, until my skin on a thumb's downstroke was smooth as an oiled plum. It took ten years off and brought more light to my eyes, which, on top of the crackling lightning storm in my gut and in my knees, were already blazing. Just shaving with those razors, the perfect geometric system of it, the straight line at each sideburn flawlessly aligned, all of it providing me the flying confidence of another time, and off I went into the cold evening taking with me one of Tess's sanded walking sticks leaning against our front door. Fuck her. Walked to town, rakish as a slick pirate with my smooth face and queen's scepter, 501s and work boots, favorite faded flannel, defying the cold, unafraid of the speeding buildings at my back, carrying our forests to the sea, knowing it would be the trucks, the madmen and the trees to suffer. Went to The Alibi certain I'd find the farmer's daughter, waited with my Beam rocks humming at the bar alongside two guys drinking Bud longnecks not saying a word, drooping over their stools like dough wrapped in denim, the black

Naugahyde pads invisible beneath them, but she never showed. Not a woman to be found for all the hours I sat there drinking, rapping my knuckles against the wood in rhythm to whatever they played on the jukebox—Patsy Cline to Pearl Jam and back again. One of the doughboys gave my hand a sidelong look or two and I thought please try me, give me any reason at all and I'll tear you both to shreds, but they gave me no reason, left after a while, and then it was just me until the place closed down. When they were gone I missed those two fat men and wished I'd had something to say to them. I left the scepter, walked home on our side of the road looking straight into the blinding white eyes of those screaming animals racing towards me, and all the way back I was trying to remember where I'd put my father's ammo box.

77

Today the morning sunlight was flashing through our bedroom windows and in it I saw my mother. She was sitting on the front step of our house in Capitol Hill peeling apples and watching Claire and me. We were children dancing in the sprinkler. A Rain Bird. I don't know how the name returns, or where it's stored, but there it is. A Rain Bird attached to the hose and there's my mother when she was young, and us two in that summer afternoon light.

Do you remember that summer, Mom? The feeling of that cool concrete step against your legs. Watching us through the spray. Did you know, even then, all that time ago, what you were capable of, what was kept within you?

See how that awful black weight creeping through my lungs can provoke such a joyous film, such gentle images. See how that projector finally pulled me from bed.

Its light was cutting my eyes, and crisscrossing through my skull, and the noise and strobing was no longer endurable and I had to escape it.

So I found a way out of bed and into the shower and into my clothes and out onto the road. I recall none of that. Not my feet on the ground, not the water, neither my belt nor these shirt buttons in my fingers.

First there was the film, and then I was walking along the road again with my hair wet, and the pine wind cooling my burning brain. It was a nice, calm middle ground. Not like the night before, not like the morning. I came to the diner and bought a paper and a glazed donut and sat outside. I was hoping I might find the black-haired woman there, early for breakfast before the market. But no luck.

There was an article in the paper about Phillip Seymour Hoffman, who killed himself a few days before. It was John Le Carré who wrote it and he said the world had been "too bright for him to handle." That Hoffman had to either "screw up his eyes or be dazzled to death."

I tore that paragraph out and brought it home in my pocket. Maybe you either squint or you die. But really I don't think he was dazzled to death. I think he died squinting. In my experience, that's what heroin and all the rest is for. It replaces the broken filters. It prevents the trees and the sky from carving into you.

Tess and I smoked it twice and shot it once that first year in Seattle. No shortage of heroin in Belltown then. At the beginning of our American Dream, all I had to do was lean out the window. I won't go on about it except to say that its softness, the protection it provided me from my own mind, was terrifying in its warm pleasure. If not for Tess, I'm not sure I'd have ever stopped.

So I will tell you that I understand. I will tell you just how easy it would be. How reasonable. It makes such sense to me. And I don't think there's any shame in it, either.

Not the drugs, and not the suicide.

If you have a broken system, maybe it's either squint or die.

78

I don't know how many times we'd been back to see the Trampoline Girl, and I don't know how many times Tess had risen from our bed and gone alone into the early dark.

We could no longer go walking after dinner without feeling the planetary pull of that house on Vista. What for me was dread was some other thing for her.

But it doesn't matter.

Dread or not, the result is the same.

There were nights we found nothing but lightless windows and there were nights we found her bouncing on the trampoline with no sign of the professor. "Hello, Boyfriend. Hi, Tess," Anna said, and laughed as if she were fully a child.

There were nights she bounced expressionless through the screaming and we looked on, imagining ourselves silent guardians, in loco parentis.

"Good night, Tess, good night, Boyfriend."

I don't remember how long it went on. Our visits. Those walks. How many times we saw the house dark, or saw Anna smiling, or stood idle behind the white picket fence listening to the fighting through the thump and squeak of the trampoline.

There were many nights I wouldn't walk. Nights Tess went off without me. Nights I'd sit on the porch and worry about her until she came home to take her place next to me and pour herself a glass saying nothing to my nothing.

We were moving toward something. You have to see that it was inevitable. I'm sure you believe in responsibility, in free will, in making decisions. Even as you spend your life sliding back and forth on that train, in that truck, rising up and down on that elevator. Even as you do the same things day after day. Even as you murder your time while the same dull people say the same dull things about changing your same dull life.

And all the while saying, I can do what I want, I can do what I want, I can do what I want.

There was a moment when the great boulder began to roll, and nothing was to be done about it. A time when there was no more freedom, no more choice. We were a simple single fact, one foregone conclusion, the two of us, one thing, hurtling forward.

And then one night there was a black figure in a black mask standing at our bedroom window. Two eyes and a mouth. And I thought, Sam Young has come to kill us. I will have to fight. I was moving, rising toward him, sick with adrenaline, wide awake, determined and committed. But I stopped when the figure crossed from the window to the door.

I said, "What the fuck, Tess?"

And maybe she hadn't heard because of the mask, or maybe she was trying to frighten me. But whatever the case she didn't turn, and she didn't speak.

I stood naked at the window watching her walk away from the house until she vanished from view.

I suppose I'm a kind of a Quaker now myself. Sitting here at my father's table looking out over the clearing. What is this if not waiting worship?

What is the difference between Tess and God? And even you?

These are silent services. These days facing the woods are long prayers. These words, this quiet.

The television is gone, and now the telephones.

Yesterday afternoon I found my father's .45.

It was in the garage wrapped in a yellow chamois at the bottom of the dented army ammo box along with his dog tags and a carton of bullets. I sat out there at the workbench and broke down the pistol the way he'd taught me. More or less, anyway. It was a struggle to remember all the steps. I cleaned and oiled it as best I could and put it back together, which took a long time. I don't think I'd even held the thing since I was fifteen. I fed the clip, thinking of a Donald Duck Pez dispenser my sister used to love.

You wouldn't approve, Claire, would you? Of this isolation. Of my mind. Loading Dad's gun.

Get in the car and drive, right? Burn the fucking house down already. Cut and run. To hell with Tess, that selfish bitch. How can my brother have become so weak? Live your damn life. You'll be dead soon enough. Go get drunk. Get laid, for Christ's sake. Find that fine little farmer.

I can hear you yelling. I see your neck all flushed.

But what about you, Claire? Are you really living your life out there? Are you so happy with your new name, your new money? Are you so much better without us?

I laid the computer on an empty lawn bag in the clearing and shot it to pieces. Emptied the whole clip. I still feel the bursting recoil in my hand.

When it was done I tied the bag and dumped it in the trash.

The .45 is back in its box on a shelf in the garage.

But I've refilled the clip, left one in the chamber.

So the computer is gone, the TV and the telephones, the satellite dish, the radios. And with them all their chatter.

I think I'll abandon spoken language. I prefer to wait with you in silence for whatever it is that's coming.

The talons and the tar, or the other thing beyond language.

You or Tess or God.

81

The Owl on a booming Saturday night. A week after my lunatic girlfriend scared the shit out of me and then went off into the White Pine night dressed like a cut-rate assassin.

We went about our business. The trampoline kept making its wretched music, and that piece of shit kept throwing his wife into walls.

And yes, we called the police. Three times we called. Once they came. Once nothing was done. No charges. No complaint filed.

How do we know?

Seymour Strout, to whom we will shortly return.

Seymour Strout knows all.

It was the usual farce, the usual terror. We keep out of domestic affairs. We are reluctant to get involved in the private matters of the home. Private matters between husband and wife, a wife who refuses to make a complaint, who refuses to explain her injuries. A daughter who shows no sign of abuse, who claims to know nothing of her mother's bruised face, et cetera, et cetera, et cetera.

Is there a single person left alive who doesn't know this story?

The gruesome machine. Its grinding horror. For and by men. So the police were reluctant to get involved, as are we all. Tess, on the other hand, had a different attitude altogether. As you may have gathered by now, Tess had a different attitude entirely. So back to a Friday not long before we dove headlong into the darkness.

We are at The Owl. Tess out on the floor, Seymour running his door, and me, I'm working my bar. It's crowded with students, this the night before spring break begins. An Emerson tradition, one last party before the party, before flying off to Mexico or Florida or Texas or wherever else they went each spring. Nights like this I have a barback. I can't quite see him now, but I know he's there, marrying bottles, bringing buckets of ice. He's a blur. Some local kid, a townie, who nearly by definition despises the students he's serving. He's someone talented, or he wouldn't be there. The job pays too well. We can afford to be selective. I can't see his face, but I have some vague sense that he had unruly hair. I may be confusing him with someone else from another time. So many bars in my life. But who gives a fuck, right? Let's just say he's a tall, thin kid with wild curls. Let's say his name is Matt or Craig and that Seymour brought him in as a favor to the kid's father who's a guard out at The Pine. So around nine the place is humming and all of us are on. It's that feeling when all the planets are aligned. A rare and lovely thing.

I'm on the upswing. Then and now.

There is no grime obscuring my eyes. I'm calm and fast. The orders come in over the bar, and from the waitresses, Tess among them. I see all the drinks before they're made. There is no math too complicated, the world a perfectly ordered place, all systems pure.

Let's say dead center you've got two long-haired idiots who think they're both Eddie Vedder. One of them keeps raising his hand saying, "Yo, bro, yo, bro, yo."

And then you've got three guys you like on one end, who tip well, and some girls whose order you already know on the other. And Tess is coming in at the service side and she's waiting for two vodka tonics, one Jack and Coke, and three Cuervo shots. The guys you like are Coronas with Cuervo shots back and it's all coming in at once. Nights like this your filters are flawless. Nights like this you're some kind of prodigious performer, some magical dancer. You see each glass before its even on the runner and then there they are all in a line and you can't even remember doing it, setting them up: six shot, three rocks.

Ice, ice, ice.

Lime, lime.

Straw, straw.

The right hand is moving the vodka bottle on the two count from glass to glass to glass. You start the Jack pour with the other in time with the second vodka.

Vodka back to the well, Jack to the first shelf behind you.

Always return bottles to their place. There must never be disorder.

Your thumb on the gun goes, tonic, tonic, Coke.

You sail that Cuervo bottle over the shot glasses and split three from the six.

Tess gets her drinks first.

Always.

She looks at me with an expression I can't parse. It is not part of our repertoire, our silent language of the workplace. There's the smallest pause, the briefest slowing, and then she pivots and glides away.

Now the rubber runner is free for two martini glasses. Fill them with water and ice, because you have style despite the place. You pop three Coronas, the opener as easy in your hand as brass knuckles.

You deliver it all and follow with a plate of limes and salt. You smile at the guys. You remember their names. You say something funny about Florida.

They say, "Keep the change, Joey."

You mix the Cosmos in a shaker. You think Kamikaze plus cranberry. You think, very tricky landing.

Vodka, triple sec, lime.

Very. Tricky. Landing.

Because a thousand years ago that's how you learned it and every single time the order comes, for an instant, in a flash of film, you see one of those planes, one of those Zeros in black and white tearing out of the sky.

Then the vodka is a two count three times in one hand, so six. And the triple sec in the other. Then there's the Rose's. Then there's the cranberry. You dump the chilling glasses. You cap the shaker and go one hard snap. More than that is meaningless theater and you don't need that bullshit.

Now look at the girls. Look right at them and smile to say, *these are yours.* To say, *even if I'll never fuck you, we can pretend.* Because when you are like this, when you are fearless and deadly, when you have the fleeting maniac confidence, the electric rise that brought you to Tess in the very first place, then you know there isn't a woman alive who wouldn't take you to bed. And as if to prove your point, as if to prove your own invincible brilliance, you fly the shaker across each glass and there is just enough, down to a single violet drop, there is just enough to fill those three full to their brims.

They say, "Thanks, Joey," and they smile up at you because you are elevated, because you are impervious even to gravity, and they say in their secondary language, "We would do anything for you, Joey March, anything at all."

This is what it feels like out there at The Owl on a Friday night in April with the love of your life speaking strange with her eyes, when all the world is a land of perfect logic, when there is no downturn and Seymour Strout smiles at you from the door, gives you a certain nod that says he knows too that this night is a good one, that there is a secret rhythm, a secret chord, and all of us are inside of it, all of us are infected. And this good night goes on and this crowd is another single thing, which swells and deflates, swells and deflates.

Tess returns amidst some lull or another. She glides in on one of those shifts in pressure, a disturbance in the atmosphere, and she arrives with the same look, speaking that same silent phrase I can't yet decode.

I go to her and incline my head.

She brings her mouth to my ear.

It is a sublime and extraordinary privacy.

We drop below the water line. Down here the noise is muted, the crowd retreats.

She says, "The bathroom," and I follow.

This is an order I've never been given, not here, not by Tess. I abandon my post. I give the bar to the back.

There's a narrow bathroom out by the storeroom—facilities for the labor.

When I open the door she's standing, leaning against the small sink, her shoulder blades to the mirror.

"Close it," she says, giving a sharp little nod. I fall back. There's a quiet click sealing us in, and the bar noise loses its treble.

Here her expression is familiar. Lust.

Though there is something else to it I still can't translate.

Maybe it is the degree.

"Hey, Tess." Just to say her name.

The clock has started.

The ice is melting.

A towel is folded over the sink divider.

A cap is loose on a bottle of olives.

We're low on cherries.

The bar is a savage animal I've left untended.

Tess is looking at me in her new way. Or the old way multiplied and laced with some new thing.

"Joey," she says.

There's a single dim bulb hanging from the ceiling.

There's no tenderness in her face.

What I love is when she narrows her eyes, tilts her head just an inch to the left, and smiles at me with her lips closed. An uncanny expression, which contains both desire and sympathy.

This is not that.

This contains a foreign and faraway thing.

A flake of malice.

She draws her hands up the outsides of her thighs, beneath her black skirt, and bends at the waist. Her face is replaced by my own. For a moment I look at my eyes in the mirror. Then down to the curve of Tess's back.

She is upright again.

She winds her panties around her right fist like she's taping for a fight.

She reaches again and pulls her skirt up.

Not slowly.

She widens her stance. "Come here," she says.

There's no singsong in her voice. No girlish theater. "Come here."

I take the space between us. A single step. I'm looking down at her. If I were to look up, I'd see myself. I can sense that dark figure.

She moves her fingers around the back of my head and squeezes.

She looks right into my eyes.

"Suck it," she says. Stretching the s, stressing the k, making it all one angry word: SssuKit.

She pulls, but I resist. She raises her other hand, my ears now between her wrists.

She pulls and I go down.

I'm squatting but she wants me on my knees.

She pulls and I come forward off my heels.

She presses her feet against my shoulders and lifts herself onto the sink. She's still pulling. I'm too far away. I have to inch along the filthy floor.

"Fucking suck it," she says, her nails digging hard into the back of my scalp.

Then all at once she lets go, reaches between her legs and spreads herself open for me. She's so wet she's dripping onto the tile.

I fall forward into her, my knees a fulcrum, her legs over my shoulders, her thighs sliding against the soft skin of my neck.

I fall into her and press my tongue flat against her cunt, my hands on her ass, holding her to my mouth. She moans, but it is deeper than usual—in sound and in origin. Lips tight, teeth clenched.

She returns her hands to my head. She holds me hard and begins to move against my mouth.

I can feel it running down my throat. The taste makes me harder. The smell too. I push my tongue as deep as it will go. But she says, "No. Suck it."

SssuKit.

So I bring my mouth up until I feel that smooth rise. I take it between my lips, gently draw it in, move my tongue around and around and around.

Now that sound again. A kind of growl. Her nails are cutting. She's pushing with her hips, circling, holding on with everything she has.

I can barely breathe.

"Suck it," she says again. "Suck it you fuck, you fucker."

I don't stop. I can feel her close to coming. I am listening to her now. I am outside of myself. I am outside of us both. Now she is moaning higher. As if at last this groan, this tight-lipped, teeth-clenched groaning has broken her mouth open. The sound leaps an octave. I'm sure that I'm bleeding from her nails in my scalp.

"Do it, you fuck," she says.

I listen to her until she hooks her ankles together. She's

closing down on me, her thighs pressing and pressing against my ears and as she comes her voice fades.

She is soaking. She is shaking. Increment by increment, she is releasing me.

Sound returns. She lets me breathe. My mouth is wet. My chin. My neck.

She is trembling, her hands still in my hair, but gentler now. When she opens her eyes she looks down at me.

"Clean it up," she says.

When I don't move, when I only look back at her, this new person, she points to the inside of her glistening thigh.

And I do it. I do what she asks. I lick her clean.

I get up and pull some paper from a roll, and dry her as tenderly as I can. I press it against her to feel the pulsing.

I step away and watch as she unwinds her panties from her fist and slips them back on. She comes to me and runs her tongue around my lips, cleaning my mouth. She kisses me as softly as she knows how.

Then she opens the door and leaves.

When she's gone I stand at the sink and splash water on my face. In the mirror I see that my black T-shirt is scattered with dark patches.

And now, today, for you, I mark those minutes in a dirty bathroom at the back of a bar in White Pine, Washington.

I mark them as another point of change, of revelation, of no return.

82

C harlie Haden died the other day. All these deaths of people I've loved from afar. He was a tough, gentle man who refused to betray himself. We used to pay such careful attention to the world, Tess and I. Once upon a time when we had the energy for it. The rage. Who knows? Maybe Tess is out there right now, fighting some war or another. I hope so.

I hope so, but I will not search for her, or for anyone else.

You will return when it is time, or you will not return at all.

About Haden, he had always reminded me of my father and it made me very sad to read that he had died.

Do you see the difference between sadness and all that other muck?

Do you understand that it is not the same?

All day long I've been listening to him, an album of spirituals called *Steal Away*. My dad sent us that record. He wrote across the back in black felt pen, *For J and T, One of my very favorites. Especially the last. With love from your Jesus freak father.*

I'd forgotten about the inscription. It contains everything. His self-deprecation, his humility and humor, his awareness of my skepticism, his love of music, his love for us, his own shifting mind, inside of which Tess becomes his daughter. And also, I think, his sadness for having lost Claire.

I admire so much about him now. Especially that he kept his humor.

I am listening to that song he loved, *especially the last,* which is called "Hymn Medley," and I think of us in his house in White Pine.

It is the night I first arrived.

Poor boy with his life interrupted.

Poor boy suffering the cruelties of the world.

I think of him unpacking my bag as I slept, all he'd lost, all he'd given up. My father bent slightly at the waist, laying my clothes inside the drawers of a yellow dresser, him arranging my shoes on the closet floor, hanging my coat on the door hook, kissing my forehead before turning out the light, before returning alone to his room.

Towards the end of this song my father loved, this medley of hymns, is Haden playing "Amazing Grace." The bass comes in loud there for a while and the piano falls to the background. It is my favorite part of my father's favorite piece.

This is the story.

This accrual of days.

These losses.

These sadnesses.

This present.

This music.

There is never any stopping. We are always in motion. The ground is unstable, the plates forever shifting.

Charlie Haden vanishes and the world is altered.

That's a strange fact and it is one I love.

83.

At the end of that Friday, the night Tess took me into the bathroom, after we had cleaned up and cashed out, we sat with Seymour. We three around the same table as always. A bottle, glasses of ice, a pack of Virginia Slims, an ashtray stamped with the face of The Owl's owl. The manager locking the upstairs storeroom. Other waitresses leaving, laughing. The wild-haired barback restocking. The sound of him tearing open cardboard cases of beer, marrying bottles, replacing whatever was low, marking inventory with a pen on a chain. There was the music, which back then was all the Seattle stuff—Mudhoney, Screaming Trees, Soundgarden, Hammerbox, Temple of the Dog, Alice in Chains. But Cobain was our crown prince, our John Lennon and he was everywhere. So if you want the best guess, we were listening to him.

It was still the time of "Nevermind," pervasive across the land, but in a bar in Washington State in those years, it was inescapable. "Ubiquitous as harm," Richard Hugo once wrote, another of Tess's great loves.

Anyway, if you want to know what it felt like at the end of a Friday night in September of 1992, that's the best I can do. Joey March and Tess Wolff, Seymour Strout and Kurt Cobain. Come as you are, as you were, as I want you to be, as a friend, as a known enemy. On and on through the night, through our strangest, most dangerous years.

Tess was restless and wouldn't stop talking. She kept getting up and wandering the bar. Hanging her arm on Seymour's neck. The long night, the alcohol, our episode in the bath-room, had done nothing at all to calm her. Seymour and I were tired and relaxed, happy to be sitting, happy to be drinking. But Tess was moving, always moving. She the performer, we the audience.

What she was this night was nearly what she'd been becom-ing. Nearly the culmination of her changing, prowling eyes, her mask, her secret wardrobe.

"C," she said.

She'd started calling Seymour, C.

She was standing then, half-dancing with a chair. We'd been through all the subjects, all the questions. Always Tess would ask after my mother. And always the answers were the same. She was in prison. Nothing changed. Nothing discernible any-way. She seems tired. She's been a little quiet.

Seymour gave me a look, which meant, what's with her?

I shrugged.

"Don't look at him," she said. "You're talking to me."

"More like the other way around."

Tess dragged the chair she'd been dancing with over to the table and straddled it.

"I want to tell you something, C. See See Rider."

"All right." He lit a cigarette and blew the smoke at the ceiling.

"There's a girl."

"I don't want to be set up, Tess."

"Fuck. No. That's not it. Just listen, just fucking listen."

There was that old sick feeling.

"She lives with her family up on Vista. It's a nice house. There's a trampoline outside. You know it?"

He shook his head.

"She lives there with her parents. No brothers, no sisters. Her father's a professor at Emerson. Sam Young. Never heard of him?"

Seymour shook his head and glanced at me.

Tess waited until she had his eyes again. "This man, he likes to throw his wife into walls."

Seymour nodded.

She waited and stared.

"Tess, what's up with you? What are you telling me here?"

"I'm telling you that there's a man living on Vista who likes to beat his wife."

Seymour looked at me.

"He's been there, too. He knows. He's heard it. He's heard it, but I've seen it. I've seen what he does to her. I've called the police."

"*We* called the police," I said.

"It's true. Joey too. We both did. Called and went in there and did it in person."

"What are you telling me here, Tess?"

"I'm telling you that we've come to a point, C. That the police don't give a fuck. They don't do a thing about it. And they look back at you like *you're* looking at me. They say the same thing *you* do."

"And what do I say, Tess?"

"You say, why are you telling me this?"

"That's not what I said. I said, *what* are you telling me."

"It's the same thing, Seymour. It's the same *fucking* thing."

It wasn't only that she was drunk.

Seymour lit another cigarette.

"You don't know a thing about me." He dropped his matches on the table. Some of his calm was gone.

"No? Then do something about it."

He laughed. "What *should* I do about it?"

"What are you willing to do?"

He shook his head and leaned back from the table. "What's gotten into you tonight?"

"It's not only tonight," I said.

Tess ignored me. "Tell me, C. What are you willing to do?"

"About what? About this guy and his wife?"

"Yes. About them. What are you willing to do? Tell me. You willing to talk to your police buddies? See if you can convince them to give a fuck? You willing to kick in the door and scare the shit out of him? Willing to put a bullet in his head? What are you willing to do, Seymour?"

Seymour raised his chin and squinted at her.

"Hey Tess. You know where I work, right? I mean aside from this charming place? You know the kind of women I spend most of my time with? You remember that, right? And you remember how a lot of them got there?"

"You think they got there by protecting other women, C?"

"I sure think one of them did. And I also think she wishes she hadn't. I think every single day she wishes she hadn't."

"Well, I know you're wrong."

"What? She likes being in that cell?"

"I think she doesn't regret doing what she did. That she believes it was worth it."

"Worth it? To trade all these years, to trade her husband, her family, for that piece of shit?"

Tess looked away to some dark corner of the bar. "You haven't told me, Seymour. What are you willing to do?"

"Right now I'm thinking about what I wouldn't do."

He had those big hands clenched around each end of his towel. The expression of amusement, that slight smile, the detachment, was gone. Now his focus was on her and with a seriousness he used only for the rare drunk who wouldn't follow his friendly orders.

"What's that, C?"

"I'm not much interested in fighting, Tess."

She turned to him and laughed.

And now I want her to say, "Some people have to fight every moment of their lives."

But the problem here is that she wouldn't have said it. Not because it isn't hers, which it's not, but because it's taken from the book of poems she found later in Seattle. The book she loved, the book she left behind. This one here on the table, which was published years after that night in the bar.

I've been reading it. I know it's a mistake, but I don't have much discipline lately. And in with the sadness of it, the pain, there's pleasure too. In seeing her notes, her lines, her stars. The enthusiasm of a person, a self that no longer exists.

In that damp Belltown apartment, in those days when we were reading so hungrily, she found that line, which is here now, boxed and starred.

Some people have to fight every moment of their lives.

"This is mine," she said to me then.

"And this is yours, 'He feels the lights like hard rain through his pores.'"

It was a joke for us then, an affectation of our youth, which until yesterday I'd not thought of for so many years. Something from those early Seattle days when we spent our time and money at Left Bank, and Elliot Bay, Showbox and Rock Candy. When, for a brief period, I'm ashamed to report, we were writing wretched poems, and reading them aloud in cafés and bars, when we imagined ourselves artists, part of a scene.

"This is Joey," Tess said, "he feels the lights like hard rain through his pores."

"This is Tess," I said, "she has to fight every moment of her life."

Can you fucking imagine? It is mortifying and I have no excuse other than that we were very young. It embarrasses me to tell you all of this, but remember what it's like when you're that age? When you believe that you are unusual and your anger is unlike any other that has ever been. When you've not yet discovered just how boring you are. When you believe your every gesture is some kind of poem. When you've come

to town so ravenous and frightened that you believe there is
no one else in the world with more desire, more rage or more
fear.

I'm ashamed, but there is, along with all of that pretense
and delusion and self-importance, something tender and
lovely. Isn't that true, too?

I like to think of it now, of us in those days in our warm bed,
of the bookshops we thought of as our own, of our friends
then, all of whom, to a one, have dissolved. Of our life
together, our life which felt, as it had in White Pine, a thing of
such absolute solidity.

There is the time when you believe in permanence, and
then there is the time when you do not. All change is a variation on that fundamental difference.

Anyway, fuck it, I'm going to allow her to speak that sentence even if she didn't.

"Some people have to fight every moment of their lives."

And Seymour said, "I'm not one of them."

And then off they went back and forth in this invented dia-
logue, until it quickly came to the real point, the crucial question, which was:

"Will you help us?" or "C, will you help us?" or "Seymour,
will you help us, please?"

He looked at me then. "What is this, Joey? What is it
exactly?"

"Why are you asking him?"

Tess was up again lighting one of Seymour's Virginia Slims.

"What are you asking Joey for?" She chucked the pack at
him. "Your fucking cigarettes are ridiculous." She yelled it
loud and I laughed as hard as was possible in those days.
"Answer me, C. You fucker. What are you asking him for?"

He ignored her and nodded at me.

"What's this little team? What's the plan, Joe?"

"I've sworn my allegiance," I said.

"Kill or be killed, huh?" He smiled to himself and refilled our glasses. "You two are something else, man. I'll tell you what."

Tess came over to him with the cigarette burning between her lips. She sat sideways on his lap, and took the back of his head in her strong right hand.

"Will you help us?"

She said it quietly, and where the tip of her tongue caught on the filter, there was the faintest lisp.

I could see her hands in my hair. Could feel her pulling. Can see it now.

I had to look away.

Seymour said, "I'm not killing anyone. You understand me? You fucking lunatics, I'm not killing anyone."

And like that we were an army of three.

I wake to find Tess fast asleep, my heart battling my ribs. I'm up and dressed and in the truck as if by command. Ten minutes later I'm running the Spine with all the windows down, impervious to the cold, unmoved by the icy air. As the road breaks right and descends toward the prison, I get the truck up to ninety and flick the lights off. That's when the high frenzy truly begins, a pitch-black rhapsody. Mom, I am coming to free you. It is faster to skip the road entirely, I think, to veer off and sail out into the sky instead. I'll need more speed. If I can get it to a hundred and ten, I'm certain I'll make it fine. Land easy in the soft wheat. I drop the accelerator. Pedal to the metal, Dad, I'm coming for her. Don't you worry. I'm coming to bust her out. Somewhere very far away the truck is shaking and moaning, the tires whispering to me. I've got my eyes on the red needle. It won't go past ninety-seven. I tighten my grip on the wheel and pull myself up to stand on the gas. I put my head out the window and send my war cry into the night, but the road is flattening, dissolving into the prison plane.

The needle falls.

My command is gone.

The orange lights are too bright and the walls rise up too tall.

I drive off the road and nearly flip the truck

Then it's all gone.

I walk out into the field with a blanket, stretch out onto my back and wait with my mother and the receding tide.

J ack Dugan hanged himself with a belt last week. A local farmer. Nine acres of apples mostly, some berries, some asparagus. The paper says he'd been in debt for years. And now there's his picture on the front page. I'd seen him around—at the diner, drinking a little too hard at The Alibi— though until now I'd never known his name.

It was unusually hot here this morning. In the 90s and no air. There were slow-gathering clouds coming from the west and I couldn't sit still so I walked to town. I thought maybe they'd have the AC going at the diner. The sky was that luminous slate color you see only in storms and animals.

By the time I made it I was dripping with sweat and the thunder was just starting to roll. I got lucky with the AC, bought a paper, took a booth by the window, ordered bacon and eggs, toast and coffee. I could almost see Tess and my mother sitting across from me. I could nearly feel my father's shoulder against mine.

I have always loved to sit in restaurants and watch the bad weather come. When we had our bars, it made me so happy to have people use them for shelter.

'Twas in another lifetime, one of toil and blood/When blackness was a virtue and the road was full of mud/I came in from the wilderness, a creature void of form.

Another my mother sang and sang and sang.

I loved watching the umbrellaless run across the street and dive inside. That was something that made me happy. The sense that we were providing refuge to strangers. Something about the way a storm disorients and frightens people. Makes them sheepish and vulnerable. Hair soaked, makeup running, skirts blown above our waists, everything wild and out of place.

An afternoon in one of those early Seattle years when our bar was still struggling, the rain pounding, and all at once, in a burst, just the way they say, *as if the sky opened up*. The wind and water and all those people diving in for shelter, splashing through our door, it flipped the switch and then I was standing on the bar with a bottle of Jameson in my hand, another between my knees, lightning running my spine, the bartender tossing me shot glasses and I'm passing out whiskey as if the place is just a hobby for a king and not our last and only hope. I'm up there holding court, the most charming man on earth, while Tess stands by the bathrooms trying to take me down with her killer eyes. But even she can't shoot me from that sky, can't stop me from giving our money away. Me, I fall of my body's own accord, so I stay where I am, benevolent lord, pouring my drinks, bowing to the shrieking crowd.

Anyway, this morning I was feeling okay there at the diner with my family and a farmer in a red cap at the booth next to mine, both of us watching the rain starting to fall. When the thunder got loud and the lightning close, he glanced at me and said, "Big one. Hope there's no fire." I smiled and nodded and felt all right. I didn't want to talk, but I didn't want to be alone. I liked his face.

All of us, Claire and Tess, Mom and Dad, we watched as the storm passed through, and for a while I didn't want to be anywhere else.

Once it had gone, and the heat broke, I opened the paper and saw Dugan's face. I don't why he matters exactly. Just that his story twisted in me and from the start I promised myself I'd put everything in.

All of it. Whatever comes through.

86

My father called on a clear morning in October. This is in White Pine. We'd had days and days of rain. Storm after storm and then, one morning, blue sky.

Tess refused to be still. She no longer read. Wouldn't sleep. Was always at a window. Despite the gloom, the fires I lit, she wouldn't stay with me beneath the blankets, wouldn't slip her feet beneath my legs. I tried to read, but mostly I watched her patrolling, leaving and returning. She wasn't eating much and her face had taken on an angular severity, which made her eyes appear wider-set than they were. All her softness was gone, and in its place, an unmitigated fierceness. She paced the house like a fighter waiting for the ring. Tess, her constant moving and the ceaseless rain had caused me such a sense of suffocating claustrophobia that when the phone woke me that morning, and I heard my father's voice, and saw the sky, I was gone before she'd opened her eyes.

He was on a bench down at the waterfront with a bag of donuts and coffee for us both. I was so glad to be there. I think that deep comfort had to do with the relief of having him next to me right as the shell was cracking.

I was dominated by fear. Once again, the world felt precarious and fragile and I was grateful to have my father, upright, still, the way he had always been.

Constancy, kindness and faith, his greatest gifts to me.

It is what I imagine offering to my own son one day.

Steady, I would so much like to be steady.

I kissed the top of his head and sat with him. He put his arm around my shoulder. Whenever we met, after a day, or a month, always there in his face was a flash of boyish excitement. I don't ever remember meeting him, not once in my entire life, without seeing it. This expression indistinguishable, really, from that of a boy meeting his father. And sometimes it caused a pressure in my chest, something unsettling I couldn't identify. But today when I saw him, his eagerness, there was no irritation. I only loved him.

His warmth in the cool morning. The soft, round smell, Right Guard and Royall Lyme and some other thing that language can do nothing for.

There's a smell of coffee too, and of those fresh donuts. Glazed and maple.

White seagulls circling above and strutting in front of us.

"I saw Mom the other day," he said.

"How is she?"

"Seems the same. She always seems the same."

"Does she still tease you?"

He laughed. "Not for a while."

The teasing was about being a Quaker. It had been me who'd told her and it was the last time I'd seen my mother smile. I mean smile with her whole mouth, with a little glee.

"You like that," I said.

She closed her eyes and nodded her head, suppressing a laugh.

"Why?"

She shrugged. "I don't know, Joey. It's just that your father is extraordinary. The man cannot be broken. He sees peace everywhere. Calm in all corners. You and me, we see war. Not your dad. You should learn from him all you can."

"You mean you and Tess," I said.

"Me and Tess what?"

"See war in all corners."

"And not you, Joe?"

I shook my head. "Not the way you two do."

She nodded in her deliberate way, looking at me as if she were trying to work something out, trying to find a quality in my face she could not.

"What?"

"Well, you are, after all, a man. No way around that in the end. A fact's a fact."

"Sink or swim," I said and smiled at her.

"That's it, Joe. Sink or swim. Fight or die." She leaned forward and took my hands in hers. "Despite those facts, I love you. And I love that girl of yours, too."

"I know you do," I said.

"Which? Which do you know?"

"Both, Mom, both."

Now my father was talking. We'd finished our donuts, the coffee was nearly cold, the sun was up high enough to cut the air, to warm our bare necks.

"I get the impression she's drifting. Faster and faster," he said.

It was true. As if her eyes were draining out. A recession, a withdrawal. Something she couldn't help. What I kept thinking, but never said to him, was that what it was, what she couldn't help, was dying in there.

"Anyway," he said. "She told me something I don't understand."

"About what?"

"What are you planning, Joe?"

"What did she tell you?"

He finished his coffee, crumpled the cup, shot and missed the trash can across the walkway.

"Joey. Please don't do anything stupid. We've had enough. You and I. We've had enough of it all."

We watched a decrepit fishing boat kill its engine and glide into the harbor.

"I don't know what she's planning," I said.

"She?"

"Tess."

He stood up, grabbed the cup and dropped it into the can. He took his time, but when he came back to the bench, he said, "It's not just Tess."

"I have no plans, Dad. I don't know what's wrong. I don't know what's happened to her. And I don't know what she's planning."

"It's Mom, too, Joey."

"She's what? Giving instructions?"

He shrugged. "Impression I have."

"What did she tell you?"

"She doesn't really *tell* you anything, does she? But that's not the point. What I'd like, Joe, is for you to stay away from it. And I'd like for you to talk to Tess. Keep her away, too."

I thought of her looking down on the street from our bedroom window, the black mask, her visits to The Pine.

I hadn't seen him so angry at my mother in many years.

"Easy to preach crime from prison," he said.

87

One evening I went for a run down along the water-front, out past the meetinghouse and beyond to the narrow beach stretching far north toward the Olympic Peninsula.

I came home thinking Tess had gone out. But at the top of the stairs I saw her through the open bathroom door.

The water was running. She was sitting naked on the edge of the cracked claw-foot tub.

There are few images that exist in me the way this one does. That remain with its clarity. Clarity not only of shadow, color and line, but of sound and smell, of tone, texture and atmosphere.

I cannot do it justice:

There was the water thudding against the enamel, and the green, corroded drain. Up on her toes, heels raised. Elbows on her knees. Her left palm upturned and resting in her right. Her head down, eyes down. The light entering from the bathroom's single window filling the small angular space beneath the undersides of her breasts. There is a smooth, elegant line that falls from her shoulders, turns at her lower back, swells around her ass, along her thigh, turns in the dark corner of her knee, drops around her taut calf, tapers to her narrow ankle and begins again where her toes touch the floor.

There is a soft breeze stirring the toilet paper poorly torn and hanging long from its roll.

The light makes its rough end glow.

Her face is turned slightly toward me and what is absent in her expression strikes me hardest.

She is incautious. She is undefended.

I lean against the wall and feel a blow of sadness.

What is its source?

The depth of her grace, yes. And the relief of seeing this other part of her again, at last, returned. Still, contemplative, gentle. And the intimacy of it, yes. All of these.

But there is dread too.

Many years later, Tess and I took a train into Canada and somewhere along that line we stopped in a wide-open plain of snow. There was some problem with the tracks ahead. We'd been going for days and then all at once the noise ended. The chatter, the constant rattling, the speeding landscape.

All at once, the world was still. We were alone in the center of a vast white world.

This was like that.

Sudden stillness.

Space opening up around me.

A cooling of my eyes.

A slowing. The machine hissing, shuddering, shutting down. Silence.

It was just like that.

She slipped into the bath and turned the faucets with her toes.

She closed her eyes and sighed.

I waited and when it was unbearable I went to her and I kneeled on the white tiles and I washed her hair.

Neither of us spoke.

All that night the train went nowhere.

88

Fuck you, Tess. This morning, furious again, I got out of bed, dressed, ran below the sky low and heavy through the woods where the trees closed in so dark I couldn't see the ground. Ran hard enough along those deep snaking trails to burn my lungs. Looping home terrifying a feeding deer which went leaping into the underbrush as I came swooping by so close I could hear it breathe and all those branches cracking beneath its hooves and behind my eyes and when the grey light of the clearing appeared I sprinted full-blast driving with my knees just the way you taught me, Dad. Fuck you for leaving, Tess. Fuck you for quitting, you child, you coward, deserter, defector, traitor. Fuck you, turncoat bitch, you so proud and principled and sure all those years ago condemning my sister for doing just what you have done yourself. Fuck Claire, you said. Such certainty. Such moral clarity, my exquisite hypocrite, liar, deceiver, failure, renegade. Home I was sweating, pacing the deck, chasing my breath, adrenaline rolling, I wanted you back only to slap your face hard, the violence building in me, saw my palm against your skin, heard the cracking sound. And do you see how with that fantasy, that visceral hunger, I am no better than Sam Young? Another terrified man run out of language, absent imagination. Me, the usual. Me, the same old shit, clutching the same dull script. Showered, dressed, lit a fire. Usually it all subsides after swimming through the dark woods where I fight it, hammer it to the ground, but not today.

Today I could not win. I could not get it out.

Tess, I kneeled at our sacred wall of books and withdrew *The Once and Future King* from a low shelf: hardback, horizontal stripes of blue and green and black and blue, crowned lion rearing up on one hind leg, claws pawing the air, jaws open, roaring.

You are the knight, your mother wrote across the top of the third page. *Happy Birthday. October 30, 1981.*

You were ten.

I am ashamed to tell you: I burned that book.

89

The day I followed Sam Young the clouds raced across the sky while I waited in my truck hidden by shade watching both the front door and the still black surface of the trampoline.

He left his house in a tweed suit, Thermos in one hand, leather satchel in the other, got into his car and drove away. Something silver. I followed him all the way to Emerson. And then from a parking lot on foot to the great quad, into a brick building, up the stairs, along a corridor where I passed him as he stopped to unlock his office door.

I read a book on a bench and waited, followed him to a raked hall and watched from the dark back row as he clicked through slides and gave a lecture on something I can't remember. It would be helpful if I could. It might lend a little weight here, a layer or two of meaning. The story of a great battle, perhaps. Maybe I should invent something. The Barbarian Invasions. The Crusades. The Inquisition. Good and evil. Let Sam Young foreshadow his own fate.

But these are not the lies I want to tell.

I can't even remember what his specialty was.

I was looking for something in him I couldn't have described then.

It was some new version. A version we couldn't harm.

He was a stodgy speaker. The lecture hall had no charge. There were no questions at the end. I followed him to a meeting and then later back to his office where he left the door open. I waited down the hall. Students stopped by. He was friendly and patient. There was warmth in his voice. They seemed to like him. When the hour was over, we went to a café at the student union building where he ate lunch with two men and a woman. I assumed they were professors. I was too far away to listen. He smiled a lot and when he spoke, the others leaned forward. They laughed. He removed his jacket and hung it on the back of his chair. Although his hair had fallen across his forehead, he left it alone.

I wasn't following orders. No one knew I was there. I hadn't been sent.

It's that I wanted to see him in some other realm, with some other quality.

Or I wanted some further confirmation of his cruelty.

I was there looking for one thing or another.

Make him a man, or make him an object.

But more the former. I was looking for evidence. More than anything I wanted to come home and show it to her. Say, "Look at what else he does, Tess."

Tess, in our living room a few nights before, pacing before the fire addressing her troops.

Look, I wanted to say, see? He is this thing too. He is also this other thing.

After lunch I followed him to the library steps where he sat and smoked a cigarette. He tilted his face to the sun and closed his eyes for a moment.

Look, he is contemplative. Look, this is a man with an inner life.

I followed him inside the library, and into a lighted theater where he took a seat and began to write on a legal pad. A woman on her way down the aisle touched his shoulder. He looked up and smiled. The seats began to fill. A man walked to the front, made an introduction I cannot recall, and then left the stage. The lights went dark and a film began to play. I left, bought a cup of coffee on the quad, and took it to a bench.

What had I discovered? What evidence could I bring before the court? To my superior? Sam Young liked a cigarette in the sun, was kind to his students, attended meetings, made his friends laugh, allowed his hair to fall out of place, saw films.

Seemed generally liked.

Was generally alive.

What I'd come to find was what I found.

So I sat with it feeling, if not hopeful, then encouraged. It was hope without dimension, but I let it carry me for a while. Along with the coffee and the sunshine and the safety of that place.

I believed, or pretended to believe, that I might change our course. That this new information might have some kind of significance.

And then there was Marcy Harper standing in front of me.

"Mr. March," she said.

There was none of the coldness I'd remembered. Instead she smiled—warm and mocking. I was surprised by it, by her manner, by the easiness of our banter, by our affected formality.

"Ms. Harper."

"Back to campus, I see."

I nodded. "I like it," I said. "Closest thing we have to a park."

She sat next to me on the bench.

"How's your mother?"

"I'm never sure how to answer that question, Marcy."

"She's stopped writing to us, you know."

"I didn't. I'm sorry."

"Me too. She won't see me anymore."

"Did you visit her often?"

"Twice. Once alone, once with a few others."

"What was she like with you?"

"She was smart," she said, nodding to herself, "and fiery and tough, too. Full of advice, full of ideas."

"What kind of ideas?"

"Things we might do here. Ways to protest, ways to fight."

"Like what?"

"Oh, nothing revolutionary, really. Letters and marches. That kind of thing. Mostly it was just her enthusiasm, her encouragement."

"What about violence?"

"No, never."

My mother knew how to choose her generals.

"I see. Well, you can always try again," I said. "She changes."

"Maybe I will. Maybe you'll mention it to her."

I laughed.

"What?"

"Now you want my help."

"I'm sorry about that."

"No. Don't be. I was a prick."

"You were fine. Sometimes I lose my humor. It must be difficult for you."

I shrugged. "So what's next in the campus rebellion?"

"You really care?"

I nodded.

"A woman was raped in the basement of the Beta house two weeks ago. Remains under investigation. No one has been arrested. Saturday we're going to gather out front."

"Maybe I'll see if I can convince Tess to come."

She shook her head and laughed. "You're going to come stand in front of a frat house with a bunch of college girls on a Saturday night?"

"It's either that or set it on fire."

She laughed. "Which do you think Anne-Marie March would prefer?"

"The fire," I said. "The fire, of course."

There was a surprising ease between us. She had a term for what they were planning, some academic jargon, the kind of thing Tess abhorred: aggressive silence, violent passivity, accusatory presence, et cetera. I can't remember. Doesn't matter. The thing is that when Marcy left I felt that sad hope of mine bolstered. I stood on the steps of the library with the belief (or some thin version of belief) that there was an alternative and when Sam Young came past me down the steps, I followed him to his car.

Now I felt a sense of affection for this man, about whom I knew so little. This man I'd spent all day inventing. Affection as I drove behind him, tailing, counting five seconds between telephone poles, slowing to twenty on Water, feeling, by the time he disappeared onto Vista, a strange illogical love for the man I'd created.

And then a spark, perhaps composed of that contrived and desperate affection, ignited those unknowable rockets and I was hovering three inches above my torn seat, eyes well-tuned, and I hit the gas, took a turn, came up fast on him, the gearshift, so supple in my palm, was a weapon, a controller, and I raced forward incapable of error, dropped from fourth to third and that downshift noise made Claire giggle, it was on the road, in my throat and I pulled the Mariners hat down low nearly to my nose, and I was on him, my rusted front bumper two feet away, then one, then inches, and then there were Sam Young's eyes in the rearview mirror. He accelerated, tried to escape, but there was no losing me. I was expert, I was weightless, I had infinite control and I was going to stop him, Dad. It would be okay. I would save you the heartache. I was going to pull him over even if it meant driving his shitty sedan into a tree. I would change him, fix him, force a confession, take him to jail, break his arms, whatever it took to avoid whatever it was Tess was planning.

But then he slowed down.

Those red lights shining in my eyes, refracting in my windshield, exploded the engines.

And it was gone.

The dimensionless hope, the flimsy belief.

I slowed to a creep. The sedan hovered for a moment, and then shot away.

I stopped and waited next to a hydrant, with the slow flood of tar.

Now I slunk down and drove along his street.

I heard the thump and squeak of the trampoline.

There was Anna flying through the trees, and as I passed she met my eyes. She waved from midair. That familiar, expressionless face. I raised my hand out the window and spread my fingers.

She kept her mouth shut.

By the time I'd returned home, I had nothing to show, no evidence to provide. Nothing but an invitation to another protest lit by candles, to participate in aggressive silence, violent passivity, accusatory presence, et cetera.

And what would Tess Wolff say to that?

I came in and found her sitting on a front windowsill, feet flat against the floor, toenails freshly painted red.

Or so I remember it: blade of late spring light carving across her ankles.

Seymour sitting on the couch.

I poured myself a bourbon from the bottle on the coffee table, touched his glass with mine and sat next to him.

"How does it go, Joe?"

I'd forgotten it. This thing Seymour used to say to me.

Until now, I'd forgotten it entirely. Gone and then returned. Who knows what else exists in there? All that information resting dormant. Dust on water, flotsam on the surface of a still sea.

Anyway, that's what he said.

That evening, and all through those days.

"How *does* it go, Joe?"

Over that short course of time when we were friends, when we believed so fully in our own intransience, when there was no consideration of separation, no sense of time ever drawing us out into the wider world.

This tidal past rushes back so rapidly. Comes and goes so often without explanation.

I loved Seymour asking, "How does it go, Joe?"

So I tell you this to record it, to mark it down before it's gone again.

And I tell you because, simply: I loved Seymour Strout.

It matters, doesn't it? I think it must. I think the three of us mattered, in the same way that Tess and I did.

As units.

As single pieces in time.

Or single pieces of time.

I don't know if there's any distinction between time and what exists within it.

All these loves of mine. Love for my past selves, for my mother, for my father, for Claire, for my vanished Big Sur friends, for Tess, for our Cannon Beach family, for Seymour, for all those dissolved and dissolving, for those waiting within me, caught in some taut mnemonic fold, and for this physical world, I insist they are of significance.

In all their various weights and surfaces.

The only constant things within me.

So:

"How does it go, Joe?"

"Went out to Emerson," I said.

Tess turned her head from the window.

"Why?" she asked. Or without the question mark, said as if she knew.

"I needed a vacation."

She looked at me the way she always did lately—with cold suspicion. Always as if she were evaluating me, my promise. There was a fierce tension between us now, which as we drew closer to November, was nearly unremitting.

"Why were you there, Joe?"

"I needed some air."

She looked back out the window.

"It's a nice campus," Seymour said to the room.

"I ran into Marcy Harper." Keeping my eyes on the side of Tess's face.

"Who's that?" Seymour our great objective mediator.

"Student at Emerson. Tess's friend," I said.

"Not a friend. What did she say?"

"We talked a long time. Had a cup of coffee together. Apparently my mother won't see her, doesn't respond to her letters."

Tess smiled at the street.

"You know about that?"

She shrugged.

"There's a protest Saturday night. She invited me. Invited us."

"What's it for?" Seymour had moved to the floor where he now lay flat on his back.

"A girl was raped in a frat house."

We were all quiet for a long time.

Then Seymour said, "Fuck it, I'll go."

"Me too," I said. "Saturday night. She's pretty, C. Marcy Harper."

I said it to provoke Tess, but she didn't react. Seymour

laughed. "In that case I'll wear a clean shirt. We'll have to get off work."

"Fine by me," I said.

"Tess you want to come?" He was up on his elbows.

"What's the plan exactly?"

I told her, "A silent protest. Candles. Wear all black, stand in front of the Beta house."

"That's it?"

"Aggressive silence," I said.

Tess gave us her most disdainful, most mocking laugh.

"Come on," Seymour said. He poured himself another drink. "You know, we could do the same thing." He was getting to his feet now. The giant emerging from sleep. He went to the door with his glass. There with his hand on the knob, he looked down at her. "We could do the same thing. Stand in front of his house each night. Black hoods. Candles in our hands. Pretty good idea, really. Save us the trouble of the other thing. Save us the trouble of prison."

I was watching him at the door, seeing all at once, in one *fail* swoop, that he was just a kid. Maybe some new angle to his face, or a glint of fear. I looked up at him and thought exactly that, *He's just a kid.*

Tess looked up at him then. Said, "We should all go on Saturday night," as if it had been her idea in the first place. "We go in hoods, we see Marcy Harper and her friends, we light our candles. We stand in *aggressive silence*. We make sure we're *seen*."

Seymour looked at her a long moment. "Seen?"

"Being peaceful, yes," she said.

He shook his head, and then went outside onto the porch to smoke a cigarette.

I liked Seymour's idea. The three of us out there embarrassing Sam Young. Maybe we'd bring Marcy and her gang. Swarm the bastard's house night after night until it ended.

Until the reporters came. Until the police were forced to respond. Until his wife was safe. And Anna. I liked the idea of it, but we could not do both things.

It was one or the other, and Tess was moving at breakneck speed.

90.

S aturday night the three of us in my truck driving out to Emerson. The close cab. Smell of Seymour sweat, Virginia Slims and lemon oil, coffee and night air tinged with salt. Of us. One unit. One brick of time.

The Beta house was on Barry, one of four main streets that framed the campus. Here were all the frats on one side, all the sororities on the other. Five and five.

And who cares what they were called? Can you think of anything less important in the world than distinguishing Beta from Delta? Kappa from Gamma?

Fuck those people.

There is a point when fear leaves me, when rage replaces it. And when that rage fuses with the upswing and the clear light, well, then I am deadly and I am invincible. And when that fusion, that concoction, that strange combination meets the end of Seymour Strout's patience, and is joined to all the wrath of Tess Wolff, then we are an army of rare and secret power.

We are out of the cab. We are off-kilter, irritable and separate. We have not yet cohered. But it is coming. I can feel it now, here in this house, and there is nothing I cannot see.

My heart is ahead of you, my whole body.

I will bring you in soon, I will bring you to me.

In the present, in the past, in all their respective iterations.

We are out of the cab.

We are walking down Barry, Tess ahead of us. Of course. A good full step. There are the houses, Alpha to Omega, or however it went. Five and five. And on the fraternity side, people spilling off their porches onto lawns.

The sororities had no parties.

When those women wanted debauchery they crossed the street.

They said heaven was on one side, hell the other.

Marcy Harper, dressed all in black, was there in heaven. Surrounded by the others, whose faces I can't remember. Or what they called themselves. But they were there, maybe ten, maybe fifteen to begin with. Milling around when we arrived. Tess hugging Marcy as if she were an old friend, as if she believed in her methods of war. Marcy tolerating Tess, and then smiling at me, saying, "So nice to see you Mr. March." And then looking up at Seymour with the kind of nervous reserve his size and ever-changing eyes—dull to sharp, matte to gloss—provoked in people.

He and I were the only men. We stayed in the shadows, back on the second line. There were maybe thirty of us there. Two rows of fifteen by the time Marcy began distributing the lit candles, got all our hands glowing. Then in our uniforms, in our formations, we became a single entity. We held no signs. We kept our silence. We did nothing but stand and face the Beta House. Tess and Marcy front and center, side by side. We would stay the duration of a single small candle. Two hours. We would hold our ground. Say nothing.

Then we became a focal point and quickly had the attention of the street—the passersby, the people on the house porch, on the lawn. Rapid shift from invisible to visible. Stage lights thrown. The next hour you can predict. The various responses and insults. Our still black band, a solemn mass amidst the speeding Saturday night. But we stayed where we were. We kept our promises.

"What are you for?"

The first phrase I'm sure of. Someone calling from across

the street. Some drunken fool on the Beta porch. Poetry by mistake: "What are you for? What are you fuckers *for*?"

The night took on a new pressure. I could sense it in Seymour. His body straightening. Tess motionless. And who knows how much time passed?

That's the call, which threw the switch.

"What are you fuckers for?"

And:

"Who wants to see the basement?"

And:

"Which one of you whores wants a tour?"

Then:

"Tour, tour, tour, tour, tour, tour."

Then:

Laughter.

There was competition now.

Who could do what?

Who could do more?

Who could do worse?

So, someone threw an egg.

Missed.

Someone threw a bottle.

Now there was glass in the street.

"Fuck off, dyke. Fuck off, dyke. Fuck off, dyke."

Faded. Failed chant.

Try again:

"Suck my cock. Suck my cock. Suck my cock."

This one more successful. Call and response. Back and forth. Fraternity, sorority, fraternity, sorority. Men calling, women responding.

Low: "Suck my cock."

High: "Suck my cock."

Fade away. Laughter then a lull. And our formation unbroken. Candles still lit. Promises kept.

But always there is someone willing to cross the street. Rarely does he travel alone. So across Barry came three Beta brothers. Two shirtless, one in a red polo.

They were familiar to us from bars. Familiar to me and Seymour and Tess. The types, I mean.

We filtered them through our three respective lenses—barman, doorman, waitress.

We experts. We warriors.

They came on with the swagger of athletes at home.

They said, "What are you here for? What do you want?"

And we said nothing.

I can't say who of our front line looked past them, and who looked down, and who raised her eyes.

But pretty soon they were right in front of Marcy Harper. The single black woman there. A fact worth mentioning, I think. Worth mentioning that we are in White Pine, Washington, in 1992.

In any case, she didn't look away and she didn't look down. Whatever the reason, the drunk boys were over the curb now, closer, focused on their single subject.

"What are you here for?" one of them said.

And the other: whining, slurring, repeating his call as if he were demanding the answer to some crucial existential question, "What are you for? What are you *for?*"

I kept thinking, trying to keep my promise, as a way to remain calm, He's forgotten *here.* He's forgotten *here.*

Then a litany: Cunt, whore, dyke, bitch, et cetera. The usual.

Then, noticing me and Seymour, faces shadowed by our hoods, they stopped for a moment. But they found their courage again, bolstered each other, and then to us: pussy, faggot, piece of shit, et cetera.

On it went. You can imagine, can't you? The insults, the provocations, our refusing to respond.

What else then is there to do for those minds, those enemy soldiers?

So the whiner, the one in red, he put his hand over Marcy's face and he pushed. She fell backwards into our second line, into two small women who couldn't hold her. She landed on the grass, down but unhurt. And still we made no move. Someone found her candle, relit it. Up again. Back in formation. Tess stayed still. I did too. And Seymour. But he pushed an elbow into my ribs.

Which meant: If they do it again, Joe. If they do it again.

I nodded. And I knew that Tess was listening. That she was in agreement. Enough was enough. I also knew that Marcy Harper would be angry. That she wouldn't want our protection, that she didn't need it.

But whatever we may have believed then, I don't think it was ever a question of protection. We were, just like those three fools in front of us, looking for war.

So when the red shirt laughed and put his palm on her face again and shoved, Seymour and I came through the front line fast. Seymour, following his open hand, came in a single move I knew from the bar. No talk, no warning, just his big fingers open as if around a fat coffee mug driving forward to the throat. He took that boy off the curb and into the street like he was some kind of inflatable doll. Driving him back and down.

Seymour kneeling above the kid now, choking him, holding his head to the asphalt, the boy making a horrible bird sound. And then one of the shirtless ones came toward Seymour, setting up with his leg, winding, but before he could kick I hit him hard in the gut and he fell back. I turned to face the other, who was moving, but not with much enthusiasm. There had been a change in the sound. Now more of them came from the lawn to the street. No more laughter.

Tess was off her line now too, her hood thrown back, yelling in her loudest voice, "C, let him go, C."

And he did.

The boy rolling away, his hands at his throat. And now Seymour standing with me, facing the coming Beta. Who stood still waiting for the next move, the next decision, for someone else to make it. And Marcy and Tess both yelling, "Stop it. Stop. Fucking stop."

The two of them brief partners. Same goal, different motives.

Tess in performance, determined to be seen as peaceful.

Marcy in real outrage.

The choked kid was being walked away. The women continued to hold their candles.

In the lull Tess was saying, "Go back, go back."

Marcy saying the same.

We followed orders. We returned to our line. We waited. That was the end of it.

There were some trailing insults. Bluster. But nothing else.

Each of us stood our ground, kept our places. Burned the candles down.

And then we left. All of us walking in silence to someone's house where we sat on the front steps drinking beer, while Marcy seethed.

She said what you'd expect, "We don't need your goddamn protection. We don't need to be defended."

We were sorry. Seymour was quiet the way he always was after battle. Tess trying to play sympathizer and sister in arms, but getting nowhere.

Soon we said our goodbyes. Marcy Harper looking down at us from the top step as we walked away, Seymour lumbering along ahead, sullen.

And us three we went back to the truck, drove up to Lester's and got lucky with a booth. The place was packed with guards, the music loud.

We ordered a pitcher of Olympia and a pizza.

Something had been proven. Tess had made her point.

We were not suited to peaceful protest. That kind of thing didn't coincide with our vision of ourselves. Or, at least, Tess's vision. But you have to understand that there was no great system in place. No grand philosophy. None of us could have told you what our ambitions were then. It was to do with rage and love and friendship. Boredom, too, if I'm to be honest. Let us not pretend that we were noble. Or entirely so. We were kids, after all. Which excuses nothing, of course. Only to say that reason was secondary.

We were not that night at Lester's, nor at any other time, nor in any other place, talking politics and activism. Do not confuse us with movie militants in a basement room, cleaning our weapons, maps on the table. Or even with Marcy Harper's disciplined and thoughtful campus variation.

That night we ate and drank and said nothing of import. No rousing speeches were made. But now we had an immediate and certain future before us. No ambiguity. No wondering what was to come. And I think it was that feeling of certainty and resignation that drew us from the night's outrage and gloom into something brighter, into something nearly joyful.

91

I'm afraid that I have made some fundamental error. I worry that I did not look at Tess correctly. Have not. Through all the years together, and then from here, too, from afar, in all these increments of recollection.

What is the nature of this error?

I'm not certain.

Is it something to do with the way that I observed her? Something to do with *beauty*, with the effect her body had on me. To do, even, with the words themselves.

Beautiful, for one.

Think of the way I saw her in the bathroom that sad afternoon. The light on her breasts. The slope of her back, her thighs, her calves, her narrow ankles. All the rest I've described to you. The power she had. Not she, but her body. You see in those descriptions that there are no scars. No blemishes, no hairs trapped beneath her skin. All that body and so little mind. Oh, but that's not true either. More than anything she exists in me as a force, a heat deep in my spine, a turning in my chest. It is not her physical shape that stirs me most or first. And it never was, not even from the start. It is everything else: will, fire, fury, lust, intelligence, vision, heart, humor, conviction.

I am doomed to this litany, to confusion, to clichés, to dead words.

And yet, and still, the way she appears here to me now so clearly, I see no imperfection. And is that not a kind of tyranny? Haven't I imprisoned her? Us?

She becomes material so easily—whole and in parts. Her skin, her eyes, her breasts, her shoulders, her mouth, her thighs. I do not mean to do it. But there she is assembling and disassembling.

Here I close my eyes.

The falling line of her throat.

Her feet, which she did not like for their size and flatness. "Too big," she said. "So ugly."

But no, there was nothing ugly.

And I *do* remember scars.

One thin curve soaring from her hip bone. Left.

A lopsided diamond at her ankle. Left.

The start of a spiral on the meat of her shoulder. Right.

Coming home from somewhere in winter, her eyes red from the cold, nose running, hair a tangle, lips dry and flaking. Or the relentless pimples, which appeared on her chin late into her thirties. The lines at her eyes, and across her forehead. The flecks of grey in her hair.

It was all the same.

Her beauty deepened. I cannot change this, and I cannot avoid the word. For so long, I have tried to make her ugly in body and mind. But there is nothing to be done.

Through all the years we are expected to stop looking at one another, I looked. When abruptly we were no longer young. Through the panic of age, and accelerating time, and deteriorating bodies, through the shock of, the rebellion against, and, at last, the resignation to those things, I watched her. I could not stop and I wonder if there was an error there. A failing somehow. I wonder if through all that watching, I was doing her harm. If to see her always bathed in these golden lights was itself an act of violence. Was it the violence of worship? Have I, all these years, made her something impossible? Inhuman?

But then I remember my frustration, how often I hated her,

how often we fought, her stubbornness, her selfishness, her disappearances, physical and otherwise, her cruelty and blindness.

I have not forgotten how anger flowed between us for so many years. That's all there too and because it is, I believe I have loved her in spite of those things.

I believe I have loved her fairly.

92.

My father had constructed a life without us. At the meetinghouse he'd become friends with a tall, sturdy man in his seventies who had the face and demeanor of a character actor. He might once have played a noble cowboy, a wise cop, and now, while still handsome, was in fast decline. My father and Hank Fletcher, who was an easy six inches taller, walked together on the beach in the mornings. You might have confused the two for brothers. Hank, limping, hands clasped behind his back, cigarette in his mouth, and my father at his side, carrying that red Thermos full of coffee.

As far as I knew, my father had never had friends of his own. In the first Seattle days, good and old, my parents would, from time to time, have dinner with other couples, but I never once knew him to go out alone with anyone other than me, or Claire, or my mother. There was a time when he played center field in a Sunday softball league, but even then, after those games it was family picnics and barbeques, not men together in bars. His solitude, his reluctance, or incapacity, to make friends never occurred to me, not until my mother took a hammer to Dustin Strauss's skull and we all found ourselves shipwrecked in White Pine.

Reverberating loudly enough through those years, intensely enough to reach me even through my self-absorption, my righteousness and debilitating love for Tess, was the knowledge that my father was an isolated and lonely man. Even if he would never cop to the accuracy of such descriptions. Never.

Because they could be construed as weaknesses, as flaws, and he could not acknowledge such things, or even their possibilities. Not to me. Not beyond the general, the safe concession that, yes, we are all flawed, none of us is finished improving, et cetera. No more specific than that, no more damning than the broad damning of human beings of every kind, and everywhere.

To convey to you the nature of those years in White Pine, there can be no separating these three fundamental and confluent facts:

1. My mother's incarceration and subsequent change of demeanor and, of course, what brought her there.

2. My gradual understanding that my father was, save for his son and imprisoned wife, friendless and lonely in the world.

And 3. My love (measly word) for Tess.

Which is all to say that it was a surprise to witness my father's renaissance: first the meetinghouse, and now Hank Fletcher.

I would like to tell you that it was entirely pleasant. I would like to say I was big enough of heart by then that to see my father walking side by side with his handsome new friend provoked in me feelings only of happiness and warmth, but I am humiliated to tell you that this is not the case.

My displeasure, my suspicion and petty irritation was, in part, to do with the Quakers. Perhaps I was protective of my father, whom I imagined to be weakened and vulnerable. And I could not distinguish Hank from the church, even if I had no reason to be suspicious of either.

More than his newfound Quakerism was that I was resentful and suspicious of his willingness to continue his life, to live without us, to do what was foreign, and therefore become foreign.

But what do I know? Have I not proven time and again, how little I know of myself, how foolish I am, and, most important, most simply, how often I am *wrong*? Well, I am ready now, in the way I believe my father was ready then, to give myself over to the intelligences of other people, other institutions, mysteries greater, and more interesting, than the self.

I am prepared to surrender.

How many times have we read some version of it? We must abandon our rule, our dominance, our control, our charge. It is the only way to peace, et cetera.

Anyway, for the time being, now there they are, the two of them walking south along the beach. A pretty day, not too much wind, warm enough for both of them to go without hats or gloves, sun coming and going, red Thermos in hand, cigarette between Hank's fingers. And me, I'm sitting up on the promenade with the love of my life. We're eating fried clams from red baskets and the seagulls are at us, flapping their wings and screaming to one another.

In a few weeks we'll all have dinner together. Tess and I, Hank Fletcher and my dad, and Seymour. A new iteration of an old family. Another version in such a long series of years, and families.

I say to Tess, I say with my mouth full, "Ah, Dad's new friend."

Or maybe I say something worse, something vicious, or in a crueler tone, and Tess, she tells me I'm an asshole. She explains to me once again that I should be kind to my father, and then she says, offhanded, not as some great pronouncement, "Sometimes I think he is braver than any of us."

And I ask, "Braver even than my mother?"

"Yes, Joe."

I look at her then, the side of her face, grease glossing her lips. I don't know Tess to dismiss my mother ever, not in any way. She gets up and brushes her hands on her jeans. Slap slap slap. Back, forward, back. Universal pattern, universal rhythm.

She walks out to the metal railing and calls to them, "Richard, Hank." Three syllables. Another unit.

The two men turn and look up, and when they see her there, smile and shine and wave. I watch her disappear down the steps to the sand, vanishing in segments—feet, legs, waist, shoulders, neck, head. Gone.

93

My mother in prison, a dying animal. Some essential thing leaching out of her. My father shifting. The muscles around his eyes softening, relaxing, providing his face a new peace. In those days, in memory, he is so often in the distance. In the meetinghouse. On the beach with Hank. Crossing the yard, walking to the front door of his house. There is always a separating space—parking lot, sand, promenade, lawn.

Meanwhile across town: Tess pacing her cell. She is seething. She is losing weight.

Seymour is biding his time. He smokes. He gulps his whiskey down. He sweats. He eats little. Yet I have the impression he is never as drunk as we are. Always on the lookout, he is the careful one. He watches us. We make him nervous.

We are a single sick body. We are legion. Hot, sweating, trembling, hungry.

We were drinking too much. Those late nights at the bar, those afternoons on our off days, took on the mood of a lunatic militia's operational meetings. No matter the time, the location, there was always some version of the same staging, the same blocking. Seymour and I stayed seated. Tess began in some elevated position—bar top, chair back, windowsill—and progressed, eventually, inevitably to standing. This is the sensation of that time, the visual tone: Tess high, us low. Tess in motion, us still. Leader and led.

What have I not told you? What have I not remembered?

Other rapes in other frat houses. No one's surprised, of course. This we learned first from Marcy, and then from the *White Pine Witness*, proud pursuer of truth, rectitude and gun rights. I cannot remember the order of events. What we knew when, and all that. What difference does it make?

Whatever the case, this is what we came to know in those weeks before we fled White Pine for Seattle: No one had been arrested. Investigation ongoing. One rape was perpetrated by a group. A single witness had lost sleep and so came to the police. Or to the administration. The fundamental facts matter. And they are always the same. They compose the same stories, and are repeated year after year after year after year. The same violence, the same failures, the same impunity, the same verbs, the same nouns.

I am exhausted by them now.

I am defeated.

We have lost, I am sorry to say.

I am nostalgic for my old rage, my old fury, for the time when we believed we might destroy some rotten thing, some fundamental structure.

But I have given up.

The nights we drank and drank and drank. Nights we wanted to burn the houses down. Fraternity and sorority. Hell and heaven and the road between. Set them on fire. In the nights of our wild tears, our benders, we talked of pouring gasoline into bottles, stuffing them with rags.

But in the end, it wasn't fire she wanted.

94

We cleaned up for dinner. Somehow got it together. Took it easy on the whiskey. Prepared ourselves. It was a mild afternoon. No rain. Tess held onto my arm. Kept herself tight to me. I loved this always, but in particular then—for the surprise of it, for the pressure of her body against mine, the illusion of power it provided me. The illusion that I might protect her.

I think of us many years later, all of this long over, walking through Pioneer Square toward Elliott Bay, Tess holding onto me in just the same way—her fingers on my bicep, keeping me close. I remember pulling the door open for her, pressing my palm against the small of her back, guiding her over the threshold into that crowded haven of squeaking floors and crammed shelves.

What of these days? These brief moments of tradition and chivalry? Only that I liked them, and that they were not standard. I suppose that's all. That I liked when she inclined her head and pressed her cheek against my shoulder. That there were moments when we moved through the world as that kind of pair. Of tradition. Man and woman. Protector and protected. That I loved her in this way too.

That over time we were many different things.

Anyway, this day in White Pine, we were descending the hill, Tess holding onto my right arm, and Seymour to my left. All of us sober. Or mostly sober.

We cross out of shade, out of the trees where the road flattens and the promenade becomes clear. We are stepping into sunlight and it is one of those moments impossible to extricate from the season itself and all its banalities of hope and rebirth. What can I do? Spring had sprung, buds were green, we were happy, and as my father would say, must have said, Put your hand out the window, you can feel it, the warm current of summer.

Out on the promenade we met him and Hank and then all five of us went down to the beach and walked it to the far rocks. Walked it to the meetinghouse. We sat in silence and contemplation while the sunlight cut through the glass and the waves rolled in.

There were no great revelations, I'm afraid. None beyond the simple pleasure of sitting with those four people. Tess's thigh against mine, Seymour's great shoulder bumping me, my father down the pew and, beyond, Hank's white hair in and out of view.

But all this peace and simple pleasure, this silence and contemplation, did not change our course. It occurred to me, yes, and perhaps I even prayed for it then, but in the end, our hour together out on the rock on that fine day was only prayer before battle.

Afterwards we returned in a new formation. My father and Seymour far ahead, Hank and Tess and me behind. We came to my father's house, the garden planted for spring. Inside, the table was already set. The living room smelled of ocean and frying onions.

There were bottles of his good Washington wine on the table. There was green salad and garlic bread and a tray of lasagna on the bar. Once everyone had been served we took our seats and my father stood.

"To families," he said, "new and old and in between."

When I leaned across Seymour, extending my glass toward my father's, he said, "In the eye, Joe, in the eye," and when I looked up, I felt a shock, a shot of pain or sadness or anger. Or love. I'm not sure. It must be a common experience. You must know it, must have felt it in the course of your life, that unsettling, visceral response, that distinct emotion we feel upon looking directly into our parents' eyes. What is it exactly? I suppose it must vary. We must each of us see many things, many combinations—longing, love, disappointment, need, frustration, possession. Is there not some universal experience? Do the eyes of all parents contain some basic and common ingredient? I believe they do. I believe they must. At least when they're turned directly on us, when they come in perfect contact with our own. Well, whatever the case, time slowed, and there were my father's soft eyes full of love and warning, fear and reproach.

But this is all fabrication, an illusion, a trick. An eye is an eye is an eye.

And we were off. Seymour and my father laughing together, and Hank with his toothy cowboy grin, and I thought, Why not? Why not love him, too? Let my father be happy, grant him his new friend, his new pleasures, his new routines, his church that is not a church, his walks without me along the beach, his beatific smiles and shining eyes.

So peace was made official without war having ever been declared.

I was insatiable that night. I ate and ate. All three of us did. We'd been so cold all the time, half-starved, living on whiskey and peanuts, and here was hot food and a safe room.

I went outside to get some wood from the pile.

I looked in at the glow of our father's home and I thought of you, Claire.

I thought of us at our table in Capitol Hill when we were kids, when Mom was a nurse and Dad was a carpenter. Outside, listening to the ocean, the sounds of Dad's new life, our new life, and I could feel you. Can now. First your left arm around my shoulder while you dug your fork into my piece of pie. Then the way you smelled as a kid, which was the smell of your bedroom, which became the feeling of the floor where we used to play, the cream carpet and the lines we drew through it with our thumbs to create borders for battles, circles for marbles. And then I began to feel you not as a physical thing, but as a tone, the way all the absent exist within me.

And there was Mom too, laughing, and she was saying, "Are you crazy? Are you fucking crazy?"

I don't know why. There is no secret meaning. It was one of those flashes. Another clipped from the reel. She is at the table leaning forward over her plate, shaking her head, looking right at someone, and she is laughing so hard, saying, "Are you crazy? Are you fucking crazy?" Then she too became tone, not the one I'd been carrying with me in White Pine, not the frozen milk color, not the unoiled metallic sound, not the smell of industrial floor cleaner, but the old one, the good one I took with me to school, the orange moon, the match light, the coffee, the gasoline.

I stood out there with my former family, waiting, drunk, watching the two worlds, cradling a stack of split logs in my arms until I heard my name and I came back. I built the fire up and we all moved over from the table to the couches and the brown corduroy chair and the worn-out rag rug. We finished off the wine, Hank revealed a bottle of scotch and everyone cheered.

"I guess you're not much a Quaker, after all," I said to him because I couldn't help myself, because when I drink I'm no good, or wasn't, or because I was still angry, or because I was still a child, or for some other reason I can't explain or even understand.

Stupid for so many reasons, not least of which is that plenty of Quakers drink to their hearts' content.

Anyway and as always back to the flow of time, and its dull

markers: action and event. To the floor of my father's house one warm spring evening in White Pine, Washington, where rape was in the news, and Anna Young flew through the trees while her father hurled his wife against kitchen walls.

"Leave it, Joe," Tess said. So I did. I relented, gave Hank a break, and the band played on and the scotch was poured and I rested my head in her lap and listened to the ghosts.

They were everywhere that night. Singing and whispering from the branches, from the blood in Tess's thigh, from the fire, from my father's hands, which moved above me, from the rug beneath my back, from the floor lamps transplanted from my childhood to that foreign town no longer foreign.

And all night my father's eyes appeared like entities separate from the man himself, singing: *Do not debase yourself, Joseph March. Do not give in. Do not break.*

Or they were only the blurred eyes of a drunken man, with no message, no meaning at all. But I will tell you this: Late in that cool night, we sat on the front step together and my father said, "I hope that you are smarter. I hope that you are gentler."

And what he meant was*, more gentle than your mother, more gentle than my wife.*

"How do you know?" I asked. "What we're planning."

"Seymour," he said.

He put his arm around me. "You think I don't know what it is, Joe? You think you two are the only people who understand what it's like to want to destroy someone, something?"

By *two*, he meant my mother and me.

"No," I said, though at the time I think the answer was, yes.

"I'm asking you. I'm saying please, Joe."

He was holding me too tightly. His hand on my shoulder. As so often, I wish I could tell you that it was a moment of tenderness and change. But what I wanted was for him to let me go.

The Royall Lyme, his wishes, his strong fingers, they all made me want to run. Made me want to fight. His admonitions, his pleadings. They made me want to go *to* war, not away from it. I do not know why. I do not know why I wasn't gentler, why my father's soft voice instilled in me a desire for violence and destruction. For the opposite of what he asked. I don't know why that is.

Was it really so simple as an adolescent instinct for rebellion?

Before we went back inside, he said, "I love you, Joe. I love you very much."

And I said, "I love you too, Dad."

And I did love him. In spite of it all. In spite of the anger he caused me. In spite of the claustrophobia. In spite of knowing I would do precisely what he did not want.

If ever there'd been a doubt, now I was sure.

But I told him I loved him, and it was the truth.

T ess handed out black balaclavas, we stuffed them into our pockets and left headquarters after sunset.

Those masks were all we carried. No wallets. No identification. No keys.

Well, Tess, she had a backpack.

We walked up the hill and turned on Vista. The porch light was on, but the house was dark.

When we returned home that night Seymour asked, "What if they're on vacation?"

Tess stared at him. "No," she said as if it were her decision.

It was the second week of March, the second week of spring break at Emerson. The three of us had taken it off. A vacation, we said. Down to Cannon Beach. Told the bar, Hank, my father.

As per instructions I'd rented a house, sent the money, used our names. The keys came in an envelope along with a few photos, a stapled packet of directions. Not right on the ocean, but an easy walk. A view of the water from the upstairs bedroom. Blue whale weather vane on the roof.

The next night it was the same thing. Nobody home.

Our victim would not cooperate.

Tess broke a rocks glass against our bedroom wall.

But a few nights later, as soon as we came around the corner, we heard the springs.

Tess made a noise I've never forgotten. Half sigh, half moan. Relief and resignation.

We picked up our pace.

Up ahead Anna was falling through the branches. Her small face appeared featureless at first. A pale oval surrounded by rising black hair.

"*Anna*," Tess said, as if she'd spent the whole week searching for her.

The girl looked at Seymour and said, "*You're* big," grinning as she lifted off.

"Did you go away, Anna?"

"Went to see my uncle."

Something about that chilled me.

I thought, we should have a dog, we should have some reason for walking this street. It's a terrible plan. Anyone can see us. Someone will call the police.

But Tess said, "Joey, do any of these fucking people call the police when they hear what goes on in that house?"

The next night we returned later. It was dark out. Clear and cold and full of stars. No clouds, no rain, no moon.

Again, the trampoline sound.

We came around the bend. I could feel the thing. All of us could.

That's how I remember it.

Or how I'd like to: A falling in our hearts.

Tess stopped before we came into the edge of light. Anna flew through the night. She didn't see us, or she pretended not to. We said nothing. We waited and listened.

Then there was the sound we were hunting: clatter and screams. Sam Young's low voice, then a full and heavy thud. Tess drew the straps of her backpack tight. She reached into her pocket and pulled out the balaclava.

Then her face disappeared.

I put mine on.

So did Seymour.

We marched in a column. Ovals for eyes, circles for mouths.

We followed Tess to the back door. She turned the knob. We followed her in, passing through a darkened living room—two lit candles on a sideboard—toward the bright kitchen.

Tess point, me middle, Seymour flank.

Then we were crowding the kitchen. Sam Young, who was standing above his wife, turned to us carrying a vile expression of hatred.

He took a step back and said, "What the fuck?"

The woman was sitting against the white oven. Her black hair fell forward over her eyes and there was blood smeared from her nose across her cheek.

She looked like Anna. Or Anna looked like her.

Outside the trampoline went on—high and low, high and low.

When she saw us she brought her hands up to cover her mouth and nose.

We followed Tess deeper into the kitchen. I stood just to her right.

Sam Young was frightened now. The anger was gone.

He tried, but seemed so suddenly frail. "What do you want? Get the fuck out of my house."

Tess slapped him. He took one step toward her, and I hit him clean. I was waiting for it. An even right cross to the mouth.

Just like my father taught me. Straight from the shoulder. Use your hips.

It had nothing to do with why we were there. I did it only because he moved at Tess. I would never learn. There was pain in my wrist, worse for the old injury.

At first, I was so even, so calm.

Sam Young was on the floor. He didn't get up, but he was conscious. His lip was bleeding.

"Sit there." Tess nodded at a chair, which had been tipped over.

When he didn't move, Seymour did it for him. Then the three of us were standing side by side in front of the man.

Now he was seated at the small kitchen table. I think we expected more talking.

"Why are you here?"

It occurred to me only in that instant that I wasn't sure of the answer. I mean that I didn't know what Tess would do exactly, or what she'd hidden in that backpack.

Then my heart started to go and I felt that first hot flush of power.

Tess hit him again. This time with her fist. I could tell it hurt her. It was the first time she'd ever hit a person like that, straight on with a closed hand.

She may have broken his nose.

His wife whispered, "Leave him alone." And Tess spun as if she might attack her too, but after a brief hesitation she left the kitchen, returned with a small green blanket and spread it over the woman's lap.

Something about that gesture set Sam Young off.

"Get the fuck out of my house," he said, but his voice was desiccated and feeble.

"Why do you do it?" Tess asked.

"Please," he said. "Leave us alone."

"Why?"

Sam Young stared into Tess's mask.

"Well," she said, "it doesn't matter."

I wished Tess wouldn't talk so much. I thought, *surely he recognizes us. Surely he knows who we are.*

Then he screamed, "Fuck you. Get the hell out of my house." His voice broke. It was all panic.

I thought I heard the trampoline noise stop.

Maybe across the quiet neighborhood a dog barked. It was that kind of scream.

"You've got a daughter, you've got students," Tess said quietly, unfazed, practiced as a cool mafia thug.

She unslung the backpack. She removed a camera and took

Sam Young's picture. When the flash went off, he closed his eyes and kept them closed. Then Tess turned it toward the woman.

"I'm sorry," she said, and took that photograph, too.

With his eyes still closed he whispered, "Please get out of my house."

I thought he might cry, but he didn't.

"Put your hands on the table," Tess said.

He wouldn't so Seymour did it for him. Then there they were, flat on the smooth laminate.

Some of his knuckles were cut and swollen.

When I saw that, I lost my pity again. I tried to keep it, but I couldn't.

Tess took another photograph.

"Are you sorry, Sam?"

He didn't answer.

She asked again.

"Fuck you."

I watched him at Emerson on the library steps smoking his cigarette in the sunlight.

"He's sorry," his wife said.

"Shut your mouth, Roxanne," Sam Young said.

Tess put the camera away.

He pulled his hands from the table.

"Put them back." She said it in a different voice.

He stood up fast then. Last-ditch. But Seymour yanked him down by his hair.

I was trying to see Seymour's eyes. I wanted to know where he would stop. And what he would allow. I thought maybe Sam Young's knuckles had pushed him over. Maybe the string was nearly snapped.

"Put them back," Tess said again. He did.

Tess removed a hammer from the backpack and Roxanne began to cry.

"Shh," Tess said, "shh."

Seymour looked up at Tess and said, "Hey. Hang on—" He nearly named her, but stopped himself.

The woman, Roxanne, Anna's mother, wiped her eyes with her sleeve and looked first at me and then at Seymour. Said, "Don't. Please."

Seymour stood up straight and released Sam Young's wrists, who, even after being freed, didn't move. I thought I saw something go out of his eyes.

"Will you stop, Sam?" Tess was leaning over him.

"Yes," he said. "Yes."

"No," Tess said. "No."

She ripped the telephone off the wall.

Then she took a sock from the backpack and stuffed it into his mouth. It was white. One of mine I used for running.

Seymour had backed away from the table and up against the oven, his pillar of a thigh inches from that woman's head. There was a sluggishness to him now. I thought, *at any moment he will slump down, wrap his arm around her shoulder.*

My heart was coming on fast. I saw straight through his mask, watched him until the black wool was replaced by his lonely face after closing, four whiskies in, standing beneath the neon owl, gazing off into the night, and it was that face abruptly projected upon Seymour's balaclava that flicked the true starter, flung me over the restraining wall and right into space, hurtling at full speed. I thought, *I have to protect him, too. I have to protect all of them. All of us. Even Sam Young. I* thought, *I will save all of you,* and then I dove. Took Sam Young by the throat, Seymour's move, drove backwards so the chair toppled and I had him bracketed against the floor, my hand a copper pipe clamp, climbed him and, like a high school bully, pressed my knees against his biceps, brought my face right up to his, close enough to smell the alcohol through my mask. He was so hot beneath me and the heat spread through

my skin like a terrible disease, flowing from his body into mine
and all that time I was speaking to him through my mask saying I-don't-know-what only that I couldn't stop talking, that I
was pushing those sentences right into his mouth and were it
not for that sickening heat between us, the threat of his disease,
I might have murdered him right then, might have crushed his
windpipe, might never have unclamped his throat, but it was
too terrible, more terrible than the tar itself, and somewhere
very far away Tess was calling to me, and Seymour too, whose
hands were at my shoulders, where his fingers pushed into my
skin and muscle and all the way to bone where it all died.

He yanked me to my feet and there we all were standing
again with Sam Young somehow back in his chair, and choking and crying and begging for mercy.

I was so tired.

It was gone into air now.

I had no prayer of saving us. As always and forever.

Tess was talking. She was furious. "Asshole," she said, or
something like it.

But it is Seymour I hear most clearly.

He said in a quite voice, "It is enough."

I had never heard him sound like that. So beaten, so
depleted.

But Tess said, "No, goddamn it."

And I'm sorry, Dad, but I went where she told me, I did
what she asked. I stood behind Sam Young and I held his
wrists with all the strength I had left in my body.

Seymour said it again and stood right up to her, but she
didn't break, didn't blink, only stared blankly into his chest.
Just biding her time.

Seymour said, "Mother*fucker*," and ripped the hammer
from her hand. It crashed and went spinning across the floor.
He leaned over to me then, put his mouth to my ear and said,
"Joe, yes or no?" But I didn't answer, I didn't move, and after

a few seconds he bent down, helped Sam Young's wife up from the oven and walked her away from the kitchen.

Tess continued on as if all was according to plan. She said, "Make a fist, Sam," and Sam Young made two.

She picked up the hammer.

I kept my eyes open.

She swung hard.

There was just no mercy in her for that man.

She went in order.

She did it four times on the right, one for each knuckle, and she did it as if he weren't sobbing or struggling against my weight.

I remember the sound. I promise you that. I remember the sound. His cries. Hers. All those bones crunching under the force of her hammer blows.

All that noise—muted and razor-clean.

Tess, the sound is what never recedes.

She moved on to his left hand, just like she was dropping sinker nails into a plank: one, two, three.

Smell of urine and bitter sweat.

Then noise in the living room and I went toward it.

In the candlelight Seymour was sitting on the couch, his mask still covering his face, and Anna, next to him in her pajamas curled up on her mother's lap, crying, and Roxanne with her eyes shut saying, "It's okay, baby girl, it's okay."

I met Seymour's eyes.

Anna looked at me in my idiotic mask. "Are you the police?"

I shook my head. "Sort of," I said. "Not exactly. Sort of."

She sat up then and wiped her nose. "You're the boyfriend. Why are you wearing that? What are you doing? Is my dad okay?"

Then Tess came tearing into the room, backpack on, frenetic and pale. Her mouth open, eyes frantic, gaze glancing off each of us, still looking for war, but when she saw Anna, she froze like a frightened buck, relaxed her fists and drew a quick breath.

When at last she moved, she kneeled and touched Anna's cheek. She looked up at Roxanne, who remained blank. And' then Tess, gentle mother now, said in her quietest voice, "It's all all right. It's fine. It's all okay. It's a game. Just a game."

"Liar," the girl said, acid in her voice.

Tess stood up then and, as if she hadn't heard it at all, bright as she could muster, said, "Good night, Anna Banana."

96

The three of us were out on the street.

Tess, me, Seymour. We peeled off our masks, walked away from the house. My face wet. Cool air on my skin.

We returned home. There was no sense of relief, of satisfaction, of pride. All that ferocious determination departed from Tess.

Something had broken.

In our living room, she looked at Seymour with a frightened openness I'd thought was impossible.

"Are we going to jail?"

I'd never seen him so angry. He shrugged as if anything could happen. He wouldn't speak. He drank and smoked and stalked around and shook his head. I thought he might attack her, so I kept myself coiled, not that I'd have been much good if it had come to that. Anyway, I watched him opening and closing his hand until at last he walked away.

When he'd left, Tess said, "I'm so sorry, Joe."

I locked the front door and we went upstairs. I drew her a bath and helped her undress.

There was blood on her sleeves.

I put her clothes in a plastic bag the way you're supposed to, then I came back, turned off the lights and sat next to her on the cold tiles.

She took my right arm with both her hands and held it against her belly beneath the water.

There was blood on her wrist.

She said, "I love you, Joe. I love you so much."

"We'll go away," I said. "Okay? I promise I'll protect you. I swear to God, I swear to God I will protect you, Tess."

She dug her nails into my arm and began to cry in a hard way I'd never seen. I watched all her fury and conviction dissolve into simple sadness.

It was many years before we saw Seymour again.

97

It had run out of her. This woman who had forced me to my knees on The Owl's bathroom floor, who had stalked our streets at night, lectured us with such humor and ferocity.

Our capricious general, the leader of our misguided campaign, was lost.

She was so disappointed by our debacle, in herself, in her heart.

She could never say why it vanished, but I believe that what she thought was both a hunger and capacity for violence was something else entirely and swinging the hammer, punching that man, had neither provided the satisfaction she'd expected nor the energy for future campaigns. Whatever had so possessed her was now absent.

And I, at least, understood that kind of desertion.

The colonizing forces inhabit us without warning. They desert us in the same way.

I know no better way to say it.

The beasts arrive, the beasts vanish.

I suppose it is like lust, like passion, like love.

We turn a corner and are confronted. All those mythic stories of what happens without warning.

It is something like that.

Like alcohol without the bottle, heroin without the needle.

There is no vessel of delivery. It comes from within.

It works in both directions. What arrives without warning. What leaves.

In the morning she said, "It's disappeared, Joe."

And after a while of sitting with Tess in bed, seeing what was missing from her eyes, I was sure she was right, that as quickly as it had come, it had vanished.

Not so much her anger or indignation, but desire. It was the desire she'd lost.

"It makes no difference," she said. "What have I done but terrify a little girl and risk Seymour his job, and send us all to jail?"

But I wasn't frightened that morning. Now, at last I was able to take care of Tess. She allowed me to hold her. She allowed me to speak. She listened.

I said, "You were brave to do it. You humiliated him. You broke his hands. You did a thing no one else would have done and maybe he stops. Maybe when he sees the photographs, when he reads your letter."

"What letter?"

The letter we'd never write with the photos we'd never develop folded inside, the letter saying we'd be watching, that if he ever hit his wife again we'd know, that we'd send the pictures to the college, to the *Witness*. We'd paper White Pine with them. I told her that when the police came, we'd say it had just been us two, no Seymour, that we'd been walking past and heard the screaming. We were protecting a helpless woman and her child.

"And the hammer, Joe?"

"What about it? There's no crime in carrying a hammer."

"And your mother? When they find out who your mother is?"

I said, "The police aren't going to come, Tess. You'll see. No way they call the police."

"It's gone," she said. "Just like that."

"What is?" I asked, even though I knew.

It went on. Her voice going softer and softer.

I said, "I know what it is for a thing to arrive and disappear so fast. Tess, it's been happening since before I met you."

98

Seymour wouldn't pick up the phone, so just the two of us drove down to Cannon Beach. I'd often imagined proposing to Tess out there in the shadow of Haystack Rock, of returning to the place where I fell in love with her, home to our motel, our exultant origins, but I hated being back there in that colorless town.

We were fugitives. All the shine was missing. There was no way to recover. No way to reclaim our former selves. This was something we the March family well understood.

Now Tess was learning the same and I hated that more than anything else.

I am on my back and Tess is holding onto me as if otherwise she might fly away. I say, "It will return. There are different ways of fighting."

I tell her we'll start over and find those ways, but she doesn't answer, just digs her fingers in, hangs on tight.

Though we never did and that was fine with me because all I ever wanted for my life was to live with Tess in a quiet place. Somehow, even before I met her, I think all I ever wanted was to walk with her in the woods and make love and listen to music and read our books and maybe someday have a child.

All I ever wanted was to construct a life of peace and good systems. To assemble a tender world with her, to nail it together and make it beautiful and organized and safe. And that world would be our fighting back, would be our war against the fools and the cowards, the bullies and the tyrants, the bird and the tar.

All I wanted was to build a fortress, to create a kingdom with my love.

For me that would be fighting enough.

But it never was for Tess. Not in White Pine, not in Seattle, not here on the clearing. From the moment she walked out of Sam Young's house she believed she had lost some vital, irredeemable thing. In swinging that hammer Tess discovered she was not the warrior she'd imagined herself to be. Nor was she the warrior she wanted my mother to be. And all of that manic enthusiasm, her obsession, her desire, was, all at once, gone.

99

We returned home to White Pine worse than ever. The following days we hid out at home and tried our best to return to our previous life, our previous selves. But it was impossible.

I never told Tess, but I was sure that any minute we'd be arrested. I dreamed of Sam Young sneering at us from behind two sturdy cops.

But they never came. The television says not to change behavior after committing a crime, but we never went back to work. We drew the blinds. We drank too much. We barely ate. Tess clung to me as if I might protect her. She had cruel nightmares and woke me with her trembling.

We stayed in bed and read the paper, but nothing was reported.

As if we'd never been in that kitchen.

I said, "You see? We're going to be fine."

Of course, that wasn't the entire problem.

"It's that I don't ever want to do it again," she said. "I thought he would be the first, Joe. I thought it was only the start."

Tess went to see my mother. I don't know what happened there. She wanted to go alone.

When she came back she said, "I told her what I did. I told her I couldn't do it again, or anything like it. She was cold. She didn't say anything. I'm sure she'd thought I was one kind of person and now she knows I'm another."

I went to see my mother myself.

I told her we were leaving.

I said, "Why would you be cruel to Tess?"

She smiled. She seemed drugged and sad. The early prison charisma was gone. She took my hands off that awful table and raised them to her lips.

One of the guards turned his head.

"You'll come back and see me, Joe?"

"Of course," I said.

I wanted to shake her back into her first self. Or into whatever version had raised us. The self that sang to me in the mornings on the way to school, that drove too fast, said, "Sink or swim, fight or die." The woman of all that light and fire, so severe, so tender, so funny, so sure of her place in the world.

I said, "What happened? How are we here?"

She took a long breath, fixed her gaze on my hands, and said, "I don't know how. There was just that woman, those kids. Then that man, Joe, that goddamn man."

Her cheeks were flushed. She pushed a strand of hair back from her forehead.

"Afterwards, for all this time, I thought, *somehow I can make it mean something*. The letters. The visitors. Tess."

"Look at me," I said.

She refused and kept on talking. "I thought all of us could make it matter."

She shook her head, glanced up, and when I saw the blue of her eyes, I said, "Sometimes I'm on fire and the world is so perfectly clear and I am so bright and alive and I can't stop moving. And other times, other times I'm just the opposite. I wake up and I'm so miserable I can barely see. I can't move at all. I don't know what it is or where it comes from."

She squeezed my hands tight.

"Do you have that, Mom? Does any of that happen to you?"

She sighed and looked at something behind me while I studied her mouth. I waited for her, for some absolute conclusion, some explanation, a final answer, a last and crucial bond. I waited and waited. I waited until I thought I would take her shoulders in my hands and shake it out of her but when at last she returned, she only said, "Me, Joey Boy, I can always move."

100.

We packed the truck and left our home. Not much ceremony. Perhaps we passed by my father's place when we drove out of town, but I don't remember it that way.

We pulled off to the side of the ridge road. We looked down on White Pine.

We found the roof of what was no longer our house. We found Vista and the trampoline. We found the college and the meetinghouse. We found Lester's and, in the other direction, the prison surrounded by those dazzling green wheat fields.

Then we drove out to the highway and left as if we'd never lived there at all.

101

Once we lived in a motel in Cannon Beach, Oregon. Once we lived in a white house in White Pine, Washington. Once we lived down in Belltown. Once in a pretty apartment in Capitol Hill.

Once we moved to the country.

And for a time we told ourselves we were still warriors. In those years after White Pine, before we became business owners, before we became *entrepreneurs*, we said we were radicals and artists. We would organize and write poems and songs and perform them and spend our time in dark clubs listening to *angry* musicians play *angry* music.

And we would call all of it fighting. Art our weapon and all that nonsense.

Neither of us believed in any of it. Sam Young was a poison, our crime a festering gash. Tess's passion turned hollow. Her conviction was still gone.

We went to D4 and High Dive and Rock Candy. We saw Mudhoney and Hammerbox, Nirvana and Sound Garden. In the smoking dark we flung ourselves against all the others like us while King Cobain hid behind his hair.

We told each other we were angrier, wiser, and more serious. We insisted we had done something to prove it, to earn it. We were not posing. We of experience had blood on our hands and somehow that terrible fact would mark us as people of distinction.

We were furious and drunk and stupid, and sometimes still

we were terrified the police would come crashing through our door.

In our damp apartment we slept badly and stayed in bed late watching the ships come in off the horizon, listening to gasping trucks leaving the market. We tried so hard to convince ourselves it was all part of our revolution, that we were still at war and living this way, afraid, broke, adrift, in possession of our cold secret, was all a form of battle.

But it didn't last long.

I was always only in it for Tess, and Tess had so terrified herself that it was just a matter of time before all that pretense would become a kind of venom, a reminder of another person, of what she had lost.

One night at Showbox, we watched a woman onstage take a circular sander to the steel bra of her bandmate. Sparks scattered over the crowd. The drummer played in time. "I am not my body, I am not my body," the singer sang.

Tess, she'd had enough.

She took my hand and pulled me out of there. She said, "I'm done, Joe. Fuck these people."

And *that* was the end of it. We gave up the clubs. We drank less. Our vigilante days formally ended. Just like that. In a weary word.

I never believed I was any kind of artist. I was no revolutionary.

It's just that I was in love with Tess Wolff and I'd have done anything she wanted.

Claire, it was night when Dad died.

Or early morning.

Seven years after Tess and I left White Pine for Seattle, his heart stopped beating.

Hank said, "He went in his sleep."

But how can any of us be sure? He might have been wide-awake, staring at a circle of blistering paint. He could have been praying. He could have been drafting a letter.

Dear Joey, Dear Tess.

And for all I know, *Dear Claire*, too. Did he write to you? He must have and I want to believe that you read his letters, that you too keep a stack of them bound in some drawer.

His ragged box of stationery was open on the kitchen table, strapping tape neatly reinforcing the corners. There was a roll of stamps. A couple of blue ballpoint pens.

Hank found him in the morning.

He'd gone over to meet Dad for their walk, but there was no answer. He'd brought two large coffees from that new place they liked on the boardwalk. A bag of donuts between his teeth.

Not that there's any evidence of this.

It's just the way I always see it: Hank outside the front door, a cup in each hand, knocking the brass kick plate with the toe of his boot calling, *Richie, Richie, up and at 'em. Richie, Richie, rise and shine.*

T ess and I were home in Seattle when he called. We had to be at the bar early that morning to meet an investor and were irritated to be disturbed.

Tess pulled the phone under the covers, said, "Hello, handsome," and pushed it at me, the cord cold against my ribs. "Hank," she said.

And then his weak and cracking voice: "Your father died, Joe."

No euphemisms from Hank Fletcher. No bullshit from that man.

I gave the receiver back to Tess. She returned it to the cradle.

Half-conscious, she said, "What's new in White Pine?"

I didn't answer and she fell back to sleep.

The talons dug deep into my throat, sharp into my heart. The tar spread with vicious speed. It was everywhere. It was ruthless. I kept thinking the same thing.

I don't know how much time passed between that phone call and the moment Tess turned on her side and rested her warm palm on my stomach.

"What is it? What is it, Joe?"

I thought, this is an irrevocable thing. This is a thing that cannot be altered.

I began to speak to myself with a new formality, as if I were a lecturing professor, an expert of the absolute.

I don't know if I spoke out loud.

I couldn't shake Sam Young. I wanted only to think of my

father, but there he was clinging to me, striding across his wet lawn.

"Joe?" Tess was sitting up now.

I did not want to tell her what I had learned. I thought, *Is there any way to defend her from this?*

"My father died," I said.

She began to cry. She lay next to me on her side with her head on my chest and her legs wrapped around mine. She was quiet, but she was shaking.

I said, "I wish I'd been kinder, Tess."

We stayed together like that all morning.

It was an irrevocable thing.

104

W e drove down to White Pine and stayed in my father's house. His landlord was generous the way everyone in his later life seemed to be.

She said, "Take your time. What a lovely man he was," and gave me a plate of peanut butter cookies covered with foil.

We went to the prison to see my mother, who had already been notified of her husband's passing. She was frail and whatever had been left of her first or second or third self was now gone, but she was not impassive. She was affectionate with us both. She cried for my father and said that he'd been to visit her just a week before, that he'd seemed so well. He'd told her about his trip to Seattle, about us two, about our life there, our apartment, our bar, how proud he was. He had told her about the house, that it was the same, that he missed us all in it.

She leaned across the table and held our hands.

We told her that he'd been cremated. There would be a service, we'd asked permission for her to attend and it had been granted.

"No," she said. "I can't do that."

"Look at me," I said. She raised her eyes. "It'll be Sunday morning. They'll bring you there, they'll take you home."

"Joey," she began, "Listen."

I stood up fast. My eyes fell into inordinate focus. I heard Tess say my name, but she was so far away. There was a pressure on my shoulder. It wasn't Seymour, but once it might have been. I wanted to tear the ceiling down. Rip the bolted bench from the floor. I wanted to break the fucking walls with it. I pulled but nothing moved. I had lost again. The lights hummed their indifferent tune. Everything so goddamned secure, so flawlessly locked in place. With my vision recoiling, the fight leaching away, I hit the table with my open palm hard enough to silence the room, to set a bruise creeping out from my thumb.

"Goddammit, you will be there," I said giving in to the hard pressure on my shoulders. "It is the only thing."

She nodded and when I was sitting again, said, showing me her hands, "All right. Okay, Joe. Okay."

Tess took a frozen pork chop from my father's freezer and bound it to my hand with one of his Ace bandages. It smelled of Right Guard. She didn't say anything about the prison, or the way I'd behaved, or my mother, but it was clear she was exhausted by all of us.

We slept in the spare bedroom, squeezed together in that tiny bed where once my father had put me to sleep. We separated his things—to trash, to Goodwill, to keep. Tess chose a thick grey cashmere cardigan, which had once been my grandfather's. I kept his lined Levi's jacket. His duffel bag. We kept his Wagoneer. Otherwise, there wasn't much to hold onto really. Photographs. Papers. Books. The record collection. Some clothes. Some wine. The ammo box.

The booze we gave to Hank, who came to see us on our first night carrying a pizza from Lester's. We gave him an umbrella, too. A good black one with a polished-oak handle.

Hank said my father had begun discreetly using it as a cane.

106.

Yes, we called Claire.
We left messages, but she did not respond and she did not come home.

I know you want more than that—explanation, resolution. But some people, regardless of blood, choose to live in other ways. What more is there to say? I have tried to grant her this without anger, without contempt. I know no better way to love her. It is what my father did, and would have always done.

I tried to hate her, to cling to the wound, to protect myself with it, but it did me no good.

She was lost to us, like so many other people we'd known through the course of our lives.

What difference does it make that she is my sister, that she was his daughter?

What difference does blood make?

Although lately I have wondered whether I missed some signal, whether all those years ago, in looking so carefully at my mother, I ignored Claire.

Was she too possessed by the bird and the tar? Is she still?

If so, perhaps this is her way of fighting.

We all have different methods of waging war.

You want reason and resolution, I know. Clean systems. As do I. As did my father. As do we all.

But time goes along anyway.

There is nothing to be done.

The service was out at the meetinghouse on a Sunday morning. There was little difference between this and any other meeting of Friends, except that I stood and spoke, except that I carried a squat brass urn, except that it was more crowded than usual. Hank said it was evidence of how much the people of White Pine had cared for my father. Guards and bartenders and waitresses and college kids from the new café.

There was little difference except the crowd and the urn and the presence of my mother, who sat back by the entrance flanked by two guards. It was the first time in many years that I'd seen her in sunlight. She was so small there between those massive men, beneath that vaulted ceiling, with the great ocean and giant sky outside. For such a long time I had seen her always in that terrible visit room, in that sickening fluorescent light where the perspective was always the same—woman to chair, woman to table, woman to wall, woman to guard.

She kept her shoulders hunched and her arms crossed. She watched the ocean as if she were trying to find some specific object out on the water.

Her skin was pale, so fine. There was so little fat on her body. So little muscle. I thought of her filters. I thought, they must be so much worse than mine.

There was nothing to defend her from the blitzing light, the roar of all those people pouring in, whispering and shifting in their seats, the waves, the creaking building, the wind pushing against the glass. I saw it all driving into her, passing through her rice paper skin, swirling behind her eyes, swelling and twisting in her chest.

I wanted to protect her. Wrap her in a blanket. Cover her eyes with dark glasses.

I wanted to say, I know what it means when the filters fail. I understand. But you sink or swim, I wanted to say, Mom, you fight or you die.

Though now, I have to allow for the possibility that I was wrong, have been wrong all this time. Perhaps my mother knew nothing of tar and filters and all the rest of that bullshit.

Perhaps my insistence on some magical correlation between us is only wishful, an invention without evidence. Perhaps in the end there is no shared beast, no common fog.

108

Some of them watched the vicious killer in the back of the meetinghouse, the mad widow at her husband's funeral. It was difficult for me not to tear their pews from the ground, difficult not to fling those tourists through that glass. But Tess squeezed my hand, she kept me still. As always, she knew before I did. She knew and I stayed where I was.

Someone rang a bell.

Then we were all quiet.

We waited and we listened for God.

After a while, I stood. I had to break my hand away from her.

I didn't see it, but I know she dropped her head in fear, in fatigue.

I said that my father had found a home first in White Pine, and then at the meetinghouse. I said that he had found friendship and peace in both places and I believed he had been happy when he died. I said that he had been the strongest, most courageous, kindest man I'd ever known.

I can't remember what else. I'm sure there was more, but believe me, it was inadequate.

I was just trying to fill the room with words.

I looked at my mother, who smiled at me in a way I hadn't seen for many years. What was it? Pride? Certainty? Maybe it was simple tenderness. Maybe it was love that I saw.

Seymour gave me a nod. A greeting, but also, I thought, I hoped, a gesture of approval and encouragement. He was sitting toward the back, not far from my mother. He was heavier, softer. He'd lost a lot of hair. There were none of those frightening angles left in his face.

I saw a young woman, too. She was the right age, had the right eyes. She seemed to be alone. She could have been Anna. Might have been.

Whoever she was, when the service ended, she was gone.

We walked down to the beach. Me and Hank and Tess and my mother and the two stony guards who allowed her to stand in the sunshine with her wrists unbound.

They allowed her to bend at the waist and remove her shoes and socks.

The tide was high and the wind was blowing strong offshore. I took the top off the urn and shook the ashes free. They blew across the sand and scattered and dissolved over the water.

That was it, the end of my father's funeral, the end of my father's body.

My mother was so bright in the sun. She was wearing a pair of jeans and a white sweatshirt. They'd run a piece of webbing through the belt loops and tied it tight with a tidy bow knot. I try to imagine what it must have been for her, after nearly nineteen years locked away, to smell the ocean, to feel the cold sand against her bare feet, the wind on her body, the warm light. To be, all of a sudden, in one fail swoop, in the center of the whole whirling world.

She closed her eyes and cried. I don't know if it was for my father, or because she was overcome by sensation, or because she wasn't free. She began to walk toward the water, but the guards held her back. Maybe they were afraid she'd drown herself.

Tess said, "Come on, let her feel it, goddamn it, you assholes."

But one of them was already kneeling at my mother's feet, slipping her shoes on, while the other was closing the cuffs.

We followed those three up past the promenade to the prison van. And then they drove her away.

In the evening we had dinner with Hank. We invited Seymour, but he didn't come. I don't remember much else. Not in terms of event, or language.

I do remember the physical world, but really, how many more descriptions of the vast ocean and blue sky can you possibly endure?

109

We returned to Seattle. We went on living. The odd thing is that I recall so little of that time. It is an indistinct shape, a hum of years.

We owned a bar, we bought another. Both thrived. We worked hard. We were making more money than either of us had ever imagined. We were good at what we did. We provided health insurance. We hired more women than men. We paid a wage better than any bar in the city. There was no miniskirt obligation. We had no tolerance for assholes. We had good bouncers, though none better than Seymour Strout.

We were always on patrol.

We ran our empire the way we wished to run the world.

And that, I'm afraid, was the sum total of our activism.

These the remnants of our war.

Time passes. It smells mostly of beer and whiskey and searing meat. It is a smear of sensation. It all blends.

It does not have the sharp edges of our earlier lives.

On a Sunday morning, our sacred day of rest, I brought Tess breakfast in bed. I put a ring in the center of a pat of butter. I pretended to read the paper. I heard her knife against the metal.

I said, "Tess Wolff will you marry me?"

She said, "Joe, Joey, Joseph, it would be my honor. Yes."

She put the ring in her mouth, sucked it clean, let it fall from her tongue into my palm, and I slid it onto her finger. We spilled our coffee, and made love and were engaged, but we never married.

The years went on. We were making our fortune.
Time was blurred. It was overwhelmed by minutiae.
Or composed of it.

110.

We benefited from our fortune—of circumstance, of class, of education, of race, of our intelligences in their various and respective forms. We replaced passion with work. We replaced desire with work. We were never lazy. We bought property. We were never punished for our crime. We were savvy. We began with a little money and we went on to have more of it. We divided and filled our days. We killed our time. From the moment we abandoned our dreams of war and honor and good, there were tasks to complete. They were to do with the bars. They were to do with the people we knew, with our home, with our possessions. We took our store of time and used it to tend to the life we were constructing. We bought clothes and wore them. We saw doctors. We had our teeth polished. We bought food and we ate it. We bought a new car. We argued about its color. We took it to be repaired. When it was empty, we filled it with gas. We washed its body, its windows. We liked to see it shine. We liked to see the needle on full. We bought so many objects. Thousands and thousands and thousands of objects. We talked about them and celebrated them and argued over them. We arranged them in our minds and on our shelves. We put numbers in columns. We put art in frames and hung those frames on our walls, in our bars. We gave gifts. We made donations and called them acts of principle. We cleaned our skin. We gave things away. We bought new things. We gambled and won. There were periods of satisfaction, and of pleasure. There were periods of frustration and of exhaustion. The tar came and went. As did Tess's patience.

111.

W hat remained of those lost days of fire were books. We continued to read. We said to each other, "This is good, this is extraordinary, you should read this." We said, "This is very bad, what a faker, what a fraud."

It's easy for me to recall those years. Even if they blend. Even if I confuse the shops, the streets, the shelves, the authors, the weather, the months, the years, the lines we loved.

Even if I confuse poems for prose, prose for lyrics.

Tess Wolff hidden away in a good corner of one bookstore or another, the rain beating down outside as always. I'm bringing her something from some other section, a book I wonder if she's read, or one I think she should, or a line I want her to see. I'm coming through the store in a hurry.

"Wait," she says, holding her hand out to me. "Come here," she says.

I come and take it and she whispers.

Sometimes the line, sometimes the whole poem.

Tess, I am here in the present praying and you are out there in the past whispering:

And if it happens that you cannot
go on or turn back
and you find yourself
where you will be at the end,
tell yourself
in that final flowing of cold through

your limbs
that you love what you are.

I have her book on the table. I have all her brackets and
stars. I do not remember when she found it. Or where. There
is just the poem and a building which may no longer exist.

There are lines at the corners of her eyes. She has lost something in her cheeks. Her skin appears thinner, drawn tighter
over her bones.

She is no longer young.

That's all it is.

Just that she is no longer young when I find her tucked in,
secreted away.

She says, "Here, come here."

She whispers.

She hated loud people.

"Will you please shut the fuck up, please," she said to a man
chattering to his wife. Not *said*. I should say, *asked him*. "Will
you?" As if she truly wanted to know the answer, so that she
could decide whether to stay or go.

The man and his wife stared. Affronted. And then left.

You see? It wasn't that she'd gone totally cold. It wasn't that
she was dead. She was still a fighter. There was still some shit
she would not eat. It's just that it wasn't the same. It's just that
she was unhappy the way people are when they fail so completely to do what they expected they would.

You might say, yes, like anyone, like every single one.

But no, I cannot see it the same. It was different with her. It
was more. It was worse.

The afternoon that Tess found this poem, after she whispered those lines, it was toward the end of our life in Seattle.

Yes, I'm certain of it.

And after she'd finished reading, she looked at me, shook
her head and said, "But I don't, Joe. Goddamn it, I don't."

112

Once, years ago on a city bus in Seattle, a lunatic woman turned to me and whispered right into my ear, "You want to know what it's like? It's like a furnace between your legs. All your life it's burning, burning, and then, snap, it goes out. So now you know, asshole."

I've never forgotten it. Her breath on my ear.

A thing possesses you and then it's gone. There's so much pain in that desertion. It's not, as you get older, that you miss your young body, your smooth skin, your strong back, your lean legs.

It's that you miss desire.

Better to be a hideous man on fire than a handsome man drowning.

What am I saying? That it's difficult for all of us—growing older, time, all the rest. But for Tess it is different. It is worse.

Truth be told, I have found the feeling of desire slipping away to be a relief. When I was young it was tyrannical. I wanted everything always. A generic and scorching desire for more. Sex above all. But later, when it subsided, that blazing furnace beneath my skirts, I was grateful. I was at peace.

All I want to say is that while it's difficult for any one of us, for Tess it was harder, it was unbearable.

And I understand.

Because of my bad filters. Because of the way I am inundated by sound and light, I believe I know what it was for a thing to hurt more than it should. For it to overwhelm and submerge and drown a person. And because I know, and because I love her as I do, I am tolerant in ways many others could not be. Or so I insist, so I have convinced myself.

Listen, Tess is a pain in the ass. Let us not pretend she is otherwise. Petulant, impatient, selfish, erratic, arrogant, unhappy. For all my shifting selves, my precious longing, my pathetic nostalgia, let me please say, Tess was a terrible pain in the ass, and it would have been so much simpler, so much easier to go off in search of someone else.

But it wasn't what I wanted. Never. It wasn't that I was *sticking it out*, either. I want no prize for *hanging in there*.

It's just that in spite of it all, I loved her.

It's just that I do.

113.

It was six years between leaving White Pine and seeing my father again. Six years to the day, and a year before his death, when he appeared in the afternoon. He knew a bar's drowsy hours of calm—after lunch, after closing—and so, with his great passion for ceremony, timed his entrance accordingly.

He is pacing the sidewalk.

He is waiting until precisely three o'clock.

He is striding through the door.

In those six years we spoke only a few times, and that was early on. Tess and I often called, but after a while he wouldn't answer and wouldn't call back.

But he sent letters. He wrote of his deepening love of God. He was thinking of us. He hoped we were well, that we were happy.

We wrote in return that we hoped the same for him.

We sent our sanitized news.

He wrote to say he missed us at the meetinghouse.

He wrote that he and Hank Fletcher went each Sunday, and afterwards they walked for hours along the beach like two old friends. *Well, we are friends, and we are old.* He said that he was reading more and more about the Quakers. He would include lines from those books, carefully copied out for us. Often they had to do with violence and pacifism.

He didn't understand that Tess and I had surrendered. Laid down our weapons. He believed we were still out there with hammers in our belts, balaclavas hidden in our coats.

We still have the letters, a neat stack of them in a blue Adidas shoebox, which once contained a pair of Tess's running shoes. Size nine and a half.

This morning I put on my parka, sat outside in the sun and read through them.

The clearing is covered in a thin sheet of fresh snow.

There are more than I remembered. Twice a month he wrote. Like paychecks, each is dated the first or the fifteenth. My father and his patterns. He seems to write slowly and not in his carpenter's scratch. The words are printed, composed of small open characters. Many of them are written on college-ruled paper, which strikes me as so sad. I see him alone at his kitchen table, writing in some notebook he's found in a bottom drawer, carefully tearing the perforated paper. Probably it's to do with my own notebooks. My father at his table, me at mine. The impressions our pens make on those deeper pages.

Later, he graduates to stationery. Not with his name printed on it or anything so fancy, just smaller, higher quality sheets of paper bordered in grey, folded and sealed into matching envelopes.

Each letter begins, *Dear Tess and Dear Joey.*

I think of my father as a boy. The photograph of him sitting in the bed of a pickup, tailgate down, legs dangling over the edge, his chin up, trying to look tough, but grinning anyway. Old jeans and muddied boots. I think of that boy in school learning to write letters. Learning the word *salutation.* His teacher passing through the classroom handing each student a stamp. The taste of glue on his tongue.

Dear Mom and Dad, They're making us write letters today. How are you? I hope you are good. I am fine.

Each of his letters, of these here in the shoebox, are perfectly organized. Just as he learned when he was young, his father's truck in a California onion field. When his own father was alive to elicit a grin from his son, to point a camera and release its shutter.

Each the same: date, two spaces, our names, our full address, two spaces and then *Dear Tess and Dear Joey*.

I have been thinking of you both, he often writes. He tells of his walks, of his growing friendship with Hank. *I am building furniture for Jon Brockett, who owns Lester's now. An inlaid walnut dining table.* He writes of a desk he's made from a good piece of oak. *I'm making cabinets for our mailman. A storm came through and lasted three days. I thought the waves would take the meetinghouse, but in the end just a few cracked windows. You should have seen the sky the next day. A woman from work is giving puppies away. I'm thinking about it. Strangest things you've ever seen. Australian shepherd mixed with chimp. Maybe I'll keep one. They'll surely be the ugliest dogs to walk the planet!* He adds that exclamation point, which strikes me now as such a gentle gesture. So much of that little boy still in him. It's difficult for me not to cry when I see it there. *Did you know James Dean was a Quaker? Went to see Mom. Wasn't very talkative. Went to see Mom. She didn't look well, I'm sorry to tell you both. She's lost more weight. I've spoken to Seymour. He says he'll check in on her. Says he'll make sure she's eating. But what can he do? What can any of us? There is only faith and prayer and kindness. And forgiveness, too. Some kids from Emerson opened a coffee place down on the boardwalk. It's nice. There's a little stage and they have live music sometimes. I went with Hank the other day. We're far too old, but no one seemed to mind. They were very nice. Hank brought a flask and made our coffees Irish. I hope it survives. It'll be rough for them in winter. You two could have done something like that. Hung around. I read this the other day,* "The meeting house is not a consecrated edifice, and if there is anything holy about it, it must be the lives of the people who meet there." *William Wistar Comfort said that and I thought it was so beautiful, and*

that you two might as well. It's people who make a place sacred,
not the opposite. Something to remember.

And so it went. The local news. The weather. Hank. My
mother always in decline, quieter, thinner. Her slow remove.
And often a line or two from something he'd read. There was
never any mention of Sam Young, or what we'd done, but I
know that he knew. I know he'd heard it all from Seymour,
whose confession, I imagined him believing, was a kind of
absolution.

My father his priest.

My father who had twice lost his own family.

My father, then father to us all.

114.

D ear Joey,
     I'm writing to say that we miss you here in White Pine,
     and have since you left so suddenly. I hope you won't
mind me writing. I hope you won't think I'm crossing the line.
Sometimes I start to feel like a stepfather only partially accepted
into this uncommon band of yours. Not, of course, that your
father and I are in love! Wouldn't that be something? No, but
you must understand what I mean. We've become such close
friends, your father and I, and I can't imagine what that must be
like for you. I do worry that you see me as an intruder or, at the
very least, look upon me with some suspicion. I understand and
I'd do the same. So I'm writing to say that I come in peace and
that you needn't worry. My friendship with your dad has been a
great blessing. The fact is that men our age (and I'm being generous to myself here given that I've got your pop by nearly ten
years) don't often make new friends, or know much about
friendship at all. It's lucky then that us two lonely old guys found
each other when we did. I hope that it's some comfort to you to
know that we look after each other. I've wanted to say that for a
while now, and I missed my chance to do it in person. Or maybe
I just chickened out. Well, whatever the case may be, I wanted
to tell you that I'm here in peace and that I've come to care about
your dad a whole lot.
     The other thing is that I know you've been calling and that it
must be very difficult not to have him pick up, or call you back.
I want to tell you that I've encouraged him to do it. And I've

encouraged him to visit you both there in Seattle. The problem is that he knows about your adventure, what happened before you left. He and Seymour had a few beers together up at Lester's and as far as I can tell Seymour told the whole thing. So knowing what he does, he's been struggling. That's what he tells me. He just can't stomach it. He says it has to do with being a Quaker, but I think just as much it has to do with your Mom and all that. I hope I'm not speaking out of turn. Maybe I'm wrong and maybe this isn't my place. What do I know? But really I think he's just frightened, Joe. He's afraid of all sorts of things. If you look at it from his side, you'll see. What with his wife where she is, his daughter too, and you and Tess, of course. Everyone gone, and everyone in danger. That's how he sees it, anyway.

I guess that's all I've got. I wanted you to know that I'm working on him. I'm trying to get him to pick up the phone, or better yet just drive up to see you. More than anything at all, I want you to keep in mind how much he loves you. I don't know if you can imagine it until you have a son of your own, but I hope you'll try, and I hope you'll believe me.

Yours sincerely,

Hank Fletcher

115

I sent Hank a warm letter in return. I said that I'd try my best to do what he suggested.

I saw my father at his kitchen table looking out at all of us: Claire disappeared across the ocean, my mother in her cell, barely speaking, barely eating, me and Tess in Seattle rampaging in the dark, in basements, building our bombs, sharpening our knives, in secret communion with his deadly wife.

So when he appeared all those years later at our bar at three o'clock in the afternoon, the old army duffel slung over his shoulder, I looked up from my lunch and saw him, perhaps for the first time in my life: a tall man, nearly sixty, short hair still thick, but gone entirely grey, slim, strong, handsome, brown eyes somehow too large, and too gentle for his worn carpenter's face.

When Tess saw who it was, this man standing in the entrance like Steve McQueen silhouetted in a saloon doorway, she screamed and ran and jumped on him. He dropped the duffel to the floor and held onto her with his eyes closed.

When she let him go and turned to me she was crying.

I embraced him as fully as I could, without the usual hesitation and my immediate desire to be free of it.

We walked him through the bar, which I should tell you was flawless. We had taste, Tess and I. Whatever our problems then, we were proud of that place—of its style and success— and it made us both happy to show it to him. He loved to see our lives, our life together. And I know that he was relieved to discover its normalcy, its distinct absence of weapons.

It makes me smile now to think of what he'd imagined—some grimy dive with an anarchist's laboratory in the back room.

Always polite, he'd arranged to stay at a hotel, but we insisted that he spend the week with us. Even if we all knew the city well, and he better than either of us, we played tourists. We went to see a Mariners game, to Elliott Bay where he found a copy of *The Journal of George Fox*, to Left Bank Books where Tess introduced him to her friends. We went down to the fish market, and walked along the water. We showed him our first apartment, a building that was by then condemned to become a tasteless glass-and-steel complex called Alabaster Court or The Ivory Lofts or some other bullshit. We went to the top of the Space Needle, where he told Tess about the March family's first trip to the San Juans. He came to the bar in the evenings to eat and watch us work.

On the day he left we crossed the park from our apartment and found our old house on Auburn Place. This pilgrimage was something I'd always avoided, and when my father suggested it, I wanted very much to refuse. But there had been a change: in me, in him, in time, something I'm not sure I can identify. Maybe it was just that I was older, or that I was under the illusion of having become an adult, or that my father had begun to appear to me as a child.

The grass in the park was wet, from dew or from rain, I can't remember, but I see us three walking side by side, my father in the middle, his arm around Tess. There are a few people out there running their dogs, but otherwise we're alone in the quiet morning.

It is one of those scenes, a perfect image so fixed in my memory that it must be wrong.

Could it have been so silent and empty?

Weren't there children chasing each other between the swings?

Trucks driving past?

Yet, I sit here at our table, and I look into this clearing and I see us: father, son, Tess, sweeping through Volunteer Park. I hear our footsteps. A German shepherd galloping past.

We are so sharp there in this clearing that I don't need to close my eyes.

We are on the other side now, on 15th, walking along Highland.

I am dizzy.

Then. Now.

I feel a strange lightness behind my eyes.

This tripling remove, this my childhood neighborhood, where once we lived, where Claire and I were kids. This very corner, Highland and 16th, where my mother once protected me from the Carlson brothers. There in the clearing she is standing in the middle of the street. Hair whipping around her shoulders, across her face, twisting at her throat. Eyes wide and those boys in front of her, straddling their bikes. She is screaming, *Look at me.* She is moving toward them. There is that car behind her now. See that fat chrome bumper. *If you ever*, she says, *touch him again.* She is bent at the waist, her hands on their handlebars—a red fist on each—the wind is blowing harder, her hair is snapping at their cheeks. *So help me God. You touch him again.* Her eyes unlike anything they've ever been. The driver blows his horn. She faces the car. The Carlson boys pedaling fast as they can. They're gone and still she is standing in the street. The wind at her back now. She stares at the driver. *Mom*, I say. *Mom.* She turns. Comes, bends to me looking up to her from the curb. The man rolls down his window. *Crazy whore*, he spits, driving past. *Crazy fucking bitch*, he screams.

She lifts me from the curb into her arms, even if I'm too old for it, too heavy. I am terrified. Of the Carlsons. Of the man in the car. Of her. Of the wind. She looks at me. Really looks.

Joey, she says, and pinches a blade of grass from my lip. *Joey*, she says as she carries me to the house. My chin is on her shoulder now. She says in my ear, to herself, *Those little fuckers, those little shits.*

Right there on that corner, here in this clearing.

We were all there once. As enduring as the yellow fire hydrant. We were all there. Me and the man in the car and the Carlson brothers and my mother, my wild savior.

We turn left onto Auburn Place East and I feel a pulsing within my head.

Is it my brain doing that? I am dizzier.

Once I lived here with my family. My parents in their bedroom. Claire in hers. Me in mine.

Golden wood dust floating in the light hair of my father's arms.

There was my mother's wide tortoiseshell barrette on the coffee table.

There was a way to make it a catapult for paper clips.

My purple bike on its side in the yard. Chrome tire caps. White Huskies handlebar pad.

All of it at once a single sense. It moves in me as we walk the block.

How do I explain this?

As if an entire childhood exists in a lone sensation. It is in my chest. It is in my mouth.

This is what I mean by tone.

Do you understand?

I am drugged by it.

It is everywhere.

It possesses me.

I am no longer on the street.

I have not met Tess Wolff.

My mother is a nurse.

Claire is ten years old.

My father is in his shop working the belt sander.

There is dinner.

There is school.

There is the park.

There is nothing else in the world.

"This is where little Joey grew up," my father says, and puts his arm around me.

We stand across the street, looking at the house.

The sensation has turned to pain. I don't know what it is made of.

Who knows its composition?

For a moment I'm afraid I may fall. I lean against my father.

"Joe," he says, "can you believe it?"

I shake my head.

"That was us four. Right there."

I nod.

"Takes your breath away," he says.

It does that. It does that, but also it does something worse. Something below the breath, something meaner.

Tess crosses the street and knocks.

I don't want anyone to answer.

I don't believe my father does either. I believe we're both praying together. Me and him. Waiting, watching Tess at the clean white door, the shining brass knocker.

No response.

She turns and shrugs and off we go back across the park, across the drying grass, to our apartment, and my father's truck.

Tess wraps her arms around him. She kisses his cheek.

"Drive safely," she says.

I hug him tight.

"I'm proud of you, Joe," he says, "whatever you've done. I love you always, kiddo. I'm sorry for all these years."

He climbs in and fastens the seat belt.

As he drives away he extends his hand out the open window.

Maybe he watches us in the rearview with our arms around each other.

Maybe he watches us disappear.

There he goes.

He is waving. He is feeling the air.

116.

This morning running through the snow my footfalls made no audible sound. There must have been six inches on the forest paths. The high boughs held piles of it. I went an hour deep, stopped then and waited on a dead tree for my breathing to slow. There it seemed as if I were the only moving thing. No wind. No animals. The sun filtering through the pines. The silence was an ecstasy.

I think I may return and make a camp. Make a bed.

Hike in with a sleeping bag and tent. The .45.

By the time I was out of the shower it was snowing again. I turned on the radio and made toast and coffee. A poached egg the way my father taught me—four inches of boiling water in a pan, a teaspoon of vinegar.

Last night I dreamed of Tess fucking another man. She was both old and young. Bent over the table, he was behind her, his face blurred. Only hers was clear. Of course, it's not the first time I've seen some version of this in my sleep. What is unusual is that it didn't upset me. Not while I was dreaming, not when I woke. And it doesn't upset me now. Certainly, I take no pleasure in it, but neither was I chained to a wall, fighting to get free, to stop it, as I have been before. Last night, we watched each other. I made no effort to move.

The snow fell harder. Not in my dream, but here at the house. I lit a fire and lay on the couch and listened to the radio. I'd run for two hours in the cold. My body was so tired, but my mind was sharp and constant.

After a while the woman whose voice I like came on the radio and began talking about Schumann's *Dances of the League of David*. I knew nothing about him, or his dances, and I thought, here, listen, idiot, maybe you'll learn something beyond feeling. But as she spoke about the music in her odd radio cadence—removed from meaning, emphasis on all the wrong words—I fell asleep. Every now and then the piano would become frantic and wild and I'd wake up, but as soon as it turned gentle, I was out again.

Then in the early afternoon, as if someone had driven an adrenaline shot into my thigh, I was on my feet, my mind rushing to catch up to my body, which was already naked beneath the shower, and when the two things fused I was flying, dressed, walking the road, in search of the farmer's daughter. The beginning of my new life, the first mark on my fresh-scrubbed slate. Twice a week they set up their stands in front of the public park and there she was sitting in a white plastic folding chair, beneath a red canopy, third table from the east. The winter market is jellies, jams, pickles, whatever the fuck else they can preserve in a jar. Cakes and pies, too. Cheese and honey, which is what she was selling, little pyramids of each laid out at her narrow wrists, and I came to her if not in the way I first glided to Tess, then with the same spirit, the same glittering clarity. There was her father standing over by one of the heaters talking with another man in a red knit beanie, pouring Bushmills into their coffee cups. She raised her eyes and smiled in a way I liked—lips together, knowing, expectant. Just as if she'd been waiting for me all day and here I was, her missing person. I was giddy with my blood crackling like that, my heart still shifting up gear after gear and her light eyes spinning my stomach, her pretty skin causing a buzzing in my legs, just the way it feels before I sprint the clearing.

I said, "What are you doing here?"

She laughed. "I'm here twice a week."

"That I know. I mean in this town."

One step away from *a girl like you in a place like this*.

"Same thing you are, I guess."

I was looking at her feeling the same good radiant power, that absolute confidence and courage, in pure possession of myself, and yet, still, there was something faded about it. Some absent element.

Maybe it's age.

Or maybe, Tess, I'm getting better.

I said, "My name's Joey."

"Beth."

"A pretty name," I said, though I didn't think so at all. You barely have to move your mouth to say it. A weak sigh of a name. I could still feel the fatigue, a far-off, subterranean stream, but I went on.

She gave me her hand. I took it and said, "Short for Elisabeth?"

"No. Just Beth."

I nodded like I knew something about her, but I was only hoping the rise would come on stronger to obliterate my hesitation.

"Where's your wife?"

I smiled. "She's not my wife. Anyway, she's gone now."

"Gone?"

"Yes."

There was that chemical thing between us. Even if it was low-grade, I liked feeling it again.

A young couple came to the table and stood behind me while their son cried and, by his teeth, clung to his father's jeans.

"I'll let you get back to work. Meet me for a coffee when you're done."

"Maybe. Aren't you going to buy something?"

"What should I buy?"

"Cheese or honey." She lingered on the third word, gave me that smile again.

"Honey," I said, playing along, but my heart wasn't in it. The engine was stuttering out.

At the diner I sat in a booth by the window and waited with a cup of coffee. In a near lifetime of rising and falling, I had never felt that undercurrent slipping along beneath the high. It was a modulating, evening force, an unfamiliar sound—distant, quiet and calm. Which was neither tar nor bird, but was something else like caution or, perhaps, even reason.

I waited, light and sharp, listening to it, feeling its watery counterweight. Beth arrived so lovely, her long black hair bulging and bound to her neck by a blue scarf, her cheeks pink, and then I wanted to stand on the table and sing to her, wanted to lift her up and run. Go down on my knees. Marry me, Beth.

But somehow I stayed where I was.

Not somehow. It was the fade. The exhaustion. It was the new sound.

She sat across from me and we drank coffee together. Beth was funny and brash, confident and intelligent. She held the honey jar in her hands and told me about her life here. The farmer was not her father, but her brother. Was married once, too young. With her then-husband, had once owned a restaurant in Portland. Had once worked a cruise ship. Had come here where her brother owned a farm with his wife who'd died in a car accident half a mile away and now she was thirty-six years old amidst a life she'd never expected in a diner on a cold night in the foothill farmland of northwestern Washington smiling her ravenous closed-lipped smile.

All was as it should have been—the snow beginning to fall outside, the upswing, the chemicals crackling between us, the relief of new company, the hot kick of fresh desire.

She said, "Show me your house."

We walked out to her truck and in the air I laughed, felt the gears shift up again, internal, external. She drove us out of

360 · ALEXANDER MAKSIK

town, along the highway, turned where I told her, and then there was our house at night, lamp on in the living room, yellow porch lights, white spot upturned to the alder where those red-tailed hawks had built their nest.

"Oh," Beth said when she saw the house. "It's beautiful."

I can't remember the last time we'd had anyone over, shown what we'd made to someone else, and I liked doing it. Even if it was thin pleasure. I lit a fire and then left her in the living room standing before the bookshelves while I went for the scotch she'd asked for.

Her coat was thrown over the white easy chair where Tess loves to read.

I handed Beth the drink.

"You live in this house alone?"

"Lately," I said.

"What a waste."

I took her out to the deck where we looked over the clearing, the soft light of the house reflecting in the new snow.

"What's out there?"

"Forest," I said.

"No neighbors?"

"Not in that direction."

I was watching myself slashing barefoot through the light and snow, breaking the dark, even line, dissolving into the woods. The wind blew the clouds away to reveal an eyelash of moon and because of it I moved so that I was behind her. I couldn't feel the cold. I wanted to push her hard against the railing. My mouth was so close to her neck.

"Joe," she said. "Come closer. I'm freezing."

I wanted her with the old savage violence. Or the violence I imagined I once possessed. Or I tried to conjure it. Wanted to use her body. Wanted to be vicious. Tear into her. Detach myself from feeling. I could have risen straight into the air.

"Joe. Please."

I pulled her back against my chest, but I was gentle. The tidal lust ran out of me. I kissed her neck. Breathed in deep. She pushed back and moaned.

I said, "Come inside."

In the living room she bent over and unlaced her boots. I liked seeing her there, long black hair trailing the floor. The rise came on stronger, the weird fatigue was nearly faded. It was quiet as flowing blood. Then I wanted to dance. I turned on the radio, but it was that goddamn classical woman, still droning on about Schumann.

Beth was sitting on the couch watching me. She'd pulled her sweater off. Now she was wearing only a T-shirt, light yellow, and jeans. Lust again. I wanted her turned around, white knees on the khaki cushions, wrists bound behind her back, clamped in my fist. I wanted to leap over the coffee table, tear her clothes to pieces. I would be what I had never been. Somehow I would deliver this frantic wildness, which then in an instant felt as if it were near its death, or, at least, its severe dilution.

She stood and took my hand. "Give me a tour."

I showed her the office absent its computer.

The bathroom where I hide and block the light.

I took her here into this room, flipped the lights.

There was the oiled .45 resting on its chamois, a yellow square atop our shining table. I'd turned it three clicks to the right. You see? Despite the distance in time and space, between this table and our Cannon Beach motel room, you see how I still cannot resist a romantic tableau?

She hesitated. Stiffened. I imagine her wishing she had on her boots.

She nodded at it, asked, "Worried about something?"

"It was my father's," I said, as if that explained anything.

She gave me a look that reminded me so much of Tess.

What was it exactly? Fear. Wary appraisal. I'd kept Tess back all night long, but now it was too late.

Beth said, "Why's it out?"

"I was going through his things."

I was so tired, so ground down. My charm was fading. I wanted Tess home.

Prayed for it right there. Maybe out loud.

She said, "Are you okay?"

I told her I was. I could barely keep my eyes open.

There was no one else.

"You look sick."

"I'm just tired," I said.

She nodded and went for her boots, her sweater.

Said, "Maybe we can do this another night."

Her coat, her scarf, her hair, pulled and spun and bound.

There was Tess's look again.

"You know where to find me," she said.

I don't know what she meant.

Invitation or statement of regret.

117

Every few months we'd drive down to see my mother. Or I would. Or Tess. And always the report was the same. She was getting thinner. She was getting older. She was getting weaker. She had less to say.

I know you're tired of this. You want my mother to find God. Want her to appear bathed in golden light, a look of profound peace upon her face. For her to be pardoned, released, restored to her old passion and verve. Free.

You want us reunited with Seymour.

You want Claire returned and reborn having seen the error of her ways, so full of explanation and regret.

You want a long grateful letter from Anna. You want her grown up, an undamaged young woman of real independence and intelligence.

You want Sam Young crawling to our doorstep broken and heavy with remorse.

You want Hank laughing at our dining table.

You want Tess to return home.

You want us happy and married with lovely, joyful children.

Or perhaps not that. Maybe you're sick of Tess and wish that I would just, for the love of fucking Christ, go sweep Beth into my arms. Or someone.

Or is it me you're sick of? Me and all my weeping, my weakness and wretched devotion, my broken *filters*, whatever the fuck *they* are, whatever *that* nonsense is.

Maybe you're rooting for Tess to find a true revolutionary,

a constant man with high ideals and a good beard, who wears fraying rope bracelets, his long hair loose beneath ragged-brimmed hats, who is devoted to the cause. A man who will never, not for a single instant, tire of war and ambition.

Ah, but no matter what you want, I will give only what I have.

But why not lie? Why don't I invent these things you want? It would be so simple to construct warm reunions, moments of sweet revelation, tender letters from White Pine, a jubilant, lantern-lit dinner around a long oak table in our green clearing.

It is to do with some foolish idea of honor.

No good prayer, no true love letter, no great eulogy may be composed of lies.

Isn't that right?

I insist it must be.

118

It takes so much work to run two bars. It requires a constant presence, a heightened energy. It is both theater and sport. All the ritual preparation. Two shows a day. Us against them. So unpredictable. So often on the edge of chaos and disaster. It is physical work. It takes a toll. And after all those years, we were sore and we were tired. Our bodies hurt. My lower back. Her feet. Then my knee, then her shoulder. We had been doing it half our lives. Maybe it was more.

As a remedy, we began to take short vacations. Out to the San Juans, to the Olympic Peninsula, into the mountains around Leavenworth. Nothing far, nothing exotic. No cafés, no cobblestones. Maybe Tess would read about a little lodge somewhere and we'd stay there, or we'd drive until it got dark and stay wherever we could find. Anyway, we always had blankets in the back and neither of us minded sleeping in the truck. It was just the silence we liked. Just the emptiness of those places.

Even if we were restless for different reasons, even if our respective discontent was born and made of distinct materials, the quiet served us both the same.

It was during one of those trips that we saw the sign staked right outside the mailbox.

For Sale.

The land.

Or, this land.

I am there now. Or, I am *here* now. Here atop our little hill, looking out across that same perfect clearing into the dark woods.

Dear Tess, Dear Mom, Dear Dad, Dear Claire,

I am writing to you from the house we built on the land we found by the side of the road one late autumn afternoon.

It wasn't a shared fantasy, wasn't something we'd been working for. It wasn't meant to be our next move, or our next life. But we stopped at a sign next to a mailbox and we turned down a long dirt driveway. There was a soft wind coming from the west. And all those pines looked so blue.

So we bought it. It didn't take very long. It wasn't very expensive.

Then we sold our bars. Not to some local who owned a good restaurant down the street, but, I am ashamed to tell you, to a *hospitality group*. Owner of restaurants and hotels throughout the country. There were other offers, but none remotely comparable. None that even entered the same realm.

"If we do this, they will kill them," Tess said, so full of contempt.

It was true. She was right. There would be branding and mission and dress code. Everything would be standardized and made efficient. Every shot would be measured and accounted for. There would be new language imposed. Scripts to be learned. Our people would have to speak like cheerful machines. All collective, all continuous: How are we enjoying our burgers? How is everything tasting? Are we still working on that?

Problems would become *concerns*. Customers would become *guests*.

"Fuck these people," Tess said.

But even Tess, Tess of our later years, could not turn away from that deadly black figure printed at the bottom of the page—a single number, which held such power, so much promise and possibility.

We fought for the health insurance to remain, for a baseline hourly wage well above minimum. We won those battles anyway. Not that it was any consolation to either of us.

And just like that, just like everything else, with shocking speed, we were wealthy. I don't want to overstate it. We hadn't sold an oil field, but for us, for the small life in the woods we said we wanted, we had plenty of money.

119

If ever I was an ambitious man, I cannot remember him. Yes, there was general fire, desire for experience, for sex. I wanted to consume all that passed before me. But that was a state of youth, *the* state of youth.

But beyond those years? No.

I never wanted to be great. I never wanted to prove myself to the world. I had no fantasies of standing triumphant before a crowd. I never wanted to be anything in particular.

Neither astronaut nor fireman. Neither cop nor assassin.

Now my single conscious ambition is the same as it's been for so many years.

I want only a life with Tess.

You may ask, well, what have you done? What have you done with your life, Joseph March, and I will very happily tell you that I have loved my family, I have loved Tess Wolff.

And for these things I feel no shame.

But is this why she left? Have I suffocated her? Am I absent some vital thing, some essential American element? A passion for empire and celebrity? Do you think somehow it was murdered along with Dustin Strauss? Did my mother shatter something in me as she was shattering that man's skull?

Or perhaps I would have wanted more had my father been some other kind of man. Or if I had a stronger, more constant mind.

Well, whatever the case, here I am and there we were in our new house in the woods. And as with the bars, here, too, we were makers and masters of our own diminutive kingdom.

Put this here, put that there and when all was done, every cup in its cupboard, then at last we would begin. Then we would be provided with what? Peace of mind? Stillness of soul? Yes. That is precisely what I expected.

But I should also admit that there was some aspect of imprisonment, too.

Yes, I was trying to bind Tess to me.

Yes, I thought that here in the woods, I might fully and finally possess her.

Yes, within the confines of our house, our land, our perfect keyhole, the dense forest would eternally attach us together.

Like some kind of fairy tale witch, I would keep her here.

Was this house a prison? Was our clearing its yard?

Is that what I have done?

120

Claire, she was in the yard.

Out by the west wall, just at the very edge of that little field they have. You can see it from the back end of the parking lot. No matter the season, it's mostly dead brown, but in late spring there are bits of green near the basketball courts.

It was Seymour who called.

It wasn't protocol, but he'd become a captain by then so he took his liberty and did it anyway.

"Joe?"

I hadn't heard his voice for so long.

We were on our deck. I'd been for a run. The sun was out and I was half-asleep on one of our new lounge chairs. Tess was potting flowers.

The phone rang, the one with all those megahertz.

She went inside to get it and when she returned said, "It's Seymour."

She pointed the handset at me. I see her looking down, her terrible expression, and most of all, and as always, her eyes.

Seymour told me Mom was standing on her own. She was there, not doing anything in particular. The guard who saw her fall said she was looking toward the east, her back to the yard, but that he didn't know what she was looking at, or if she was looking at anything at all. Seymour didn't want to go on, but I pressed him. I wanted to know exactly.

For me, but for you as well.

If you ever come by here. In case you ever ask.

"The guard said, 'It was like she'd been shot. One minute she's standing and the next she's on the grass.'"

She was sixty-four years old, Claire.

I'm glad she didn't clutch her chest, or stagger, or cry for help.

I like to imagine her facing the sun.

I like to imagine her looking through the fence, beyond the walls.

Who knows? Maybe she had her eyes closed. Maybe she was absent from herself entirely. But I will remember her with eyes open, her face full of sunshine, looking at something very far away.

I think of Dad dying as if falling into water.

I think of Mom vanishing quick as light.

I suppose we're fortunate. No protracted illnesses. No suffering for our parents. Both of them gone so quickly.

121

We returned to White Pine and stayed in a motel. Tess was tender with me, but very quiet. In the evening we got pretty drunk and then drove over to Lester's to meet Seymour, we took the same old booth.

I saw him come in with a large box under his arm. He was bald now, and had lost a bit of weight. I watched him make the rounds. It was still a guard bar so he knew everyone there.

It was hard to imagine him then as anything else, but once, I swear to you, he had been so entirely different.

He made his way over and sat down next to Tess.

"C," she said, and began to cry.

He put his arm around her and she slumped into him, pressing against all that soft flesh.

He reached across the table and shook my hand. "Joe," he said. "I'm sorry, brother."

I was glad he spoke that way, still a bit of the young soldier left, my long-gone friend.

We shared a pizza and drank too much. There was little talk of the past, and certainly no mention of Sam Young.

Seymour pushed the box across the table. In it were packets of my mother's letters. Four of them. From me, from my father, from Tess, and then from her fans, Marcy Harper among them.

Her wedding ring. Some clothes.

And my mother herself, who'd been burned to ash and

poured into a plastic bag, which had been sealed and fitted into a small white cardboard box. There was a printed label stuck askew to the top of it: Anne-Marie March.

In the morning the three of us drove out to the beach below the meetinghouse and shook her ashes into the wind with some sentimental hope that she would return to my father, or he to her, or both of them to God, or whatever it is one hopes for the dead.

And because we couldn't help ourselves, or really, because I, forever my father's son, couldn't help myself, we drove slowly past his house. There were purple pig lilies in the garden and a boy on the front step with a yellow Tonka truck upside down across his knees.

We stopped on Mott Street and watched for a while, but only saw a shadow pass in the upstairs window.

There was no sign of the Night Gardener.

At the Young house nothing moved. The trampoline was gone.

We didn't visit Hank. I can't remember why.

We dropped Seymour off at the prison.

"See," he said, leaning down to us and pointing to the far basketball court, "it was there. She was right there."

We returned home with my mother's wedding ring, and her packets of letters. Home where we pulled weeds from our garden and cut the grass and wildflowers when they grew too high. Home where we ran a damp cloth over all our smooth surfaces.

It was then something changed in Tess. Or changed again. My mother's death had provoked in her some of that former fire and panic, unearthed the old desire. She spoke less. Was remote in her old way. A new heat and charge to her.

We'd been home a week or so when I woke in the night to see her dressed and standing by the window in the moonlight. I called her name and she came to me and sat on the bed. She moved her fingers through my hair and kissed my forehead.

"Sleep, sweetheart," she said. "I'm not tired."

I closed my eyes.

"I'm not tired at all," she whispered.

I woke again hours later as she was climbing back into bed, her skin so cool and smelling of night. She pressed her back to my chest.

I trapped her in my arms. I locked her ankle with my heel. "Where have you been?"

She moved against me until I was inside her.

"I went for a walk."

"In the forest?"

"There's so much light out there," she said.

"I would have gone with you."

I moved my hand between her legs.

"I know."

"It's dangerous, Tess."

"It's not," she said. "It's fine."

She broke free and rolled me hard onto my back.

"What could possibly happen, Joe?"

Then she was on top of me, her hands pinning my wrists.

"Will I be torn apart by wolves?"

She laughed. Her teeth were on my neck.

She let go and rode upright, her hands on her breasts, nipples between her fingers. I watched her moving above me, her open mouth, her eyes closed, her hair swinging forward and back, face flashing dark and silver in the moonlight.

She was loud that night, and after she'd come, fell asleep almost immediately.

124

There were many nights I'd wake to find her vanished, or slipping back into bed.

There were days she barely spoke at all.

And then, in an instant, Tess was gone.

I'd been to town to have my father's Wagoneer serviced and when I returned the house was empty and on this table, here in the middle, held down by a white bowl of berries, was her note.

"I am too various to be trusted. But I am safe and I love you. T."

That's all.

One of those lines she'd always kept around, stolen from a novel she loved, followed by her tired cliché of meager reassurance.

125.

Over the time she's been gone, nearly a year and a half now, I have often thought that had I just paid closer attention to her marginalia, to her stars and underlines, to all her bits of paper tacked to so many walls, I'd have saved myself a lot of trouble, and a great deal of pain.

Those scraps might have served as warnings, rather than thin decoration.

Well there are many ways of being held prisoner.

It may be that we can reassemble a person this way. Or, really, assemble them correctly.

God knows I have tried.

Surely there is a formula to be written, an algorithm to be employed. There must be a way to input all of the variables and have returned to us the woman herself. If we take the library of a true reader, as Tess is, and evaluate all of the books, plus all of the markings, would we not have some fundamentally truer version of that person than if we were to do the same with her spoken language, or even her letters, her journals?

Take all of those well-ordered books there on our great wall of carefully crafted shelves. Take the texts themselves, and then add to them whatever has been inscribed in their first pages.

Tess Wolff. Seattle. Washington. 1995, for example.

Add then the drawn lines—vertical and horizontal, doubled and tripled, plus their various flourishes—finishing hooks, upticks and down, plus power of pen stroke—depth of impression, plus considerations of paper stock, plus all the notes and stars, asterisks and brackets, exclamation points and question marks, plus stains and bookmarks—blood and coffee, insects and flowers, photographs and train tickets and sand. Take all of it and I am certain that out of the right machine would come the very truest portraits.

We are so much better told by the sentences of others.

It may be that I am doing a better job of telling your story than I am of mine.

After my mother died they made a film about her. They stood outside our old bars. They went to London to find Claire. All of us refused, so they turned our desire for privacy into a subject of suspicion. Enigmatic Tess, rich and glamorous Claire, shy Joseph. Richard the good Quaker. Anne-Marie March: hero or madwoman? They put Claire in black-and-white ducking into a clean white Mercedes. They filmed the prison and played their music of doom.

It was a despicable film, but we watched anyway. It was the first time I'd seen you, Claire, in such a long time.

So many years gone. You were a woman in a black business suit. A stranger. Serious and pretty.

We left Seattle for this place where we were to start a family, where we were to be at peace, where we were to find relief from our terrors and our passions. But one day I returned home to find the house empty, and Tess replaced by a slip of paper.

And now here I am, a man alone in the woods writing to Tess and to Claire, to my mother and father. To you.

I am trying to hang on to order, to believe in it, but now that I have told you everything, I'm afraid I'm beginning to spin away into some foreign and frightening land.

I can feel the frame shuddering.

I am rapidly approaching the present.

I have come to the end and she has not returned and I do not know what to do next.

What should I do? Tell me, please.

Now that I have realized our nation's great dream. Now that I have pulled myself up by my bootstraps and worked hard and made of my life what I could. Now that I have money and quiet and a good place to live, what do I do?

What do I do if the love of my life has gone, and my parents are dead, and my sister has shunned me, and my friends have dissolved?

What do I do if I have come to the end of the story and there's nothing else to tell, what do I do next?

There is no way to change the will of others.

The whole thing is falling to pieces.

This story, this eulogy, this letter, this prayer. The foundation, the frame.

I am running out of energy. I am running out of faith. I can no longer understand the system. The logic is faulty.

What good are more anecdotes, more stories of our great love?

One more.

I will tell you one more. I promise it'll be brief. And then I'll let you be.

Just the recollection of a few hours of a single day.

We were in this house. A wild storm was blowing through. We were trapped inside. We were drinking. We were listening to music.

Tess closed her eyes and began to count backwards from fifty.

"Hide," she said.

I was in the entryway closet where we kept our coats. She was calling to me, singing my names, and I was laughing from cabin fever or love or bourbon or joy and I couldn't stop. Soon she yanked the door open, and when she saw me there giggling like a little boy, she began to laugh and tackled me to the floor and we kept on like that until we had no more left. There were boots and shoes and sandals all around us. She reached up and pulled my father's old down parka from its hanger and covered us with it. Her hand above us on the sleeve. I pulled the door closed. The wind and rain and thunder were shaking the house.

We stayed on the floor for hours, breathing, bundled in the pitch dark listening to the storm.

128

I have written you across time.
I have written you across my life.
I have gone to town.

I have taken care of the garden.

I have called Seymour, who is getting married.

I have called Hank, who is hanging on.

I have left messages for my sister, who still refuses to respond.

Perhaps one day, Claire.

I cannot fully explain it, but somehow I understand you. It is perhaps healthier to turn entirely away. Begin again from nothing. If I were capable of it, I think I'd like to do the same.

No matter how you live, there are casualties.

I have tried. I have tried to rid this house of its detritus. But there are objects I cannot burn. I don't know why that is. The books remain on their shelves. There are still matchbooks, feathers, champagne corks, photographs.

Despite my efforts, there is all the usual crap.

I want to burn the whole thing down. But I don't get very far.

The devices are easy.

My own clothes are easy.

I have fantasies of dying like my mother did. Leaving so few objects behind. It thrills me, this prospect. Give everything away.

Leave nothing behind but a pistol and a paper box of ash.

A legacy of bone.

I see the box, square and white on this table, and I feel calm. My own ashes here as a centerpiece. I feel chills of pleasure to think of it. Such clean simplicity.

And yet I cannot even take the books from the shelves. I can barely rid the house of anything that holds her mark.

The other night I sat outside with matches we'd kept from some lodge in Leavenworth. I burned them all at once on the deck, and only felt regret.

And now when I see the black mark on the wood, I think of them, and then of our room there, and then of Tess on a mountain path in the snow.

I dream of Tess in all the ways a person dreams: nightmare and vision, fantasy, hallucination and reverie.

It is no good.

You see how I am stuck?

Even if I have tried so hard to do so, even as I keep the .45 in front of me. I cannot rid myself of hope. And perhaps that's what nostalgia is. Perhaps that's what it is to be sentimental. An inability to abandon hope.

Look at my father. He died with a heart on fire, so full of faith in all of us, and our pure and fertile futures. He died believing we would all be happy, Tess and I and Claire. Seymour and Hank. Perhaps, even, my mother.

When I burn the feathers and the matches. When I burn the books, and all her fragrant clothes, the photographs and all her notes, that is when you might truly worry.

129

I want you to know how it ends. Or how it ended for a while.

Just like that.

Suddenly.

Out of thin air.

The way my life has changed over and over again.

I go along and then there is horror.

I go along and then there is wonder.

It was late afternoon. Cool. A soft wind blowing through the apple trees. Hundreds and hundreds of high white clouds racing through the sky. Sunlight flashing across the house. I'd collected green beans from the garden and was sitting outside with a basket of them snapping off their ends. There was a cardinal flitting around, returning again and again to the same branch. I was talking to him. He was singing to me, cocking his head in that sweet cardinal way—human and questioning like an old man, half deaf. When he took off for the woods I looked up and there was Tess.

Is Tess.

Is Tess.

Is Tess.

As sudden as my mother's temper, as sudden as my mother's death, there was Tess at the edge of the clearing just as I had dreamed her. Well, no pistol, no saber, no stallion, but otherwise, just as I had dreamed her.

She was wearing jeans and a white T-shirt. Over it, her ragged army surplus jacket. The sleeves rolled up. Her hair cropped short again.

There was a dog at her side.

I was still, basket between my bare feet.

She was coming toward me, talking to the dog. The animal stopped first, raised its head and barked. Then Tess looked up. Both of them with a similar expression—heads canted at the same angle, gaze on the same line, mouths slightly open. Both were tense, muscles coiled, ready to spring.

And you know what I saw? Watching Tess Wolff in her boots and army jacket? The strangest thing: I saw my mother sitting on our front step in Capitol Hill in a red summer dress, the fabric drawn loosely between her knees, a blue bowl of cherries to her right, and she was pushing the pits out, dropping the flesh onto a white plate to her left, while Claire and I played in the spray of our Rain Bird.

I had been injected with the image, the needle slipped straight into my brain.

And it was not Tess who made me think of my mother.

It was me.

Or it was me through Tess's eyes.

I might have been wearing the same dress, dropping green beans into my lap, smiling at my knight errant returned from battle.

She stopped.

She was only a few yards away now.

Her skin was deep brown. Her hair gone greyer.

I saw her sailing some subtropical river.

Against her tan face, those green eyes appeared exaggerated, lit from within, the lines at their corners deeper, more beautiful.

Tess stopped, but the dog kept coming, tail down, head down, all curious submission. I reached and once he found me friendly, he began to wag what was left of his tail and nuzzle my leg. He flopped at my side and rolled over.

It was an Australian shepherd, barrel-chested, black and white and grey with one of those milky-blue eyes.

"What's his name?"

"Zeus."

She smiled at me.

The dog looked at her, his head hanging upside down off the step.

She was still too far away to touch, standing in her boyish way, hip kicked to the right.

I said, "Is this as close as you're coming?"

She came near enough so that I could see the down on her arms. And then enough to touch. She pressed her hands against my thighs. She pulled herself forward by her nails until her balance was gone and she knocked me back and I had the full weight of her body.

"Joe," she said, "Joe."

It is not possible to translate into language what it was to feel her against me.

It is not possible to describe what it did to my skin, to my eyes, to my blood.

I can only tell you what I have always known, and what I knew again with such pure certainty: I would give anything for the full heat of her body.

There was nothing I would not do to have her.

No. *Have* is the wrong word.

There is nothing I would not do to be in contact with her. I would do anything to see her move, to listen to her speak. I would do anything to be near her.

Whatever she asks. Whatever she wants. No matter what.

There is nothing I would not do. Do you understand me? There is nothing.

I have given up.

We went to bed and I did not want anything else.

I did not want to know where she had been.

I did not want to know how long she would stay.

I wanted nothing else.

I have given in. I have given up.

We went to bed and I did not want anything more.

I have abandoned all of it: logic, control, and system.

In those first days I held onto her with such fierce and desperate strength.

We pressed so hard against each other. We were trying to make some seal, some perpetual lock. We were trying to make some absolute and final joining.

For nearly two years she was gone.

Now Tess is here. When I wake she is next to me.

E very morning I run through the cool forest. Sometimes with wild brightness, sometimes dragging behind me the tar and the bird.

And when I return home Tess is there on the deck in the sun with her books.

In the evenings we cross our clearing and walk together along the elk trails while Zeus charges ahead.

L ast week we drove all the way out to the coast and spent a thunderstorm getting drunk in the back of the Wagoneer while Zeus cowered and farted between us.

After the rain passed, we had the beach to ourselves. All three of us were delirious with joy, chasing seagulls, running in circles.

The wind came up in the late afternoon and we all lay on our bellies watching the sunset. Tess the sniper, we her spotters.

132.

Perhaps I will ask where she has been.
Maybe I will ask what she has done.
On the other hand, one must surrender entirely.

L ast night on the couch, Tess tucked her feet beneath my legs. Zeus was asleep between us. Our owl was calling from the woods.

I wanted nothing but for nothing to change. I wanted nothing to change and for nothing to change to be my reward for faith, for insistence, for staying alive, for fighting so hard against the dark, for surrendering, for seeking out that other thing, which is neither tar nor bird, which is neither beast nor object, which is beauty, which is love.

I wished for nothing to change, but if wishes were horses, Joey Boy, beggars would ride, and the night went on and on toward morning, and now as I sit here writing one last time, I see Tess at the edge of the clearing, her back to the house, Zeus panting at her side.

She is out there looking into the forest at something I cannot see.

Acknowledgments

I am grateful to the following people for their generosity, intelligence and faith:

Caroline Ast, Natalie Bakopoulos, Joe Blair, Ryan Bloom, Laura Bonner, Jon Brockett, Diane du Périer, Patricia Escalona, Jenny Gersten, Francesca Giacco, Pilar Guzman, Leslie and Jon Maksik, Paula and William Merwin, Greg Messina, Michael Reynolds, Grant Rosenberg, Barbara Seville, Stefan Schaefer, Colombe Schneck, Eric Simonoff, Rachael Small, Daniel Smith, Tara Spencer-Frith, Françoise Triffaux and Christian Westermann.

I would also like to thank The Corporation of Yaddo for twice providing me shelter, peace and friendship.

ABOUT THE AUTHOR

Alexander Maksik is the author of the bestselling novel *You Deserve Nothing* (Europa, 2011) and *A Marker to Measure Drift* (Knopf, 2013), which was a *New York Times Book Review* Notable Book of 2013 as well as finalist for both the William Saroyan International Prize for Writing and Le Prix du Meilleur Livre Étranger.